Praise for *After Happily Ever After*

D0170085

"In Leslie A. Rasmussen's debut novel, a woman finds herself reanalyzing her life and her marriage when her daughter is heading off to college. Smart and funny, *After Happily Ever After* is an exciting debut."

—Laura Dave, international best-selling author
of *Eight Hundred Grapes*

"Leslie A. Rasmussen has written a story that most women can relate to in one way or another with compassion and love. *After Happily Ever After* is a wonderful read that will not disappoint. I highly recommend *After Happily Ever After* to women both young and old."

—*Readers' Favorite*, five stars

"*After Happily Ever After* is a road map for every empty nester whose marriage has lost its spark. You can't help but see yourself on these pages."

—Adrienne Barbeau, actress and author of *There are Worse Things I could Do* and the *Vampyres of Hollywood* series

AFTER HAPPILY EVER AFTER

After
Happily
Ever
After

A NOVEL

LESLIE A. RASMUSSEN

SHE WRITES PRESS

Published 2021
Printed in the United States of America
ISBN: 978-1-64742-014-7
ISBN: 978-1-64742-015-4
Library of Congress Control Number: 2020912073

For information, address:
She Writes Press
1569 Solano Ave #546
Berkeley, CA 94707

Interior design by Tabitha Lahr

She Writes Press is a division of SparkPoint Studio, LLC.

In memory of my father, Howard Rieder, who was an amazing writer and my biggest fan. He was also the master of quiet sarcasm, and Jewish guilt, so I know if he was still here, he'd have nudged me to dedicate this book to him. Dad, I'm listening, but I would've dedicated it to you anyway.

AFTER HAPPILY EVER AFTER

I zipped my jacket up to the top of my neck, which still didn't keep the frigid air from whipping through my body. The sun hadn't come out in two weeks, and I was beginning to wonder if we'd ever see it again. As I cursed myself for parking so far away from the bank, a handsome man wearing a New York Yankees baseball cap was walking toward me. His face was lit up by a smile. A smile so warm that it looked as if it rested on his face even if no one was around. As he got closer, the sun suddenly peeked out from behind a cloud. Was the universe trying to tell me something? Could this be the man for me? Would this be the day that something exciting finally happened? My heart began to race, and I saw my brand-new life in front of me. This man and I would spend all our time together, laughing, antique shopping, and having amazing sex. It would've all been perfect. . . .

If I were not already married.

CHAPTER 1

———◆———

At 5:55, I rolled out of bed and caught my reflection in the mirror above my dresser. That mirror was my enemy. It pointed out all the new wrinkles that had been born on my face while I slept. I was not taking to the idea of aging gracefully . . . gracefully.

The room was lit only by the glow of the clock. Jim was happily snoring and was no closer to waking up than our basset hound, Theo. I had five minutes before I had to get Gia up for school. She was going to be just as happy to hear my voice as I had been to hear my mother's when I was a teenager. My feet jumped as they touched the cold, hard wood. Where the heck did I put my slippers? I walked through the dark room, feeling my way along the furniture. I made it past the footboard on the bed, and just when I thought I was safe, I stubbed my toe on the dresser. Damn those slippers! I bet they were laughing at me.

"Gia, it's time to get up," I called through the pain. I didn't feel bad yelling when Jim was still asleep; he could sleep through anything. Hopefully no one would ever break into the house and try to stab me in our bed.

After a moment, teenage mumbling echoed down the hall as sleep escaped her seventeen-year-old body. I shed my pajamas and wondered how the heck thirteen-year-old me had morphed into the body of a forty-five-year-old woman. Like most women, I'd resigned myself to the fact that it was out of my control. Or was it? If I started going to the gym again, I could tone up my floppy belly, my sagging underarms, and my ass that was creasing below my thighs. As I got in the shower, I decided to either give it a great deal of thought or push it out of my mind. I stood under the warm spray, letting it soothe and care for me. I would happily stay here forever.

"Mom," Gia called as she charged into the bathroom as if she'd been left out of something. Forever was not living up to its reputation. I turned off the water, grabbed my robe off the floor, and wrapped my wet hair in a terry-cloth turban. Her five-foot, six-inch lanky frame dwarfed my five-foot-two compact self.

"What's the weather like today?" She was wearing a silk shirt that barely hid the fact that she hadn't put pants on.

"We live in Connecticut and it's winter. What do you think the weather's like?" I asked.

"It's winter right now, but at some point, it'll be spring."

"You'll get a warning. Spring doesn't really 'spring.'"

"Mom, you're so funny."

"You need to finish getting dressed. The last time I checked, your school required pants," I said. She rolled her eyes. Eyes I would've killed for. She had lush lashes that curled upward, except for a few in the corner that curled down. At my age, my lashes were either falling out or turning gray. Long eyelashes were wasted on the young.

When she ran off, I threw on a pair of mom jeans and a white hoodie and pulled my wet hair into a pink ponytail holder. Someday I'd find the motivation to update my wardrobe. Before making

Gia breakfast, I tried to wake Jim up. Not because I needed him for anything, but because it bugged me that he could sleep through all the commotion. I coughed loudly, but he didn't move. I faked a belly laugh; still nothing. I gave up and went downstairs.

Fifteen minutes later, I was sitting across from Gia, enjoying a cup of coffee while she scarfed down a bagel with cream cheese. She pushed a paper across the table, not noticing the dab of cream cheese on its corner.

"Can you sign this so I can get out of third period and go see my college counselor?"

"If I don't sign, would you have to skip college and live with me forever?" The phone started ringing, but I ignored it.

"Not going to happen. I just hope I get into UCLA. I want to go to California, where it doesn't snow and there's sunshine twenty-four hours a day."

"If you really believe that, I don't have to worry that you'll actually get in."

"That sounds like something Dad would say."

"You were blessed with parents with a great sense of humor."

"I meant it's annoying that you both make the same bad jokes." She wiped the cream cheese off the paper and then licked it off her fingers. The phone rang again, but after two rings the person hung up. "Can you just sign this?" Gia asked, holding out a pen.

"Fine." I took the pen and signed. "You can't fault me for loving you so much that I don't want you to leave."

"Do you love me enough to let me stay home from school tomorrow?"

"Nope, that's where my love draws the line."

She took the pen back from me and stuffed it in her backpack; then she looked up at the clock on the microwave. "I gotta go." She let me kiss her goodbye, and I followed her to the front door.

I watched as she walked across what would be our grass if it weren't completely covered in fresh snow. Her heavy backpack weighed her down, causing her to stride awkwardly. As she crossed onto the sidewalk, she dropped her lunch, and in one fell swoop, picked it up. I yearned for the little girl who always turned back, wanting to see me wave one last time, but this young woman didn't give me a second thought.

When I quit my job seventeen and a half years ago to stay home and raise her, I told myself publishing would have to wait. I was sure I'd go back to my editing job when Gia entered kindergarten, but she was such an anxious kid that I needed to be here when she got home from school. And now seventeen years had flown by, and in a short time she'd be gone, and I was going to be alone.

I closed the front door because my fingers were getting numb, but I continued to watch her out the window. When she got to our corner, she walked toward a boy who was leaning against a black Honda Civic that was parked at the curb. I assumed it was her new boyfriend, Jason, although she still hadn't let me meet him. His dirty blond hair was shaved on the sides and slicked up and over with gel. The style teenage boys wore so they could avoid getting haircuts very often. I didn't know why he had to drive her when we lived only three blocks from school. Well, I did know, but I didn't want to think about it. I opened the door to get a better look at him, when he began tapping on his horn. I'd hoped a daughter of mine wouldn't put up with that kind of behavior, but she smiled at him and got in the car. I could tell he was the same kind of boy I used to go for in high school. The kind that was full of himself. The kind that always broke my heart.

I went back upstairs, and as usual Gia hadn't bothered to close her bedroom door. Her room was its usual mess, her wicker hamper lying in the corner on its side. Half her clothes were hanging from the rim, the other half scattered on the floor surrounding it. Was it really that difficult to put dirty clothes in a hamper? When she was four, we used to play a game together to keep her room neat. Barney the dinosaur has not been given enough credit for all the good he did in my house.

The next thing I knew, I was singing, "clean up, clean up, everybody everywhere, clean up, clean up, everybody do your share." After I finished my solo, I realized I'd picked up all her laundry and was now carrying it downstairs. I'd read the books, I'd heard the experts. I knew I should've left it and had her do it herself, but those experts weren't coming to my house and listening to her whine that she had no clean clothes.

I was halfway down the stairs, when Jim called out from the kitchen, "Maggie, have you seen my keys?" I stayed put, hoping he'd find them, although I knew he wouldn't. This was a dance we'd been doing for the past nineteen years. The keys were probably on the kitchen counter under the huge pile of *Psychology Today* magazines. The magazines he never had time to read. The magazines I kept quietly throwing out when he wasn't looking. I heard him tossing things around, and I knew in his haste he was dumping stuff everywhere. I had to find his keys before the hurricane moved from the kitchen to the living room.

When I walked into the kitchen, Jim looked at me hopefully, as if I'd been sent from the Promised Land to help him. "I can't find my keys, and I have a client coming in early," he said, pushing his bangs off his forehead. I sighed as he started looking in the appliances. Did he really think they'd be in the toaster oven? I glanced at the hook near our back door that we'd put in for this exact purpose, but his keys weren't there. I moved the pile of magazines and handed him his keys. "Thanks," he said, letting out a huge breath.

"Do you want some coffee before you lose the coffee pot too?" I asked.

"It's not nice to make fun of an old guy," he said.

I handed him a cup of coffee and a bagel. He tucked a napkin into the top of his red-striped polo like a bib so he wouldn't get cream cheese on it. Jim's hair had almost no gray in it, which pissed me off. Although today I saw a few white hairs peeking through the stubble on his face, which gave me a little satisfaction.

"I forgot to tell you I can't go to the Marksons' party next Saturday," he said. "I made an appointment with a new client."

"On a Saturday evening?"

"It was the only time he could come in. You can go to the party though."

"Forget it. I'll skip it." I got myself a bagel and sat down to have breakfast with him when his cell phone rang. His ringtone was "Ride of the Valkyries" from his favorite scene in *Apocalypse Now*. I hoped he wouldn't answer and we could have breakfast together, but that wasn't the case.

"Hello. . . ." He listened a moment. "Okay, try to calm down. Just tell me what's going on. . . . I know you think she's stalking you, but she's your mother, she's eighty-five, and she's in a wheel-chair. You'll be safe until our appointment at nine." He hit the end call button and turned to me.

"What're you up to today?" He asked this as if I might be hiding some secret, exciting life and today might be a new adventure. Part of me wanted to say I was going to Vegas to lose all our money and start a prostitution ring, but I figured he'd just ask me to pick up his favorite cookies on my way home.

"I'm going to Brooklawn this morning." How could he not remember that I go visit my dad at his assisted living facility every Tuesday?

"Oh yeah, sorry. I've been a little distracted."

"What's going on?"

"It's work stuff." He put his dish on the sink and left his mug on the table, as if he'd forgotten we had a dishwasher.

"I know, but it makes me feel bad when you shut me out. For a while now it's seemed like your mind is somewhere else, and I keep bringing it up, but nothing changes."

"You're right. I'll try harder, I promise."

"Okay," I said, wondering if this time he'd hear what I was saying.

Jim picked up his briefcase and went to the hall closet to get his coat. As he put on his gloves, I said, "Gia's not going to be home tonight. Do you want to try that new gastropub?"

"I don't know. I might be too tired." He walked toward the door and put his hand on the knob.

"Has Gia mentioned her new boyfriend to you? I don't think I like him," I said, putting his mug to my lips and drinking the last drop of his coffee. Jim's shoulders drooped as he realized his great escape was going to be held up.

"Can we talk about this later?" he asked.

"Why can't we talk about it now?"

"I don't want to get stressed out."

"I'm stressed. I thought we could share it."

"You know I don't like dealing with this kind of stuff before I go to work."

As a psychologist, Jim listened to his patients and helped them solve their problems, yet I was often left to deal with ours by myself. He'd come home to a place where our problems had been magically fixed.

He kissed me on the lips lightly, so lightly I felt a brush of air and the slight hint of a cinnamon raisin bagel on his breath. He opened the door to the garage and called over his shoulder, "Love you."

"Love you? Where's the *I*?" I said.

"Okay. Love, *I*." He was delighted by his comeback.

"Get out of here, before *I* kill you," I said.

I found myself twirling my wedding ring around and around; it had been on my finger for so many years. Sometimes it was hard to remember my life before marriage, when the biggest decision I had to make in the morning was whether to have a Café Americano or an iced green tea before picking out a cute outfit and heading to my job as a senior editor at Shier and Boggs publishing. My best friend, Ellen, still worked there and got to have deep conversations with interesting people, and I got to scrub melted Rocky Road ice cream off my counters.

I raised the shades in my kitchen. The morning light danced in the room as it reflected off the snow. I had lived in Shelton, Connecticut, my whole life. When I was a kid, there were about twenty-seven thousand people, and now there were more like forty-one thousand. Our town had gone from mom-and-pop shops to Targets, Staples, and Starbucks, although we still had a few quaint cafés and a lake where everyone fed the ducks. We also had one independent bookstore, *Written Words*, which had been here since I was a kid. When Gia was four, I took her there to hear a man in a Sammy the Whale costume read stories. She was so scared of the guy—and all whales for that matter—that when her grandmother gave her a toy stuffed whale, she freaked out. Needless to say, she's never been to SeaWorld.

Shelton was only forty minutes from a big city, yet our house backed up to the woods, woods that seemed to go on forever. When I looked out my back door, it often felt as if I was alone in nature. It was a feeling of peace yet also loneliness. I marveled at how the tall, barren trees covered in snow would bend down ever so slightly. And the ground free of footprints, except for the occasional raccoon that had run across the fresh powder to dump over the garbage can and spread wrappers from the chocolate that I denied eating. How I longed to leave my own footprints in the snowy woods. They were so inviting. Sometimes I thought about walking out my back door through the leafless trees. I would disappear for a while. Not forever, but at least a month. I wondered how long it would be before Jim or Gia noticed I was gone. Would it be today? Tomorrow? The next day? Would they notice when they got hungry and I wasn't there to get them dinner? Would they miss me?

The phone rang again, and I knew I couldn't keep ignoring it. "Hi, Mom," I said.

"How did you know it was me?"

"We've talked about this. Your number comes up on my caller ID." I wanted to say no one else would call repeatedly this early in the morning. How many weekends did she wake up my whole house?

"Why didn't you answer the other two times I called?"

"I was busy getting Gia out the door."

Mom was like the Energizer Bunny, up early and always moving. When she was younger, she never needed to diet; her hyperactivity kept her in shape. She was a young seventy-five-year-old, and only the creases in her hands revealed her age. "I wanted to tell you I bought the cutest dress yesterday," she said.

"That's nice." I began tossing moldy strawberries from the fridge into the trash.

"And I wore it to lunch with Cayla and Jill."

"Great."

"They loved it. Said I looked ten years younger."

As I moved on to the expired yogurt, she began describing the new restaurant they had gone to. I moved from *oohing* and *ahing* into *uh-huh* mode. Mom went on to tell me about every dish she and her friends tried and how the chef came to their table and told them he had just gotten out of the hospital after a gallbladder attack. When she started talking about the waiter's sister, I closed the fridge and told her I had to go, I had a lot to do. She said she understood and didn't want to keep me.

As my finger hovered over the End Call button, she asked, "When was the last time you talked to your brother?"

"I don't know."

"You should talk to him more. You're family."

"I really don't want to discuss this."

"Fine, but someday it'll just be the two of you. So, how's my granddaughter?" she asked.

"She has a boyfriend."

"How nice."

"I'm not sure this guy has the best manners."

"I remember the boys you went out with in high school. Talk about rude. There was that one boy who'd come over to pick you up, and he'd never even say hello to us. What was his name?" I knew exactly who she meant, but I shook my head, even though she couldn't see me. "When you were young you were a terrible judge of character." I wanted to drop the phone down the garbage disposal, but instead I took a swig of hot coffee directly from the pot, hoping it would burn my mouth so badly I couldn't blurt out the twenty curse words I was thinking. "Your father kept saying you were a smart girl and you'd be fine. Thank God you found Jim when you did. He really straightened you out."

"I really have to go, Mom."

"Are you sure? We're having such a nice chat."

I had never been so sure of anything. "Dad's expecting me. Bye."

After I'd hung up, the sound of the ticking clock on the mantel became so loud it was all I could hear, that and my mother's voice in my head. Over the years, I'd tried to ignore it, or pretend it didn't affect me, but it did. Even at my age the things she said made me question my judgment, so I tried to avoid her.

I got in my car and turned the volume on the radio up full blast to drown out the noise in my head. After ten minutes and a handful of judgmental stares, I arrived at Brooklawn. With its celadon siding, white columns of ledger stone, and circular driveway, it looked more like a quaint hotel than an assisted living facility. An American flag and a Connecticut state flag blew in unison. Even though I'd been coming here at least once a week for the last nine months, every time I walked through the doors, a feeling of melancholy washed over me. I wanted to go back fifteen years to when my dad was a vibrant and active prosecutor with no health issues. I signed in and then made my way through old people with walkers trying to mow me down. I saw Julia, my favorite nurse, walking toward me. Even though she was in her mid-thirties and had a thick blue streak in her hair, I wished she were my mother. She'd comforted me when I cried the first time I saw my dad alone in his room, and she'd stood up for me when one of the doctors caught me sneaking our dog, Theo, in to see him.

I waited while Julia stopped to help an elderly woman who had her shirt on backward. She had the woman raise her arms over her head as she turned the shirt around, being very careful to keep it pulled down so the woman could maintain her dignity. As the woman walked away, Julia waved me over.

"Hi, Maggie. I know you're here to see your dad, but can I ask a favor?"

"Of course," I said.

"Mrs. Cryer needs someone to listen to her news report. Could you drop in on her?"

"No problem," I said. I had become familiar with many of the residents. Mrs. Cryer was ninety-six and convinced she was

Walter Cronkite. She liked to report the news every morning . . . the news from 1962.

Julia went back to work. As I walked down the long hall, the smell of bleach and cleanser permeated my nostrils. Dad had a private room at the end of the hall, with a hospital bed, a dresser, a well-worn navy club chair, and a side table. On the side table was a Victorian lamp, the one Mom kept bringing over to my house, even though I kept saying I didn't want it. On the dresser were three pictures: one of Mom and Dad on their honeymoon, where Dad's wearing a sombrero and Mom's laughing hysterically; one of Jim and me and Gia in New York City; and one from my childhood of Jerry and me, where Jerry's smirking at the camera. Mom thought she was only going to be able to have one child, so she told anyone who'd listen about her miracle baby boy. Jerry still smirks whenever you take a picture of him; he took that miracle thing too much to heart. Jerry and I were six years apart, and he was stubborn, meticulous, and a loner, which also explained why as an adult he could rarely maintain a relationship with a woman for more than a few months.

I kissed my fingers and touched the mezuzah that Mom had put up on Dad's door. A mezuzah is a Jewish symbol that signifies God's presence. Dad wasn't religious, but he believed in traditions, so every home he'd lived in since he was born had one.

He was wearing charcoal gray sweatpants and a navy T-shirt that said, *A GOOD LAWYER KNOWS THE LAW . . . A GREAT LAWYER KNOWS THE JUDGE.* His silver hair was combed far enough back to reveal a very high forehead. A forehead I'd inherited, which was why I always wore bangs. Dad was sitting in his club chair intently focused on the television. Pat Sajak of *Wheel of Fortune* was calling out letters, and a professorial-looking man was trying desperately to solve the puzzle. "A Blast from the Past," I called out as I came up behind him, kissing him on the cheek.

"Show-off," he said. When I was growing up, Dad and I watched *Wheel of Fortune* together almost every night. Mom nor Jerry ever tried to join us. Mom was usually in the back room sewing or reading a book, and Jerry was on his Atari. I'm not sure if that was their choice or ours. During the commercials, we'd talk about my classes, which boys I had crushes on, and whether Whitney Huston or Madonna had a better voice.

"How's my favorite daughter?" he asked.

"I'm your only daughter."

"That you know of."

"Very funny." He was slumped to one side of the chair, so I reached my hands behind his lower back and pulled him up so he sat straight. Or as straight as I could get him with him being dead weight. Dad had Parkinson's disease, so sitting upright wasn't easy. He gazed blankly into the distance while I pulled him up and didn't say a word. I wondered if he was embarrassed that he couldn't control his own body well.

"Hey, you want me to sneak you in a chili dog next time I come?" I asked. His face looked a little thinner than the last time I was here.

"Sure, but don't tell your mother. She likes me to eat healthy."

I promised to keep my mouth shut, which was easy because when I talked to my mother, she did most of the talking anyway. I told him that Julia had asked me to go see Mrs. Cryer for a few minutes.

"Mrs. Cryer's loony," Dad said. "In the dining room the other day, she told me the Boston Strangler was on the loose and headed for my room. I told her I'd just hit him with my walker, and she said I'd do more damage with an AK-47." He laughed at his own joke, but the laugh caught in his throat, and he started coughing. I looked around the room for a cup of water, which I found on a side table, and held the straw up to his lips. In the last few months, his shaking had made it harder for him to hold a cup himself. I hated seeing my strong dad reduced to needing help with such a simple task.

Mom and Dad didn't tell me at first that he'd been diagnosed with Parkinson's, because they knew I'd worry. Then, a year ago, he started falling a lot, and one day when he fell in the kitchen, Mom couldn't get him up by herself. She called Jerry, and Jerry called Jim and me. When we got to their house, they confessed how often Dad had been falling. We got them to agree that they needed help. I wanted them to hire someone to come into the house, but Dad refused. They couldn't afford twenty-four-hour help, and Dad didn't want my mother to be his caretaker. He saw what it had done to his own mother when she took care of his father for the last five years of his life. His mother ended up an angry, bitter woman who resented his father. Dad never wanted that for my mother, so we moved him into Brooklawn, and Mom spent almost every afternoon with him. I never asked her what it was like to sleep alone after all those years.

I kissed Dad on his cheek and told him I'd be back soon, although I didn't get back to him as quickly as I wanted. After listening to Mrs. Cryer go on and on, I was cornered by another woman who needed help getting a knot out of her yarn so she could finish her great-granddaughter's sweater. When I finally got the knot out, she pointed out another one. After twenty minutes of new knots popping up, I figured out that she was tangling them purposely so I would stay and talk to her. Finally, she fell asleep, and I snuck away. The number of forgotten seniors here made my heart ache and scared the hell out of me. Would I be left all alone in a facility someday? Would Gia ever come see me? When Dad moved to Brooklawn, I told Jim that if I got to the point of having to go into any type of nursing home, he should leave a large quantity of sleeping pills on the counter and go out for the day. He said if I could get to the counter by myself, I probably didn't need a nursing home to begin with. I thanked him profusely for feeling my pain and knowing what I needed to hear.

When I finally got back to Dad's room, a nurse was helping him steady himself on his walker so he could go to the dining room for lunch. I felt bad that I'd been away for so long, but Dad was happy to see me again and asked me to join him for lunch. He loved showing me off. I told the nurse I'd take over and made sure he was steady on his walker before we began a very slow progress toward the dining room. For every step I took, he shuffled two while I waited.

I spent an hour eating a lunch of baked cod amandine, sweet potatoes, and dry green beans and listening to a medley of the elderly telling me how adorable I was. Nothing lifts your spirits more than feeling as if you're a teenager when you're over forty. I settled Dad back in his room and told him I was going to head out.

"Your mom said you haven't come by the house lately," he said.

"I've been busy, but I'll try to get over there."

Dad was always the peacemaker with my mom and me, but he should've been more concerned about his relationship with Jerry. Dad had trouble connecting with him, so he put all his fatherly efforts into me, which didn't help the situation. Mom felt bad, so she had tried to become both mother and father to Jerry.

A half hour later, I was turning down my block when I realized I didn't want to go home. I didn't want to do any more laundry. I didn't want to wash any more dishes. Or walk the dog. Or cook dinner. Since Gia started her senior year, and would be leaving for college soon, I'd been struggling with how I was going to find a new purpose to my life. There were plenty of people who would've been happy to *not* have to go to a job every day, but right now I wasn't one of them. If I had a job, after she left, I'd have a place where I could still feel important. At forty-five, I was insecure, and I worried whether I'd ever get back into the work force, and at the same time, wondered if I really wanted to. My mixed-up thoughts depressed me. And then I remembered something that made my day even worse. I'd offered to volunteer at Gia's school to set up for Winter Carnival. Oh, yay, I'd get to be with moms who lived to boss people around.

As I turned the car around and headed to her school, I drove past a Dunkin' Donuts. If I were going to get through the rest of this day, I needed a sugar fix, and a donut would make me so much happier right now. Besides, I was already late, so what were a few more minutes? Ten minutes later, I walked out with a powdered sugar donut in my mouth and two glazed ones in a bag.

The first thing I saw when I walked into the gym was grown women standing in groups like high school cliques. In the center of the room were the high-powered moms who were doctors and lawyers. They were handing out clipboards to the rest of us peons. When Gia started kindergarten, I'd tried to make small talk with them, but they snubbed me when they found out I didn't "work" for a living. They had no idea how hard I worked, and I resented them and felt inferior at the same time. The thought of spending the afternoon with these women made me so anxious that I was already sweating through my shirt.

My friend Heather was standing in a corner with her head bowed over her phone as if she were doing something very important. She hated these things as much as I did.

"Hey," I said.

"Shh, I've been here ten minutes and they haven't noticed me yet," she said. I don't know how they could have missed her. She had blond spiky hair and was wearing pink cowboy boots.

Amy, a five-foot-ten model-looking pediatrician, approached us. "Can you go help with the decorations?" she said to Heather, who shot me a look. Then she handed me a bunch of clipboards. "And you get to work on the silent auction." She said this as if I'd won the lottery. As Heather and I went to do our slave labor, Amy returned to her friends to sip coffee.

For the next half hour, I got to decide opening bids on luxury items. There was an aromatherapy session at a spa, which I thought about bidding on until I realized it was for a dog spa, and Theo was not the pampering type. There was also a basket filled with David Spade movies, and a surgical tummy tuck with a belly button reconstruction. Finally, something I could've used, but there was no way I was putting my real name down on that one.

I'd volunteered for three hours, but after two, I'd hit my limit. I walked over to where Heather was hanging up streamers. "You want to get out of here?" I whispered.

"They're not going to just let us leave. We have to come up with a good excuse," she whispered back.

"I'll say my mother needs me to take her to the doctor," I said.

"That's good. I'll say my kid's throwing up in the school bathroom."

Heather put down the streamers, and we loudly made our excuses to the coffee klatch. No one said anything or even acknowledged we were leaving, which was probably for the best, since when we got into the corridor, I noticed I was still holding three clipboards.

CHAPTER 2

Friday afternoons had always been my favorite time to spend with Gia. We'd see movies, get facials, or grab a late lunch. The only thing I hated doing was clothes shopping with her. It was like trying to tweeze a stray hair from your eyebrow, only to find it isn't a hair, just a drop of mascara, and now you're bleeding. Today was no different. In each store we went into, she tried on ten outfits before settling on one or two shirts. I could really have used a glass of wine. Or some chocolate. Or a glass of wine made from chocolate.

I fished my phone out of my purse and called Ellen. I had a feeling I'd be waiting for Gia for a while, but I got her voicemail. "Hi, it's me. So, I'm stuck outside the fiftieth dressing room in two hours waiting for Gia . . . okay, maybe it's the tenth, but I was hoping you were there to talk me out of running out and leaving her here, which I think is child neglect, but she's going to be eighteen soon, so I'm not sure. I was also going to ask if you had any ideas of how I could get Gia to open up to me about her boyfriend, Jason, but I guess I'll just have to go solo on this mission. Talk to you soon. Oh, and I also have a blister on the bottom of my big toe. Bye."

As I hung up, Gia came out of the dressing room, giggling uncontrollably. "This is the ugliest shirt I've ever tried on." She was wearing a peach shirt with large ruffles down the front. The ruffles moved up and down as she twirled around in front of me. I shook my head and laughed. "It looked better on the hanger," she said.

"No, it didn't," I said.

As she headed back to the dressing room, a saleswoman told her how lovely she looked in the shirt. Obviously she was on commission.

A few minutes later, Gia came out with a pile of rejects. "I'm not sure where to put these," she said. She handed me the clothes one by one, and I automatically began putting them back on hangers. Wait, what was I doing? I stopped and handed her everything back.

"You can hang them over there," I said, pointing to a clothing rack that had half a dozen things hanging from it.

Gia walked over and hurled the clothes over the bar, dropping the hangers on the floor. "Maybe I should apply to work here over the summer. It might be fun," she said. I was about to tell her that if she worked here, she'd be the one cleaning up those clothes, but I decided it would be more worth it to see her face when she found out. She walked through the store and found a rack that she'd missed the first time around.

If I was going to bring up Jason, now was the time. I needed to lead up to it very slowly. I had to be like a series of stealth missiles quietly soaring overhead ready to explode on her when she least expected it. I started by asking her how everything was in school, which seemed subtle. She gave me a noncommittal *fine* and moved on to a rack she'd already scoured, as if it were the first time she was seeing the clothes. While she was distracted, I asked how her friends were doing. Again, I got a noncommittal "fine." I hated that word, *fine*. It gave you no real information. I still used it with my mother. Gia began to ogle a shirt. I looked at the price tag and almost had a heart attack. "Do you like that?" I inquired, as if a hundred dollars for a shirt was something we did every day.

"Yeah, but it's really expensive."

"It is, but I can think about it."

"Really?" she said giddily, her eyes lighting up.

I was never going to pay that much for a T-shirt, but I wanted her to talk to me the way she used to. It was not my best parenting moment. "How's Jason?" I held my breath and waited.

She held on to the shirt as if it were a newborn baby that she was afraid would slip from her grasp. "He's good."

Good was movement. I went in for the kill. "Are you guys doing something this weekend?"

She moved to the jewelry counter, and I followed her. "Yeah, he wants to take me to see some new horror movie."

"Did you tell him horror movies give you nightmares?"

"Of course not. Besides, I don't get nightmares anymore." Three months ago, she wanted to sleep in my bed after watching *Gremlins*. She continued, "He loves horror movies. He takes all his girlfriends to see them."

"Has he had a lot of girlfriends?" I tried to sound as though whatever she said was no big deal.

"I don't know." She tried on a choker and looked at herself in the mirror. "He dated a bunch of girls from school this year."

A bunch of girls? School had only been in session five months. The only sane part of my brain was saying, *Don't lose it right now. This could be one of those teachable moments.* I told her that relationships should be give-and-take, and if he was a good guy, he'd understand if she wanted to do something else, but all she cared about was whether he liked her. Red flags were waving wildly in my head, and I wasn't doing a good job of hiding my displeasure.

"Why are you getting all crazy?" She put the choker back.

"I'm not getting crazy. It's just that right before I met your father, I dated someone who decided I needed to learn about wine to be sophisticated. Even though I was only nineteen and didn't like wine back then, I still did what he wanted. I learned about all the different types, how to harvest the grapes, and how to properly taste it. Before I found the confidence to tell him to take a hike, he dumped me for a girl he thought was more refined. They were married until he found out she was refined with every guy she met."

"Why are you telling me this?"

"To show you what can happen if you don't stand up for yourself. When I liked a boy, I did whatever they wanted. I gave up who I was, and the boys didn't respect me. I don't want you to make the same mistake."

"I get it, but I'm not you," she said.

"I know, I'm just giving you some advice."

"I don't need advice." I thought that when Gia became a teenager, I'd share my experiences with her, and she'd learn from them and avoid getting hurt the way I did. Finally, I was getting the chance, and she didn't want to hear it. "So what if I let him pick the movie. You let Dad pick the restaurants we go to," she said.

"That's not the same thing."

"Why not?"

I tried to come up with a good answer, but I didn't have one. Was I still pushing my own opinions down for a man, even if it was my husband? "Let's go." I walked toward the exit.

Gia was still holding the expensive shirt. "Wait, don't I get my shirt?"

I looked at the long line to buy one expensive shirt that I never should've said I'd think about buying to begin with. "No."

On the drive home, she was quiet. I wasn't sure if she was angrier about the shirt or my opening my mouth about Jason. When I saw Jim pulling into our driveway, I was bugged because he knew I liked to park there. Maybe I'd bring it up later.

Jim got out of the car, juggling his briefcase and an expanding folder of files. Gia jumped out of the car and ran to the front door, leaving behind all four bags from our shopping excursion. I balanced them in one arm and took Jim's jacket from him in the other while he unlocked the front door. It amazed me how many packages I could hold since I'd become a wife and mother. As soon as we walked in the house, Gia reached in the bags and took out her shirts, then ran upstairs, leaving the bags in my hands. Jim dropped his files and briefcase on the counter, opened the refrigerator, and took out an apple. I went to give him a kiss, and he was kind enough to swallow first. Sometimes when he came home, I felt like a dog waiting for its belly to be rubbed, only its owner was too tired to notice.

"How was your day?" I asked.

"Not great. I don't think anyone could be more exhausted than I am."

"I took Gia clothes shopping."

"You win," he said.

Jim and I had been together for what seemed like a lifetime. Ellen and her husband, Sam, had been determined to fix me up, because Ellen hadn't liked any of the men I'd dated. I hated blind dates, but she kept insisting this would be different, that I'd like Jim. She said if I didn't, she was going to date him, so I better go out with Jim to save her marriage. I told her I wanted to wait a couple weeks to meet him until the pimple on my chin went away. The following Saturday night I was dateless, so I went to pick up Chinese food, but the restaurant was running fifteen minutes behind on take-out orders. A man in a navy suit and a red tie walked toward the take-out counter. He moved in his suit like a man who was happier in jeans. He confessed years later that he'd been wearing a suit because all his jeans were dirty, and he didn't feel like doing laundry. As people will do when they're bored and hungry, we struck up a conversation. The next thing I knew, we were talking about more than how much we both liked kung pao chicken. I learned he was getting his PhD in psychology, and I told him about my job in publishing. He made me feel as though everything I said was interesting, something no man since my father had been able to do. When our food was finally ready, I was disappointed he hadn't asked for my phone number. When we finally got together, he told me he had kicked himself all the way home for being such an imbecile. I liked to bring it up on every anniversary.

Two weeks after talking to this man at the Chinese restaurant, I agreed to go out with Ellen and Sam's friend Jim. As I sat at the table waiting for him, I was so nervous I twirled my aquamarine ring on my pinky finger around and around until there were scratches on my skin. At least my pimple was gone. I looked up to see the hostess walking toward me, followed by the kung pao guy. Almost two decades have passed, and that man was in my kitchen looking put together and messy all at the same time. He had on a pair of khaki pants and an untucked white button-down shirt. No more suit and tie. I missed that suit and tie.

He tossed his half-eaten apple into the trash and opened the refrigerator again for turkey slices and string cheese. "It's almost dinnertime," I said.

"I'll be hungry. I'm a growing boy."

"Why don't we order Chinese? We could get some kung pao chicken."

"That stuff's too spicy, it doesn't agree with me anymore." We had become one of those boring couples where nothing was exciting. It was sad. And even sadder that I thought kung pao chicken was going to liven things up. Where was the husband who used to want to try a different ethnic food every week? Was I now going to have to settle for plain chicken and boiled potatoes?

"Did you call the plumber for the upstairs toilet?" he asked as he sifted through the mail.

"Yes, he's going to get back to me. I also went to the bank and picked up your prescription from the pharmacy."

"Thanks. Let me know when dinner's ready." A moment later I heard the buzz of the national news coming from the television.

I made grilled cheese sandwiches and tomato soup for dinner, my go-to when I didn't feel like cooking. When the three of us sat down at the table, Gia talked incessantly about some YouTube star she idolized. Jim and I barely got a word in edgewise.

As I dipped the last bite of my sandwich in my soup, I noticed our entryway was dark. Jim still hadn't changed the light bulb, even though I'd asked him three times over the last few days. I didn't want to hear another excuse about him doing it later, so after dinner I went to the garage to get a light bulb. The garage would have had the perfect amount of storage if we'd only kept the things we needed. Instead, there was junk falling out of every cabinet, and more junk on the floor. A white plastic bin in the corner was stuffed with all my high school mementos. The yearbook from my senior year was nestled between my prom picture and the tickets to the homecoming game. The yearbook had a few ripped pages from being crammed among so much other forgotten junk. I hoped the ripped pages weren't the ones with the beautiful inscription from that boy I had a crush on my senior year. I wish I could remember his name. Next to the yearbook stood a small trophy for best female performance in my high school's rendition of *Xanadu*. Where would I be today if I hadn't given up those Broadway dreams and skating lessons?

I still hadn't found the light bulbs when I saw my notebooks from when I first started working at the publishing company fresh out of college. I sat down on the dirty concrete floor and started to go through them. I found my notes from books I had liked that I had recommended to editors. I was proud that some of them had gone on to be best sellers. I'd been good at that job. I looked around at the garage that was filled with my life, the life I seemed to have lost. I wished I could go back to the publishing industry after all these years.

"Hey, what're you doing in here?" Jim asked as he came into the garage.

"Looking for a light bulb for the entry hall," I said without turning my head toward him.

"I would have changed it," he said, neither of us believing him. He pulled a light bulb out of a box on a shelf and left. After I turned out the lights, the overwhelming darkness was a relief. I didn't have to look at my old life anymore.

When I got back to the kitchen, Jim was at the table going over one of his files. I whispered, "Gia told me that Jason's taking her to a horror movie this weekend."

"Okay."

"Not okay. You know she doesn't like horror movies."

"If she really didn't want to go, she wouldn't go," he said, his nose still in his file.

"She thinks he'll stop liking her if she doesn't. That isn't the way to be in a relationship."

He opened the refrigerator, grabbed the orange juice, and took a swig out of the bottle. "She's smart and knows her own mind. She gets good grades, she's not anorexic, and she's not on drugs. She'll be fine."

"I think she's in over her head."

"I think you're overreacting."

I could feel my blood pressure rising. "What if she gets hurt?"

"Then we'll be there." He took another swig out of the orange juice bottle.

"What if she ends up pregnant?" I asked.

"What are you talking about? She's going to a horror movie, and unless it's *Rosemary's Baby*, I think we're on safe ground."

I didn't know if I was more upset by his attitude or the way he drank orange juice right out of the bottle. Maybe I was being irrational, but he should still support me. He put the juice back, leaving the refrigerator door open.

"At least she has one parent who cares," I said, slamming the refrigerator door shut with gusto.

"This is a ridiculous argument," he said calmly and walked off, leaving me fuming. Whenever he walked out on me without finishing our conversation, I turned into a three-year-old who wanted to go hit him. And now I was left standing in my kitchen, just me and the dog. Theo looked up at me, seeming to understand what a big deal this was. He was the only sensible male in this house, I thought, until he tripped on his own ears and collided into the cabinet.

CHAPTER 3

---◆---

The tapping of the rain pelting the windows got louder and louder until it reached a crescendo, and then it got softer for a few minutes. The best thing about a rainy Sunday morning was to curl up on the couch under an afghan with a cup of coffee. What could be more peaceful?

"Mom, did you wash my new shirts?" Gia yelled loudly from upstairs.

Peace and teenage girls did not go hand in hand. "They're in your closet," I yelled back. I pulled the afghan over my head and reached my arm out to put my coffee cup on the table. The phone rang, but I let it go to voicemail. It was my quiet Sunday morning, and I didn't want to hear what my mom had for dinner last night.

"Hey," Jim said, coming into the living room.

"Hey," I said from underneath the afghan. He walked out without saying another word. When you've been married as long as we have, your spouse either doesn't question why you're hiding under a blanket or doesn't notice. I'd like to think it's the former.

A loud honking came from outside. Who the heck was outside our house at eight o'clock on a Sunday morning? I threw the afghan off my head and jumped off the couch, but before I could get to the window, Gia came flying into the room. "It's for me."

"Jason could come in. We've never met him," I said, knowing her other friends would've knocked on the door.

"Not today."

"You let me meet your last boyfriend."

"I was thirteen. I needed you to drive us to the movies."

"Why are you cutting me out of your life?"

"Mom, you're being ridiculous."

"You used to tell me everything."

"There's nothing to tell. It's not like we're having sex."

"Good. I wasn't asking that, but good."

"I have to go. Jason's waiting for me." I wanted to peer at them out the window, but she would've been really mad if she saw me, so I rose up on the tips of my toes and tried to look out one of the panes of glass at the top of our front door. Damn, I was too short. I jumped up and down like a flea trying to land on a dog, but I couldn't get a good look. At least now I could skip my jumping jacks this morning.

"Did you see what Gia's doing with Jason?" Jim asked as he came down the stairs.

"No, I'm too short."

"They were making out in front of the house," he said. Why didn't I think of running upstairs and looking out that window?

Wait, now he's concerned about Gia and Jason? I was not going to give him the satisfaction of seeing me uncomfortable. "How about some breakfast?" I asked.

"It's not okay for her to do that in front of the whole neighborhood," he said.

I didn't answer. Instead, I opened the refrigerator and started throwing the entire slab of bacon into the frying pan, as if we were feeding every kid on the block. I cracked five eggs into a bowl, added milk and cheese, and began to whisk them. I was whisking them so hard that little drops of egg were spraying onto the floor. Theo was delighted as he licked up every drop.

A car peeled out, and Gia came back in the house. She sat down at the table as if it were any other Sunday morning and poured orange juice into her glass. Neither Jim nor I said anything, as neither of us wanted to get into it with her, but the quiet at the table was louder than Theo's slurping.

"What?" she asked off our stares.

"Your boyfriend just drove over here to make out with you for five minutes?" Jim said.

"So?"

"So, you shouldn't be making out in front of our house," Jim said.

"It's no big deal, Dad," Gia said, picking up a slice of bacon off the platter.

"Maggie, do you have something to add?" he asked pointedly.

"No." I didn't want to be the bad guy again.

"See, Mom agrees with me," Gia said.

Jim gave me that *why aren't you backing me up* look. I finished the eggs, and we had our usual Sunday breakfast, Jim reading the newspaper while Gia watched a bunch of cat videos on her laptop. I knew what she was watching because she described every one of them in excruciating detail. Who knew cats could be so scared of cucumbers? Before I had eaten my eggs, Gia reached for the last slice of bacon and said her friend Taylor would be picking her up in ten minutes to go to the mall. She ran off to get ready.

"Why didn't you jump in when I was talking to her?" Jim asked.

"Two days ago, you said I was overreacting, and we should let her live her own life."

"I was talking about going to a movie, not making out in front of our house."

This conversation was starting to pick up steam, and Ellen was coming over to go for a walk, so I agreed to talk to Gia later, knowing I probably wouldn't.

I had just finished cleaning up the breakfast dishes when the doorbell rang. Ellen was wearing white sweatpants, a long-sleeved white shirt, a down vest, and a fire-engine-red puffy jacket. She looked like the Stay Puft Marshmallow Man on fire. "You ready to go?" she asked.

I grabbed my jacket and gloves, and we headed out. It hadn't snowed for a few days, but it was still bitter cold, and two feet of dirty snow were piled up next to the road. The air was icy, and when I took a deep breath, my lungs hurt.

"It's so freaking cold out here. Why are you making me do this?" I asked.

"You said you wanted to start getting into shape."

"Yeah, in a warm gym." I put my hands in my pockets because even with gloves on, my fingers were stinging.

"You know I don't like to walk alone," Ellen said. "Besides, we wouldn't be shivering this much in the gym. We have to be burning twice as many calories."

We walked fast enough to get our heart rate into the fat-burning zone, but we couldn't talk and keep up that pace. Both of us were out of shape. As we slowed down, beads of sweat were settling on my skin.

"So, did you talk to Gia about the boyfriend?" Ellen asked.

"I tried, but she didn't want to hear it."

"When we first started having sex, we pulled away from our mothers too."

"She's not having sex," I said emphatically.

"Oh, I just figured."

"Are you saying she's easy?"

"Of course not, but she's seventeen. It's not that far a leap to think she's having sex."

"Well, she's not. Besides, she shouldn't be having sex. *I'm* not having sex."

"You and Jim still aren't having sex?"

"No. I think it's been only a couple of times in the last five months. When it first started, I began putting an *S* on the calendar so I could see how often we were doing it. A few weeks ago, Gia asked what the *S* was for. I told her I wanted to make sausage for dinner."

Ellen began giggling. "More like you wanted sausage *after* dinner." I started giggling too. We always found sexual innuendos hysterical. "I'm sorry, I didn't mean to joke about your situation," she said.

"That's okay. I needed to find some humor in it."

As we turned the corner to walk down the hill, a car was moving too fast and began to slide on the ice. We stopped to make sure it wasn't going to hit us. It skidded all over the street before the driver got it under control and sped off.

"What do you think is going on with Jim?" Ellen asked.

"In our marriage, there've been times he's disconnected, but we talk, and he gets better. But now when I ask what's wrong, he's vague or avoids answering. He comes home, eats dinner, watches a little television, and falls asleep. I lie there wondering if I did something wrong. I worry that after Gia leaves for college and it's just the two of us, he'll be in his own world, and I'll really feel alone."

"You're not alone, and if I hadn't lost feeling in my arms, I'd hug you." We finished our walk, and Ellen tried to give me that hug, but her arms were so frozen she couldn't lift them, so she just bumped up against me. "It'll be okay," she said.

I wished I could be that sure. She left, and as I entered the house, the heat from the living room enveloped me. I shed all my outerwear in the entryway. Jim was sitting on the living room couch typing on his laptop. "How's Ellen?" he asked.

"She's good."

"Sam and I are going to the shooting range soon."

"Oh. Okay." I couldn't hide my unhappiness.

"What's wrong?"

"Nothing. I was hoping we could do something together this afternoon."

"I'm sorry. I didn't know you were thinking that," he said.

"It's fine, forget it," I said.

"I need to blow off steam, and shooting is my way of doing that."

"Okay," I said.

"Now you have the rest of the afternoon to do whatever you want."

"I don't need more time alone."

"What I wouldn't give to get more time alone," he said.

"Wow."

"That's not what I meant." Jim picked up his keys. "I promise I'll make more of an effort, but right now I have to go." He kissed me and walked toward the door, then paused. "Did you want to come with us?" he asked hesitantly , not making eye contact.

"Not in a million years." As much as I hated being alone on a Sunday, I would've hated going to the shooting range even more.

"I'll be home right before dinner. I have to see a couple of patients later this afternoon."

"You're seeing people on a Sunday?"

"They can't come in during the week. I'm not happy about it either."

A short time later, I was walking out of the dry cleaner's loaded down with five white shirts, three ties in various shades of red, and three black suits. I was thinking how I had to find something better to do on a Sunday than go to the dry cleaner's, when I noticed a man in a New York Yankees baseball cap walking toward me. He was around thirty and attractive in a boyish, not quite adult way. As he got closer, my heart began to race. He was smiling. Was he smiling at me? Should I smile back? Why was my heart racing? What should I say if he talked to me? My heart was about to jump out of my chest when he got closer and closer and . . . walked right by me. *I'm an idiot.* Why would I ever think a man in his thirties would be smiling at me like that? I sat in my car, embarrassed by my reaction to a cute guy who didn't even notice me. I decided to go see my dad. At least he'd notice me.

When I got to Dad's room, I crept up behind his wheelchair and kissed him on the cheek. "That better be my daughter, or the nurses are getting fresh around here," he said.

"Hi, Dad." My knees cracked loudly when I bent down next to him. I was only forty-five. Would they snap off when I hit fifty? "What's with the wheelchair?" I asked. Even though it had been nine months, whenever I came here, I'd try to convince myself that he was fine and he'd go home soon. This denial had mostly worked, but seeing him in a wheelchair was not making it easy.

"I've been a little shakier today, so the nurse brought this in." He began to cough, a cough that was deep and throaty. I waited until he finished.

"Your cough sounds worse," I said.

"It comes and goes. Nothing major. The doctor said I'm fine. What're you doing here on a Sunday?"

"Jim went to the firing range with Sam."

"There has to be something more fun than coming here."

"I love seeing you," I said.

I suggested we go to the sunroom, because even though it was cold out and the clouds were blocking the sun, the room had a nicer view than my dad's. I pushed Dad over to a table and sat down on the chair next to him. The table was bare except for a white tablecloth and a flower arrangement of dried purple and pink hydrangeas in the center. A woman and her adult son were sitting at a table across from us. He was using sign language to communicate with her, so it was quiet except for the sound of Frank Sinatra singing in the background. I was never able to hear "My Way" without singing along in my head, so I was distracted until I realized that Dad had been talking to me.

"Your mother told me you don't like Gia's new boyfriend," he repeated. I could only imagine what kind of spin she'd put on this information. She probably told him I was being crazy.

"I don't know him, but from what Gia's told me, he sounds selfish."

"Isn't that the age?" he asked.

"I guess."

"I didn't like some of your choices when you were seventeen, but I had faith you'd figure it out. Gia will too."

"So, you think I'm overreacting?"

"I think you're an amazing mother, and she's lucky to have you." Hearing him say that brought tears to my eyes, which was an appropriate response, but then I started sobbing, snot running out of my nose, the whole nine yards. Nothing about that was appropriate. I put a hand over my mouth to contain the noise I was making but then realized the woman at the table couldn't hear me anyway, although her son looked at us. Their hand signals to each other suddenly got more rapid and frenetic, then stopped completely. He helped her up and took her arm, and they slowly walked out of the room.

I was trying to catch my breath, although the tears were still coming. Dad took my hand. "This isn't about Gia's boyfriend, is it?" he asked with such caring in his voice that it made me cry harder.

"I can't tell you my stupid problems when you're stuck in here."

"I'd be stuck here whether you told me your problems or not." He opened his arms for a hug, and I got up from the table and melted into him. I stayed in his warm embrace until I completely stopped crying.

When I raised my head from his chest, I saw my mascara had left a large black stain. "I can't believe I messed up your shirt," I said.

"Everyone here is half-blind, so they'll never notice." I tried to clean his shirt with my fingers, but I was only making it worse. "Don't worry about the shirt. Tell me why you're so upset."

I sat back down on the chair. "It's everything. Gia's going to be leaving for school in the fall, and I already miss her. And Jim's avoiding being alone with me. I think I bore him now."

"You're far from boring."

"I spend my days picking up his and Gia's laundry, going to the bank, and walking the dog. Why wouldn't he think I'm boring? *I'm* bored just telling you all this."

"There's more to you than what you do all day. Jim doesn't care about that stuff."

"What if he does?"

"Have you talked to him about it?"

"Yes, we've had the conversation more than once. He says he's stressed about work, and he'll try to be better, and sometimes he is, but it doesn't last. I think it's more than work, and he doesn't want to tell me." I reached in my pocket and pulled out a tissue and tried wiping my eyes, although I knew it wouldn't help much.

"All marriages go through ups and downs. Your mother and I had many," he said.

"You and Mom never fought."

"We did, behind closed doors. There were times we didn't like each other. Sometimes, I'd sleep on the couch."

"You said you had a bad back."

He shrugged. "Parents say a lot of things to their kids."

The clouds had cleared, and now the sunroom was bathed in light. "It's really nice in here," I said.

He stared out the window, then looked at me quizzically. "Why are you here on a Sunday?"

I crumpled the tissue up and looked at him. "Uh, Jim went shooting with Sam."

"Oh, yeah," he said.

He began to cough again, this time much harder. I gently patted him on the back until he stopped and got his voice back. "You'll see, things will be better soon," he said, his voice slightly hoarse. I hoped he was talking about himself as well as my marriage.

JIM

———— ·❦· ————

The gun bucks as I hit the center of the target. The feel of
the cold steel in my hands and the concentration it takes
to shoot straight are helping get my mind off my problems. It
feels good to be doing something entirely for me. Sam's talking
to me even though he should know I can't hear him through
my noise-canceling headphones. His mouth is moving, and he's
gesticulating wildly. I pull the headphones off one ear.

"What?" I ask a little too loudly because now my hearing
is off.

He pulls his headphones down around his neck. "Wow, you
don't normally shoot this well. Remind me not to make you
mad today."

"Don't worry, you aren't at the top of my list."

"And here I thought I was your best friend," Sam says.

I met Sam in middle school. I hated him at first because the
way he dressed made me think he was one of those preppy kids
from a rich family who vacationed in the Cayman Islands. The
truth was, he'd been in foster care from the time he was three,

and all his clothes came from Goodwill. My mom loved Sam because she thought he was rich, which to her meant he had more class then the other kids my age, who she was sure were all doing heroin. When my mom found out the truth about Sam, she magnanimously overlooked his previous circumstances. Even though he was only three when he went into foster care, she wondered what he'd done to get kicked out of his house.

"Want to get a drink?" I pull the wire with my target on it so I can get a better look at my prowess.

He looks at his gun as he pops out the clip. "Sure. I always need a beer after I shoot a gun."

"I wonder if cops feel that way," I say.

Sam pulls his target in and compares it to mine. A criminal would have nothing to worry about if he were the one shooting at them. "Maybe if I'd had a beer before I got here, I would've shot better," Sam says.

We leave our car in the parking lot and head across the street to a dive bar called The Dead Duck. The faded sign in the shape of a duck hanging from its beak now only says *The Dead Uck.*

Sam grabs us a couple of beers while I look for a table that might have been cleaned in this century. The moment I get the beer in my hand, I down it and order another one.

"Slow down, I promise it won't be the last beer you'll ever have."

"I'm thirsty, and it could be my last. You never know what life will throw at you." The bartender brings over another beer and I down half of that one too. After a few minutes, I pick up some darts, and from my seat at the table, I throw one at the dartboard, which is about ten feet away. My throw goes wild and sticks in the wall. Sam gets up, takes the darts out of my hand, and puts them on the table.

"Drinking and darts don't mix," he says.

"You're no fun." I slump down on my chair and pretend to pout.

"What's up? Sam asks. "You've never liked getting drunk."

I pick up another dart. "You don't like the new me?"

Before I can throw the dart, Sam takes it out of my hand, walks over to the bar, and hands all the darts to the bartender. "What's going on with you?" he asks when he gets back to the table.

"My life's a mess. I hate being a psychologist." That's the first time I've said that out loud, and it feels good.

"Since when?" he asks.

"About six months ago. I'm burned out, and I don't want to hear anyone else's problems." I let the cold, frothy beer slide down my throat. "I just want to stay here for the rest of my life and drink beer."

"And I'm guessing you haven't discussed any of this with Maggie."

"Nope. I've been hiding it."

"Not very well. Maggie told Ellen you've been distracted and disconnected."

"Great. Did she also tell her I barely ever want to have sex?" This is so embarrassing.

"No. Really? No sex? Not even a little foreplay?" I shake my head. "Hey, it's no big deal. It happens to most men. Not to me, but to a lot of others," Sam says.

"It's not that I *can't* have sex. I have no desire. I'm exhausted just getting through the day. The thought of sex seems like too much work." The bartender asks if we want another drink. I say yes, but Sam shakes his head no.

"You have to tell Maggie the truth."

"It's easier to tell her it's work stress, which is the truth. If I tell her everything, she's going to get upset and ask how we're going to pay our bills or what I'm going to do instead, and I can't take any more stress right now."

"If you think she hasn't noticed that you don't want to have sex, you're drunker than I thought."

"I know she has. It's crazy that I specialize in couples therapy, and every day I help my clients in similar situations, but I can't fix my own life. I'm a fraud." I want another beer, but I haven't had more than two beers since college, and I know if I drink another one, it will be bad. "You can't tell Ellen anything I just told you," I say to Sam, who has grabbed a handful of peanuts and shelled them faster than a monkey could. My stomach churns at the thought of how many gross drunk guys like me have had their hands in those peanuts.

"I won't." Sam throws the broken shells on the sawdust floor.

I take a peanut from the bowl and eat it. It may be gross, but at this point I'm starving. "Now, can we talk about something else?" I ask.

We spend the rest of the time talking about our fantasy football picks, wishing that Hootie and the Blowfish would get back together, and lamenting that twenty-five-year-old women consider us old.

An hour and a half later, I get behind the wheel of my car. A beautiful BMW. A car I waited years for, until we could afford it. A car that used to make me feel successful. But true success can't come from a car. My dad said success came from doing what you loved. He came home in a good mood every night. He acted as though selling insurance was the greatest job in the world, even though he didn't make much money. My dad was successful, no matter how often his Dodge Dart broke down. Why can't I feel more like him?

I still have clients to see, so it's good I'm now sober. Although I wonder if lately I'd be a better therapist buzzed. As I park in front of my office building, I notice the shutters on the windows have slats missing, the paint is chipped and faded, and the grass in front is dying. Why haven't I noticed this before? Is this building indicative of my depression? I open the door to my office, and with the lights and the heat off, the air is oppressive.

My patients are both women I've been seeing for a long time. Celia has been coming for eleven years. She's survived a divorce, a cancer scare, and a teenage son's drug addiction. She's been in a good place for the last three years and probably doesn't need me anymore, but my bank account doesn't have the guts to tell her. She curls up on my couch, adjusting a throw pillow behind her lower back. "My new husband's amazing. I've never had anyone treat me so well," she says. "I feel so lucky."

When was the last time I appreciated Maggie? When was the last time I even gave her a compliment? I doubt I make her feel lucky. My mind wanders, and I almost forget to end the session. When the light on the wall goes on, signaling my next client has arrived, I usher Celia out. I take a few moments to breathe, then I ask my next patient, Beverly, to come in. Beverly has been pushing people out of her life for years. Sometimes I wish she'd push me out of her life, because she exhausts me. I'm happy when our fifty minutes is up. I end the session four minutes early, but since the clock isn't facing her, I hope she doesn't notice. I wonder if I'm helping any of my clients or if they keep coming because the alternative of starting over with someone new is worse.

I head home and am disappointed to see Maggie's car in the driveway. I feel bad that I don't want to see her, but I don't want to see anyone. I wish I could go into the woods and live in a cabin for a few months and do nothing but regenerate.

Then maybe I'd be able to go back to my clients and not hate them all.

Maggie opens the door and greets me on the porch. "You're home earlier than I thought you'd be." She's happy to see me. I almost wish she wasn't. I follow her into the kitchen, putting my keys on the hook and my briefcase on the counter.

"How was target practice?" she asks as she pulls out various pots and pans from the cabinet underneath the oven.

"Good."

"And your patients?"

"Fine."

She takes chicken breasts and vegetables out of the refrigerator. "Can you give more than a one-word answer?"

"Sorry. I'm just thinking about the session notes I need to do before I forget everything."

"Oh," she says, disappointed. "I can call you when dinner's ready."

"Thanks." I kiss her on the cheek and walk away. I'm probably destroying my marriage with each step I take.

CHAPTER 4

———— ✦ ————

I was cleaning up the breakfast mess that was my kitchen when the usual morning phone call came in. "Hi, Mom," I said.

I let her go on for a few minutes about how excited she was that Jerry was made partner; then I lied and told her how happy I was for him and got off the phone. I wondered if she ever called him to brag about me. I was sure there was something I'd done that she could brag about.

Gia came into the kitchen to get her lunch for school. She rifled through the bag, complaining that I put in a tuna sandwich and not turkey. She also chided me for not remembering to put in Oreos the last couple of days. After her litany of complaints, she hurried out the door, forgetting to say goodbye. *Is this what I've been reduced to? A food servant? Is that even a thing?* I hated packing lunches, but next year when I had no one to pack for, I would be sad. I was going to have a constant reminder that I was a vacation mom.

I used to be an important person. My boss at the publishing house would tell me that my insights and creativity were mind-blowing. I would do research for various authors who were impressed by the intricate facts I'd find. The last time I got a compliment around here was when Gia said I did a good job braiding her hair. Not exactly what I wanted my epitaph to read.

The last time I felt significant was the day that Gia was born. I loved being the main attraction, but as soon as she popped out, it was no longer about me. I wanted it to be about me again. Our bookshelves were filled with Gia's trophies: tennis, soccer, and one just for showing up for the baseball team in second grade. I wished someone would give me a trophy for showing up. I go to every event, even when I'm sick; I have dinner on the table every night, even when I'm going out. The least I should get is a ribbon for all the laundry I do.

The phone started ringing, which was a good thing because I needed to get off this self-pitying mind merry-go-round. The caller ID told me the call was coming from my dad's room at Brooklawn.

"Hello," I said. I heard a loud thump through the receiver. "Dad?"

He had dropped the phone. There was fumbling, and I imagined his shaking arm reaching down to the ground. I hoped he didn't fall out of his chair. "Give me a second," he called out; at least I thought that was what he said, but the phone was too far away to know for sure. A nurse was talking to him, and then he was back loud and clear. "Sorry about that. I'm so clumsy."

"That's okay. Everything all right?" I asked.

"Yes, I just wanted to hear your voice. You wouldn't believe what your dumb father did this morning. I got lost coming back from the activity room. One of the nurses saw me looking at the room numbers and led me back to my room."

"You sure you're okay?" I sat down at the table and waited for him to speak. For a moment I thought he had hung up, but then he finally answered.

"I'm fine. I just got thrown that my room number went right out of my head."

"I'm younger than you, and I can't remember what I had for breakfast this morning," I said, trying to ease his worry.

"Lately, I've been feeling my age. I sometimes forget stupid stuff, but other things that happened years ago I can't get off my mind. Remember when you were eleven and fell off the bench during your piano recital?" Great, the most humiliating moment of my life he remembered.

I didn't want to talk about all the embarrassing moments of my past, and there were a lot of them. "I think that happens to everyone when they're your age," I said, which was true. Dad was still as sharp as ever.

"I guess, but don't mention it to your mother. It was really embarrassing." He asked if I had seen my mother lately, and I told him I was planning on stopping by that morning. I knew that would make him happy, and I would do anything to make him happy.

Mom and I didn't have the relationship I would have wished for, but I had come to terms with that years ago. When she gave birth to me, she had complications and was unable to hold me for four days. Dad spent hours cradling me and talking to me. I wondered if she blamed me because I never looked at her the way I looked at him. I was sure it drove a wedge between us, because I'd never been able to please her. She'd judged every decision I'd made, every action I'd taken. My father, on the other hand, had always been in my corner, never faltering in his support for me. I wondered if that bothered her also.

I didn't give up trying with my mother until after Gia was born. When Gia was two months old, my mom called and asked if I'd come over to her house and help her pick out a dress to wear to my dad's office Christmas party. I was surprised and touched that she wanted my opinion, so I used my hated breast pump, left Gia with Jim, and rushed over to my parents' house. When I got there, she'd already selected the dress and was on her way out to lunch with friends.

I pulled up to my childhood home. My parents had lived in this house for forty-seven years. Nothing about the exterior had changed, not even the paint color. From the street, I could see the window of my old room, and I pictured ten-year-old me watching the neighborhood kids playing outside on days when I was grounded.

I rang the doorbell, even though I had a key to the house. It would've felt as if I was invading her privacy if I'd used it. She opened the door with her wrists, carefully holding her hands so as to not actually touch the doorknob. This was how she was after having just handled raw chicken. Even though Dad had been in assisted living for almost a year, Mom still cooked a full meal every night. There was always enough food for five people, but except for Jerry, she didn't have people over, so God knows what she did with all those leftovers.

She was wearing her black-and-white polka-dot apron that screamed "fifties housewife," pulled taut around her large form. Mom had gained a lot of weight over the years, but she never seemed to care. Her hair, while almost completely silver, had two inches of brown at the ends. She'd stopped dying it a while ago, but it was as if those final brown strands were hoping she'd change her mind. Every time I saw her gray hair, it made me sad. It reminded me that I was getting older too, although I planned to dye my hair until I was on my deathbed.

"Come in before the flies get past you," she said, kicking the door closed and going to the sink to wash her hands. She took my coat from me and threw it on the couch. The kitchen hadn't changed much over the years either. Its warmth made me wish I still lived here, where I had no responsibilities. Then again, if I lived with my mother now, it would do me in.

The walls were still the same pale yellow as decades ago. The kitchen had been painted over the years, but she always used the same color, "Cloudless Summer." She picked the paint as much for the name as for its hue. Mom had always liked happy things. When I was young, I thought she loved yellow because it reminded her of the sun. It wasn't until I was in my twenties that I found out that yellow reminded her of the bikini that she'd worn the summer before eleventh grade. She said all the boys told her how pretty she looked in it, and from that moment on, yellow had been her favorite color, and summer her favorite season.

I hugged her, but hugging had always been awkward with us. I would wait for it to end and then feel guilty for feeling that way. I moved away from her and plopped into a chair at the kitchen table. It was the same one we'd eaten at when I was a kid. The pine had dings and scratches, and crumbs were deeply embedded within the cracks.

"I'm making a roast chicken," she said, as if I hadn't noticed.

"Sounds good."

"Do you ever make it for your family?"

"Not that often. With everyone's schedules, we can't always have dinner together."

"Family dinners are important. You need to make it a priority. I hope you're not getting takeout all the time."

"We rarely get takeout."

"Why would you ever get takeout?" She didn't wait for an answer, which was good, because I didn't have one. She put the chicken in a pan, tied its legs, and patted it down with paper towels. She treated it as if it were getting a massage, not about to be burned from the inside out. After giving the chicken a rubdown, she washed her hands again. Then she opened cabinets and began grabbing spices. Every jar in her cabinet was neatly arranged and facing forward so you could read the labels easily. She shook what looked like ten different spices over the chicken. I didn't think I had that many spices in my entire kitchen.

"You want some tea?" she asked.

"No, thanks." Having me just sit watching her cook was making her nervous. She took a mug out of the cabinet, put a tea bag in it, and put the kettle on the stove. She might have wanted tea herself, or she might have thought I should have it. What I wanted didn't always matter.

"Did your dad ask you to come over?"

"No." We both knew I was lying. The phone rang, and she pushed the button for the speaker phone. It was my father checking to see what time she was coming that afternoon. She took the phone off speaker and excused herself from the room, as if she had state secrets to share with him that I shouldn't be privy to. She was probably grilling him to see if he'd sent me to see her. I was mentally preparing what I would say when she told me how hurt and disappointed she was that my dad had forced me to come visit. I'd deny that was why I came. Then she'd say she should've known when I showed up that I didn't come there on my own accord. She'd lament how her own daughter didn't want to spend time with her. I was getting stressed; the guilt was overwhelming. These arguments were why I didn't want to come. I was an adult. I could do whatever I wanted. I suddenly realized I was arguing with myself.

She came back in the room and hung up the phone. Then she took a plastic bag out of the drawer and used it to pull the gizzard and neck out of the chicken. She wasn't talking; something wasn't right.

"Is Dad okay?" I asked.

"I think so." She picked up the salt shaker. When she didn't stop shaking it over the chicken, I got up and took it out of her hands. "He's been a little confused," she said. "He just asked me two different times when I was coming to see him today. Jerry's noticed it too."

"Dad's seventy-six, and who knows how much sleep he gets in there," I said. Mom was only one year younger, but it seemed like twenty. She had none of his health issues, tried to eat nutritious foods, and meditated every morning. The woman was going to outlive *me*.

"I hope that's it," she said as the tea kettle let out a loud whistle. She poured hot water in the mug and handed it to me. I guess I was having tea. "You never did say why you came by today," she said as she put the chicken in the oven. "What did you do?"

"Why do you think I did something?"

"Because you don't usually show up here without calling first."

I'd never shared any of my problems with her, and I don't know what propelled me to do it now. "Have you ever wondered if you made the right choices in your life?" I asked. "Like if you should've gone back to work instead of staying home with me and Jerry?"

"Sometimes. There were days I was so bored, and you two would make me crazy. You'd both argue about everything, to the point I felt like I was in Congress." She reached for a plate of cookies on the counter. Even though I saw her wash her hands after she touched the chicken's gizzard and neck, when she picked up a cookie and offered it to me, I was repelled. But not so repelled that I wasn't going to eat one of her oatmeal chocolate chip cookies. I stuffed it in my mouth. "Are you regretting your decision to give up your career and stay home with Gia?"

"No, but now that she's older, she doesn't need me the same way anymore."

"Yeah, it's in the job description. At some point, there's cutbacks, and you get demoted."

"That's funny, Mom. You were never funny when we were kids."

"You develop a sense of humor after your kids are gone. You'll see, next year after Gia leaves, you'll be doing stand-up comedy." I laughed.

She took a cookie and sat down at the table. "So, are you thinking of going back to work?"

"Maybe."

"I used to wish I'd gone back, but life kept getting in the way."

She understood what I was trying to say; maybe we were more alike than I thought. Had I been misjudging her all this time? I looked at her with fresh eyes. Here was a woman making roast chicken, something she never used to make because my father hated it. I wondered how many other things she'd given up for him. I felt this wave of connection with her, but as I reached out to put my hand on hers, she ran out of the room. A moment later she came back with a hairbrush and a mirror. She started to brush my hair from one side of my head to the other.

"What're you doing?" I asked.

"You would look much better with your hair parted on the other side." She surveyed my head as if she were assessing a dent in her car. "Here, look," she said, holding up the mirror.

"I like my hair the way it is," I said, shaking my head so my hair would fall back in place.

"But the other way, you have more volume." Mom said annoyed that I wasn't embracing her suggestion.

Same mother I was still not good enough for. I got my coat from the couch. "I need to get going," I said, heading toward the door. This was the first time I'd been happy to go for my weekly dry cleaning.

"Will you come by again soon?" she asked.

"Sure," I said, but I knew it might be a while. I didn't need a new hairstyle.

CHAPTER 5

—◦—

As I poured myself some coffee, I noticed there wasn't a dirty bowl of leftover cereal and milk on the counter. A clean kitchen meant either Gia hadn't eaten breakfast, or leprechauns had come in and cleaned up when I was in the shower. I chose to believe the latter because if she skipped breakfast and was starving until lunch, it would mean I was a bad mother. I'd been trying to get her to make her own breakfast, because at seventeen my mom made me sew my own clothes. Well, not really, but she did refuse to make me breakfast, saying I'd never grow up if she kept catering to me. Was I hurting Gia by continuing to pour Frosted Flakes into a bowl? Jim came in from outside, a dusting of snow from his jacket scattering on the floor.

"Where were you?" I asked.

"Warming up my car."

I brushed the rest of the snow off his shoulder. "Are you going to warm me up next?" I asked flirtatiously. I was trying to be more understanding about his stress.

He was staring at his phone. "I'm sorry, what did you say?"

"I said, I hope you have a good day." My understanding nature was gone.

"Thanks. You too." He picked up his briefcase and left. I was alone in my house again, not as if that was different from any other day. I grabbed Theo's leash and took him for a walk. I was planning on going once around the block, but I ended up walking for forty-five minutes. Poor Theo, he looked as if he should be on life support after we got home. Basset hounds and long walks did not mix.

As Theo collapsed on the kitchen floor, I put my purple latex gloves on and washed last night's dirty dishes. As I started on the iron skillet, the phone rang. Someone was calling me. Someone who would take me away from this drudgery. I'd even take a telemarketer right now. I took off my gloves and noticed the caller ID said "private caller." I answered anyway. It was my brother, Jerry. Why couldn't it have been a telemarketer?

I had barely said hello when he said, "I just got off the phone with Mom, and she said you were mad at her."

Since I'd moved out of her house, every time my mother thought I was upset with her, she'd have my brother call me. "I'm not mad at Mom." I turned the faucet on in the sink and put my gloves back on. I balanced the phone on my shoulder but secretly hoped it would fall into the hot running water.

"She said you were having a nice time together, and then you suddenly left."

I picked up a scouring pad and scrubbed the skillet as if it needed to be rid of evil. "It wasn't sudden. I'd been there a while."

"Well, whatever happened, it upset her. Can you try to be more sensitive? Try to be like you are with Dad." I hated when he treated me like a younger sibling. I had six years on this guy.

I had torn a hole in one of the gloves from all my scrubbing, and hot water was coming through and scalding my index finger. It hurt, but not as much as this conversation. "I'm very sensitive with her."

"You're not. Even Jim agrees with me."

Jim? My Jim? Jim wouldn't say that to my brother. At least, I didn't think he would. Then again, lately I wasn't sure I knew my husband. "When did you talk to Jim?"

"When we had lunch last week. Didn't he tell you?"

"Of course he told me." Why didn't he tell me? Why would Jim go out with Jerry when he knew we didn't get along? "I need to go," I said and hung up before he had a chance to say anything else.

My anger made me want to clean more, so I picked up the sponge and was beginning to move it across the granite counter when my elbow knocked a bottle of cinnamon onto the floor. The top wasn't screwed on, because why would anyone in my family think to screw the top back on? I pulled out a dustpan and brush, and as I kneeled on the floor and began sweeping the mess up, cinnamon dust invaded my nose and throat. I began to cough uncontrollably. Would someone find me if I collapsed on the floor from a spice-induced death? At least then I wouldn't have to deal with my husband having secret meetings with my brother, or my daughter running off to marry a boy I didn't like. That last one was an exaggeration, but I was possibly dying, so I was allowed to exaggerate.

I dialed Jim's number. "Hey," he said when he answered.

"Did you have lunch with Jerry last week?"

"Not exactly. I was at the deli, and he came in. He asked if he could sit with me."

"And you said yes?"

"What was I supposed to say?"

"How about, I can't sit with you because you're a terrible ogre who gives my wife shit." Even through the phone I could tell he was rolling his eyes at me.

"I don't know why I didn't think to say that," he said.

"Jerry said you agreed with him that when it comes to my mom, I'm insensitive."

"*He* said that. All *I* said was that you two had a complicated relationship."

"Why didn't you tell me you saw him?"

"Because I didn't want to fight about it. Kind of like we're doing now."

He was right. Why was I starting a fight when we were already not connecting? So what did I ask? "Is there anything else you're keeping from me?" I should've kept my mouth shut, but I sometimes blurted out what I was thinking.

"Did you call just to yell at me?" Jim asked.

"Of course not." I had, but I was starting to feel bad. "I called to see if you wanted tacos for dinner. I got all the ingredients at the market yesterday."

"Not really. How about that shrimp thing you make with the garlic and lemon?"

"We don't have any shrimp."

"Oh."

"I guess I could go back to the market," I said, trying to sound as unhappy as I could so he would tell me not to.

"Great, thanks," he said.

"Fine, I'll go back on the condition that you don't have lunch with my brother again."

"Got it. I'll talk to you later. Bye." He hung up, and I realized I was doing the very thing I worried Gia was doing. I was bowing to what my man wanted.

I had my keys in my hand and was heading out the door when the phone rang again. When I saw it was my mom, I let it go to voicemail.

Since it was Tuesday, I planned to go see my dad, and then I'd get a workout in before going back to the market. When I got to Dad's room, he was sitting in bed watching television. There was an oxygen machine next to him with a long tube running under his nose. He'd never needed oxygen before. Panic bubbled inside me as I thought about what would happen if he stopped breathing. How would I survive losing him? I pushed down my inclination to go to a dark place because it was adding to my overactive anxiety. I kissed him on the cheek and muted the football game he was watching. He greeted me happily, and even with his labored breathing, his eyes had their usual sparkle.

"I've never seen you using one of these machines before," I said, pointing to the black rectangle next to him that looked like a paper shredder. The whooshing coming from it wasn't loud, but it invaded my brain.

"It's nothing. I just had a little trouble breathing last night. You know how nurses are: you have a little issue, and they make you use a stupid machine."

The skin on his face was ashen, so it didn't look like a little issue. I knew he wasn't going to say much more though. "How's the football game? Who's playing?" I asked.

He stared at the television. "Uh, the Eagles and the Vikings?"

I looked at the television. "You mean the Seahawks and the Giants?"

"Oh, yeah." How could he not know who was playing, especially since the Giants were his favorite team. Could the lack of oxygen be making things foggier? He asked when Gia's history project was going to be done. He'd helped her with some of the research. I told her she had to finish by tonight. He closed his eyes.

"Are you tired?" I asked.

"No, I'm fine." He opened his eyes and stared at the television a moment. "So, when will Gia finish her . . . her thing?" he asked again.

"Her project?" I asked. He nodded. "Tonight." I leaned down and kissed him on the cheek. "Dad, you rest." He was relieved and closed his eyes again. Within moments he was breathing in a steady rhythm along with the oxygen machine. He was so peaceful. I watched him sleep the way I used to watch Gia. When I turned away from his bed to leave, he began yelling and thrashing in the bed so forcefully that he knocked his pillow on the floor. I was alarmed but didn't think I should wake him. I picked up the pillow and waited for him to be calm again, but just as I was about to put the pillow under his head, his arms began flailing so wildly that I was afraid if I got too close, he'd accidentally hit me. I placed the pillow on a chair and wandered out, feeling uneasy.

I found Julia near the nurses' station. "Is my father on any new medications? He seems more forgetful, and he was just having some crazy dream."

"He's not on any new meds, and the staff has been keeping an eye on him. He's been having a rough time, especially when he sleeps." It made my stomach lurch to hear the concern in her voice. "I'll keep you posted," she said.

I thanked her and was on my way out when she asked if I could assist a few of the residents before I left. Ever since I'd helped that one day, she'd ask me to do things for the residents. She'd flatter me and go on and on about how indispensable I was, but I enjoyed helping because it made me feel useful, and I wanted to check on my dad again later anyway. Besides, flattery always worked on me.

I spent an hour reading a few chapters of *The Bridge over the River Kwai* to two men, helping a woman write an email to her daughter, and walking three different people down to the dining room for lunch. I realized I hadn't seen Dad at any of his usual spots. He hadn't been in the activity room or movie time or even the dining room for lunch. I went back to his room to check on him, and he was still asleep. What kind of life was that for a man who used to love to golf and paint and play poker? I silently said goodbye and headed to my car.

I put my seatbelt on and turned the heater up to seventy-eight. My car's thermostat read thirty-six, and I was not going to be able to drive until my hands warmed up. As I held my hands over the vents to feel the warmth, my phone vibrated. It was my mother calling again. Since I had ignored her previous voicemail, I knew I should answer it.

"Did you get my message?" she said, not bothering to say hello. "You didn't call me back."

"I didn't have a chance." I was irritated by her tone.

"Have you seen your father today?"

"I just came from there."

"Did you notice how confused he was? Jerry asked the doctor to look into why."

"He's a little more confused, but I don't think the doctor needs to do anything yet." I didn't want to deal with her worries when I was trying to push my own down.

"I need to know if there's something wrong," she said.

Maybe Jerry was right. Maybe I wasn't sensitive enough when it came to my mother. Either way, I wanted to get off the phone. "I have to go, Mom. Gia's walking toward me." Gia was still at school, but she didn't need to know that. "Hi, Gia, I'm right here," I called out loudly. "Bye, Mom." I hung up before she could ask to speak to my daughter.

I drove to the gym. As tired as I was, exercising would give me some much-needed endorphins, and I'd eaten a family-size bag of barbecue potato chips today. It was either work out or force myself to throw up, and throwing up was gross. I put all my things in a locker except for my towel and went to find an open treadmill. When I got on the treadmill, I started moving slowly and then increased my speed to a fast walk. I hated jogging, so a fast walk was all I would do. I pushed the incline button and went up to level three but quickly brought it back down because my knees instantly bothered me.

A man was walking toward me, bouncing in his shoes like a four-year-old who was excited to be going somewhere fun. As he got closer, he smiled, and I realized it was the Yankees cap guy I'd seen the other day. He was even cuter today than I remembered. Why did I keep running into him? Maybe he *had* been smiling at me. Why had he smiled at me?

He was wearing shorts and a T-shirt with Captain America fighting some villain I'd never heard of. He had a huge tattoo on his arm with an eagle, an American flag, and a heart interwoven. It was red, white, and blue, with the inscription "Death Before Dishonor." I'd never been into tattoos before, but this one accentuated the muscles on his arm. I noticed he had a string hanging off the sleeve of his T-shirt. I wondered if I should tell him, but just thinking about talking to him made me nervous, so instead I stared at the television screen in front of me. I hoped he hadn't noticed me blushing.

The next thing I knew, the hot guy was on the treadmill next to me. Out of all the empty treadmills, he got on the one closest to me? Oh God, did I say out loud how hot he was? He dropped his towel on the floor, so close to mine they were almost touching. Then he put on earphones and began jogging. The next thing I knew, my legs had started jogging also. As he jogged faster, I jogged faster. I hadn't jogged since I'd fainted after only one lap in seventh grade. I was completely out of breath, but I was not going to show it. I wanted to look fit. He began sprinting. Holy crap, now I was sprinting. Why couldn't he stay at jogging? I was about to hyperventilate and die when I lost my footing and tripped and fell off the treadmill. I must've startled him because then he lost his footing and fell off too. He was doubled over laughing, and I was trying to sound as if I wasn't gasping for air.

"You okay?" he asked. He was breathing without a hint of exhaustion.

"I think so." I pulled my tank top down, making sure nothing was showing that shouldn't be. This cute thirty-something-year-old man was talking to me. Did he know I had to be way over ten years older than him?

He got up and then reached his hand out to help me stand. "I just joined this gym and have been forcing myself to run on the treadmill for forty-five minutes a day," he said. "I'm punishing myself for something I did in a past life."

"Then I must've done something criminal because I'm usually on this machine more than that," I said, yelling over the sound of our running treadmills. I wasn't going to tell him I hadn't been to the gym in months. He reached around me to turn my treadmill off. I worried he'd notice I was ogling him, so I forced my gaze up and looked into his big green eyes. How long could you stare into someone's eyes without looking creepy? I was running out of other places to look.

He rested his arm on the treadmill. His biceps were the size of grapefruits, and the muscles in his thighs were toned and defined. "With the lousy day I've been having, I'm happy I didn't just break something. I'm Michael." He bent over in an adorable, exaggerated bow.

"Maggie," I said and tried to curtsy, which didn't come off as cute as I wanted it to. Even though I didn't normally have conversations with strange men, the warmth in his voice made me want to talk to him more. "Why are you having such a bad day?" I asked. *My* day was now so much better.

He told me he was a writer, and an article he'd written was supposed to be in a magazine, but today he found out the magazine was folding. He worked freelance writing, mostly travel pieces, profiles of people, and human-interest stories. He sometimes taught writing classes at the community college, and someday he wanted to write a book. As the treadmills around us filled up, I shared with him how I used to be in publishing, and we discussed his writing process and what I used to look for as a senior editor. When he asked me what I did now, I faltered. How could I tell him about my boring life? I started out with the truth, about how I had a daughter and I volunteered at her school. Then I told him that I often visited my father at his senior living facility. As I heard myself talking, I realized that none of this was interesting, so I started making things up.

"I'm a freelance photographer, I rescue animals from bad situations, and I set up fundraisers for charities." I made myself sound like a saint . . . a saint who lied through her teeth.

He was impressed. "Wow, it's amazing you can still get in a workout."

Even though he was standing so close to me, my nerves had subsided. I hated to admit it, but this was fun. Great, now I was one of those women who'd get giddy when a cute guy talked to her. I hated those women; they were so obvious. I wondered if he talked to every woman in here or if I was special. I looked down and realized I'd left my wedding ring in my locker. Was he trying to pick me up? Did he think I was single? Just in case, I thought I should cut it short.

I made a show of looking at my watch. "I better go. I need to take my dog to the vet."

He leaned down and picked up his towel. "I work out most days around this time. Hopefully we'll meet again, Maggie." He exaggerated my name, or at least that's how I heard it.

"I look forward to it, Michael." I tried to exaggerate his name, but I sounded more like a dolt than I usually did. I made a promise to myself that I was going to get to the gym as often as I could, and it had nothing to do with this guy. Well, it did, but I needed to get in shape too. As I crossed to the locker room, I took a quick look over my shoulder. He'd finally noticed that string hanging from the hem of his sleeve and was biting it off.

DAD

———◈———

Maggie usually comes on Tuesdays, so when she came in my room on a Thursday, I was surprised to see her. I think she came back to check up on me. My breakfast tray is next to the bed. I left most of the scrambled eggs and half the toast. Lately, I'm not very hungry.

"Dad, you didn't eat much." She pulls up a chair next to me. I love when she visits. She asks me how I am, and I tell her I'm fine and ask what's new with her.

"I went to see Mom," she says and takes the piece of toast, spreads orange marmalade on it, and hands it to me. I shake my head, so she takes a bite.

"She told me you stopped by. How was it?" I ask.

"Fine." I can tell she's lying. She takes a bite of the eggs, then makes a face and spits them into a napkin.

"I wish you'd give her more of a chance."

"She doesn't like me."

"That's not true. She loves you." Maggie rolls her eyes. Over the years I've tried to bridge the relationship between Maggie and Dorothy, but it hasn't worked out well. From the beginning,

Maggie and I were so much alike that I doted on her. Then when Maggie was five, I made the mistake of coming home from a business trip with a turquoise ring for her and nothing for Dorothy. Dorothy said she understood and didn't need anything, but the competition between the two of them for my attention got worse until Jerry was born. After that Dorothy gravitated toward him, and Maggie felt abandoned by her. I wish I could go back and do things differently.

"I took your advice, and I switched from a PC to a Mac," she says. "You were right. It wasn't that hard to make the change."

"What's a Mac?" I ask, having no idea what she's talking about.

"An Apple?" she says, as if I'm crazy.

"Like the fruit?" I ask.

"Are you playing with me?" She laughs. I look at her blankly, my brain foggy. She stops laughing. "Are you okay?" she asks in a worried tone.

"Of course, an Apple computer, right?" She nods. "Stop worrying. It was just one of those senior moments." I try to make light of it, but I'm wondering if something's wrong with me. To calm her down, I say, "It's this place. You put someone around old people, and they act like one."

Maggie isn't convinced, and I don't like that I'm upsetting her. I tell her that I'm tired, even though I woke up not long ago. Then I close my eyes and breathe as if I'm falling asleep. I try not to move at all, until finally she kisses me and leaves. I wait a moment to ensure that she's gone, then I open my eyes and push the power button on the remote that turns the television on.

Ten minutes later, Julia comes in to check on me. "Mr. Rubin, how're you doing?"

"I'm fine."

"You sure?"

"Maggie told you what happened, didn't she?"

"Yes, she's a little worried about you." She straightens me in the wheelchair because I'm slouching again.

"It was just a momentary lapse. I could use a glass of water though."

"Of course." She pours me a glass and holds it up so I can drink out of the straw. "Let me know if you need anything else," she says.

"Please tell Maggie not to worry about me. I was probably dehydrated." I watch the nurse leave, and all I can think is *What a sweet woman. She's always good to me.* I only wish I could remember her name.

CHAPTER 6

———◆———

I called Ellen to see if she was free to meet for lunch. We decided I'd come to her office, my old publishing firm, and then we'd figure out where to go. My old office was in Stamford, about thirty minutes away, but it felt like a different universe. It was a big city, unlike our little suburb.

I hadn't been back to that office in years, because the last time, I came home depressed. My job used to be my identity, but when Gia was born, my identity became her mother. I fantasized about where I'd be if I hadn't left publishing. Would I be an executive editor by now? Or maybe I would've started my own publishing company. That used to be my ultimate dream. A dream where I wouldn't have driven a minivan. A dream where I would've gotten my hair colored when I first saw a strand of gray, not when I needed to wear a hat. A dream where Jim didn't find me boring.

Everyone at my old job used to say I was a hard worker and a fast learner. I moved from editorial assistant to acquisitions editor quickly, and then before I left, I'd made it all the way up to senior editor. I sat down at the computer and searched publishing companies to look at their job listings. Each one seemed to want more qualifications than I had. How would I compete now with people half my age who knew software that didn't exist the last time I worked? And was it realistic to think I could get back into publishing after seventeen years? Would anyone want to hire a middle-aged woman?

I felt my blood pressure rising, so I leaned down and rubbed Theo's belly, which made both of us feel better, although he was the only one who howled. Then I went on Linkedin and looked up some old contacts, but everyone I used to work with had moved to New York publishing houses, although my former boss, Lorna, still worked at my old firm. Maybe when I went to see Ellen today, she'd remember how smart and talented I was and offer me a job. And of course, she'd give me the summers off to spend with Gia when she came home from college.

As I dreamed the impossible dream, I rifled through my closet for something to wear that would make me look professional and hide my squishy belly. Everything I owned was either jeans and T-shirts or five years out of date. After a few minutes, my bed was piled with my rejects. Finally, I settled on a black skirt because no black skirt had ever gone out of style. I pulled out my Spanx high-waist control briefs and wriggled my way into them. I liked how I looked but felt like a cigarette that had been pushed back into a full pack. Now I needed a shirt because I probably wouldn't be taken seriously in just a bra and skirt. I had six silk blouses, none of which screamed *hip career woman*. So I did the only thing any middle-aged mom would do; I raided my daughter's closet. It may have been a little young for me, and a little tight, but Gia's violet lace shirt blew my silk blouses out of the water.

I was running late, but I couldn't leave without applying makeup that would take ten years off me. That may have been a lot to ask of Estée Lauder. I tried to do a smokey eye but ended

up wiping the whole thing off. I was not the smokey eye kind
of girl. Black eyeliner and champagne eye shadow would have
to do. I took a last look in the mirror and wondered who that
older and more worn woman was looking back at me. Note to
self: stop looking in mirrors.

As I drove to Ellen's office, a cloudburst and a sudden torrent
of rain hit my car. Thank goodness I had an umbrella, although
I was regretting that I'd thrown it in the trunk. As I got out of
the car, I was comforted by the busy city noises. A car alarm, an
ambulance and a jackhammer were music to my ears. The smell
of Polish sausage and churros from the cart on the street made
my mouth water. It heartened me to see the cart was still there.
When I worked here, I didn't want to take lunch because something was always going on, so I'd run out and grab a sausage and
chips. Then I'd go back to my desk and put a napkin on my lap
to protect my clothes from the grease that would trickle down
my chin after that first bite. Sometimes the grease missed the
napkin and ended up on someone's prize manuscript. I missed
those days.

I was approaching the revolving doors of the building and
trying to avoid the puddles when a woman in red high-heel
pumps pushed past me. I looked down at my shoes. I never
wore high heels anymore; I wore "mom" wedges. Wedges I was
instantly regretting, because what kind of idiot wore open-toe
shoes when there was a chance of rain? An idiot who wanted to
be taller than she was.

I shook out my umbrella and got in the elevator and exited
on the eighteenth floor at Shier and Boggs publishing house.
The paint on the walls had gone from white to oatmeal, the
couches were now chenille as opposed to leather, and the maple

floors had been stained a lighter color. Everything was different except the iron umbrella stand next to the reception desk. It was the exact same one as when I'd worked here. The one I used when my future was in front of me. That ugly umbrella stand was a symbol of all the things I could've been. As I dropped my umbrella in, I found myself caressing the stand gently. I noticed the receptionist staring at me. Did she recognize me? Was I supposed to recognize her? Did she think I was some weirdo with an umbrella stand fetish?

"Who are you here to see?" she asked.

Before I could answer, Ellen came flying through the glass door. "She's with me, Miranda," she said. Ellen walked me toward her office. "You look great. Is that a new shirt?" she asked, touching the lace on Gia's shirt.

"No, I've had it forever," I lied. Everything about her office screamed *success*. It was large with windows all around and a view of Columbus Park. There were awards for various books that the company had published in my absence. I wanted one of those awards. "Oh my God, this could've been me," I said and started to cry. I was surprised and embarrassed by my reaction, and now my makeup was starting to run. Thank God I hadn't done a smokey eye. "Your office is beautiful," I said.

Ellen handed me a tissue, and I dabbed at my eyes under my lower lashes the way those women on Dr. Phil did. "I sent you pictures," she said.

"I know, but pictures don't do it justice. Also, seeing it has reminded me what I gave up all those years ago." Ellen nodded; she always understood me. "But that doesn't mean I'm not happy for your successes," I said.

"Said the woman who burst into tears."

I smiled and finished wiping my eyes; then I threw the tissues in the trash behind her desk.

Lorna rushed into Ellen's office with her arms outstretched. She'd been my mentor and was always just a step below God to me. She was now the associate publisher. She wore a blue flowered peasant dress with brown suede boots. At sixty-three most women would look ridiculous, but on Lorna it was perfect. "I heard you were here." She enveloped me in a hug. "It's been ages."

"I know, I've really missed you," I said.

"Are you crying?" she asked.

"No, I just got an eyelash in my eye," I said, willing my eyes to dry up.

She peppered me with questions. "How's everything with you? How's Gia? How old is she now?" she asked in rapid succession and then sat down in Ellen's desk chair.

"All fine. Gia's good, applying to colleges."

"Your daughter's old enough to go to college? I can't believe it's been that long since we all worked together." She leaned back and put her feet up on Ellen's desk. "And what's even crazier is after all these years, *I'm* still working here."

"I'm still here too," Ellen said, but neither Lorna nor I responded.

"That's because you're the best publisher in town, Lorna," I said.

"No, I'm not," Lorna said without conviction.

"Can I have my chair back?" Ellen said to Lorna. Lorna removed her feet from Ellen's desk and stood up. "Maggie, you were always my favorite editor." I smiled.

"I can't believe how much I miss this place," I said. "I don't know why I left to begin with."

"Because you were nine months pregnant and couldn't fit behind your desk," Lorna said facetiously.

"But I'm not pregnant anymore," I said, hinting.

"You're lucky you left when you did. Things have changed so much," Lorna said. "Now the senior editors need to be available twenty-four hours a day. Because of social media, there's always something that needs to be taken care of. Thank God Ellen didn't have kids. She'd never see them."

"Well, my kid's almost grown and out the door," I said, hoping she'd offer me a job.

Lorna wasn't getting my hints, or she didn't want to acknowledge them. She looked at the clock on Ellen's desk. "I'm late for a meeting. Maggie, let's grab lunch sometime soon. I'd love to hear what you're up to." She gave me another one of her huge hugs and ran out with the same force with which she had entered. And with Lorna's exit, my unrealistic fantasy burst into a hundred pieces.

"I wish I could hire you," Ellen said tentatively.

"What? Oh, thanks, but I wasn't really looking for a job."

"Don't bullshit me, I'm your best friend," Ellen said. She picked up her purse, and we headed out to lunch with me wishing I could've gone home to sulk.

After Ellen went back to her office, I drove home to find Jim sitting on the couch watching one of those true crime shows. He was addicted. He'd watched so many of them that if he killed me, no one would ever find my body. "What are you doing home?" I asked.

He paused the TV. "A bunch of my patients canceled today. Where were you?"

"I went to see Ellen at her office, and I ran into Lorna. She said she wants to have lunch soon." When Jim didn't say anything, I went on. "It could be about a job." It wasn't what she said, but I wanted to gauge his reaction to me going back to work.

"Is that something you're thinking about?" he asked.

"I don't know, maybe. When Gia leaves for college, it might be something I'd enjoy doing."

"Except when you worked there, you didn't seem like you were having any fun. You used to complain about all those meetings where no one liked your contributions. And how one of the partners sometimes took credit for the books you suggested they publish."

"I didn't say I was definitely going back to publishing. I just said she might want to talk to me about it." He was making me defensive.

"Okay," Jim said and hit play on the DVR. A judge pronounced some guy guilty, and Jim jumped up and screamed, "Yes!" as if he had a stake in the case.

While Jim was doing his happy dance, the front door opened and closed quietly. Gia came in silently, as if she were trying to sneak in, which was funny because it wasn't the middle of the night. She'd started to walk upstairs when she noticed me.

"Is that my shirt?" she asked. I got so busy talking to Jim I forgot to change. I was caught, but I'd paid for the shirt, so in a roundabout way it was mine.

"I found it in my closet. I thought it was mine," I said.

"I hope you didn't stretch it out. I want to wear it when I go out with Jason this weekend." She grabbed a soda from the refrigerator and walked out. Stretch it out? I'm the same size I was when I was her age. I looked down at my body. Well, maybe not the same size, but a close fifteen pounds to it.

"She's just trying to get under your skin," Jim said. "Teenage girls have issues with their moms."

"Thank you, Sigmund Freud."

"Anytime." He playfully grabbed my butt. It startled me because he hadn't done anything that affectionate in a while.

When Gia was little, he'd come up behind me when I was washing dishes. He'd start kissing my neck, and then very quickly we'd put Gia in front of Disney's *Beauty and the Beast*, lock the bathroom door, and have sex for as long as it took the candlestick to sing "Be Our Guest." Thank God it was one of the longest numbers in the movie.

I sat down next to him on the couch. "Hey, you want to watch that Julia Roberts movie we taped?" I asked.

"Not really. You can watch my show though."

Once again, I was the one in our relationship expected to cave in, even if it was just over watching some stupid television show. What kind of example was I setting for my daughter? Jim was so engrossed in his show that it didn't matter whether I was there or not. I started thinking about Michael from the gym. I deserved more attention than the man on the couch wanted to give me. The house phone rang. I crossed to the desk to look at the caller ID.

"Hi, Dad," I said.

"Dorothy?" he asked. "Aren't you coming here this afternoon?"

"No, Dad, it's not Mom. It's Maggie." Jim muted his show when he heard the distress in my voice.

"No, Maggie was here the other day. Please come and see me, Dorothy. I miss you." He hung up.

"What's going on?" Jim asked.

"I told you he's been a little confused lately, but not like this."

"You should call your mom."

Mom answered before the first ring ended. I filled her in on what happened, and her response only made me feel worse. "I tried to tell you he's not doing well, but you didn't want to hear it." She was frustrated with me. "It can't be just age," she said. "He's been forgetting simple words, asking the same questions over and over, and tuning out while we're having a conversation."

"You sound like you've already decided it's dire. He's on lots of meds for his Parkinson's. I've heard one of the main reasons the elderly get confused is because one of their meds interacts badly with another." I was praying that was the case, because it would explain everything and have an easy fix. It was getting harder to live in my denial.

"Whatever it is, we need answers." Dad's doctor was out of town, and Dad refused to meet with any of the other doctors. He got very upset if one even approached him. He'd always been an easygoing man, so that was completely out of character for him. It also meant we had to wait until his doctor got back from Paris. "I'm going to call your dad back," she said and hung up.

As I was relaying to Jim what my mother said, Gia came back in the room. We stopped talking because I didn't want her to know about her grandfather until I had more information.

"Were you talking about me?" she asked.

"No," Jim said.

"You stopped talking as soon as I walked in."

"We were talking about something important, but it wasn't about you," Jim said.

"Yeah, sure, right." She stormed out of the room.

Jim looked weary. I patted him on the arm. "It's not your fault. Teenage girls have issues with their fathers too."

CHAPTER 7

———◆———

"Your breakfast's been sitting here for ten minutes," I yelled out to Gia.

"I was studying for a test," she said, coming into the kitchen balancing her open history book, with her notes on top.

One of the pages fell on the floor, and I picked it up. "You'd be ready for the test if you weren't always on Instagram."

She took the page out of my hands. "I wasn't on Instagram. I was going over the study guide, and I'm ready. What's your problem?" Gia was never home anymore. She was always out with her friends or Jason. Of course, I'd done the same thing at her age, but I still missed her.

"It's too early for so much yelling," Jim said, walking into the room.

"Tell that to Mom."

"I wasn't yelling," I said. Jim knew by the way I narrowed my eyes and glared at him, that he shouldn't say another word, but I knew what he was thinking: Why are you yelling at our daughter who's going to be leaving soon? Don't you want to have a good relationship with her when she goes? Don't you want her to miss you? *Okay, Jim, you're right. You made your point*, I screamed in my head, even though he hadn't said a word. "I'm sorry I was yelling," I said to Gia. "Good luck on your test."

"Thank you." She picked up her backpack and left without eating anything. I guess that was my punishment.

I asked Jim how work was going. He gave me his stock answer that things were the same. "Do you want to talk about it?" I asked. He said not really, then kissed me and left.

I sat down next to Theo, who was curled up in his bed in the corner. At least he never talked back to me. He looked peaceful until I interrupted him by laying my head on his warm body. He tried to get up, but my head was too heavy for him to move. I could have stayed there all day, but it wouldn't take away my frustration at Gia and Jim or my anxiety over my dad, and at some point, Theo was going to have to pee.

I needed to do something productive, or at least something that would distract me. I sat down at the desk and opened the mail. I hated paying bills, but that would be productive. After I watched our money fly out the window, I took Theo for a walk, and then I had coffee with my friend Heather, and we bitched about our lives. At noon I was hungry, but I wanted to try to see Michael rather than eat, and since he had said he went to the gym most days at this time, I thought I'd have a good chance of running into him. And if not, I'd go home and stuff my face.

For some reason the gym was more crowded than usual. The main area, which had all the weight machines, was surrounded by smaller rooms where they held classes like yoga, Pilates, and spin. The treadmills and ellipticals were lined up along the walls facing mirrors. Not only could you watch yourself while you ran or climbed stairs, but you had a perfect view of anyone at the weight machines. I slipped a scrunchy off my wrist and put my hair up in a ponytail, then I got on a treadmill so I could watch who came in. After I'd been walking fast for twenty minutes and thinking up excuses so I could stop, Michael came out of the room where they teach the spin classes. He was wiping his brow, and his hair was sticking straight up. Even sweaty he looked good. He saw me, waved, and headed over. I slowed down so I could talk without panting.

"I thought you said you hated the treadmill," he said.

"I do, but I need some cardio, and I'm afraid of the elliptical machine."

"Me too. I'm not coordinated enough to attempt it. Are you just getting here or finishing up?" he asked.

"Just finishing up." I hit the button to stop the treadmill, even though twenty minutes was not enough to burn even the glass of wine I had last night. "How about you?" I asked.

"One spin class is usually enough for me, but I might stick around for a while. Can I buy you a juice before you go?"

What would it mean if he bought me juice? Would it be a juice date? I'd come here to see him, but had I passed charming and funny and entered flirting? Would I have to tell Jim if I had juice? I began to twirl my wedding ring, and after what felt like a long time, but was probably a second and a half, I blurted, "I'm, uh . . . uh . . . married."

"Does marriage prohibit you from drinking?" Michael asked facetiously.

"Actually, it makes you drink more," I muttered.

He laughed, and I realized I was being ridiculous. He was a nice person who just happened to be a good-looking man who was a lot younger than me, and all we were going to do was have an innocent glass of juice.

"Sure," I said, and we walked over to the juice bar. He pulled out a barstool for me to sit on, which felt nice. Jim hadn't pulled out a chair for me since we were dating. Michael got two little bottles of orange juice and two glasses. He poured the juice into our glasses and took a drink from his. All I could think of was how nice it was that this man didn't drink his orange juice out of the bottle like Jim did.

"So, how long have you been married?" he asked.

"Nineteen years."

"Congrats. I was married in my early twenties, but we only made it three years."

"Did you have kids?"

He looked serious. "No, I have a knack for finding women who don't want them. I know you said you have a daughter. Do you have any other kids?"

"Nope, just the one, although sometimes it feels like ten."

"How old is she?"

"Seventeen."

"A teenage girl . . . that must be a lot."

"Yeah, the hormones running through my house are out of control. My daughter has this boyfriend and . . . Sorry, you don't need to hear this."

"No, I'm interested."

"It's not a big deal. Are you originally from Connecticut?" I asked, changing the subject.

"New York. I moved here to go to Wesleyan and ended up staying. My parents liked it better than the city, so they followed me out here, but it's only my mom now. My dad passed away a while ago."

"I'm sorry."

"Thanks. My mom has been living alone for a long time, but now she has diabetes and can sometimes get dizzy. She's even fallen at times, which makes me nervous," he said.

"My mom is fine, but my dad has Parkinson's. I've decided I'm not going to get old because it sucks," I said. As we finished our juice, it dawned on me that in the last thirty minutes, I'd told him I was afraid of a workout machine, I had crazy hormones in my house, and my dad had health issues. What was next, that my C-section scar depressed me?

I thought it was best if I left before I divulged any other things about my life to this man I barely knew. "Thanks for the juice, but I have to get going. I have a lot to do today," I said. My afternoon schedule consisted of trying to free the spoon that was wedged in the garbage disposal.

"Are you one of those women who does it all?" he asked.

"Yep, I'm Wonder Woman."

"And I'm Wonder Man. Is there a Wonder Man?" he asked.

"Nope. Only women are wonder . . . ful." He started laughing hard, not one of those fake polite laughs, but a genuine laugh that came from your belly and exploded out of your mouth. Jim hadn't laughed at my bad jokes lately, maybe because I wasn't making any. He had fallen in love with a young, playful, accomplished woman, and now he was left with this older, tired, boring one.

"Have a good day," Michael said and bowed again like he had when we first met. So dorky, yet so cute. I couldn't believe how easy it was to talk to this guy. Lately it wasn't this easy to talk to Jim. I wanted to stay and talk to Michael for hours, but instead I turned and scurried into the locker room. I pushed the door open and almost ran into . . . Ellen.

"Hey, what're you doing here?" I asked.

"I had a conference call from home this morning, so I don't have to be in until two."

"Well, see you later." I walked quickly past her and went to my locker. She followed me and stood there while I fumbled with it, unable to get the key in the lock. She took the key from my hand and opened it.

"Someone's having a day," she said mockingly.

"I have to get out of here now so I don't run into him in the parking lot when he leaves." I was rambling.

"Who leaves?" She waited for me to get my stuff, then steered me to a bench in front of the lockers. She sat down next to me. Part of me was thrilled that I had run into her, because I was bursting to share my conversation with Michael. This was exactly the thing you wanted to share with your best friend. But before I could say anything, we were surrounded by five well-padded naked women chatting about *The Real Housewives of Beverly Hills*. They were trying to get to their lockers, but Ellen was so focused on what I was going to say that she didn't seem to notice the abundance of exposed backsides in our faces. I, however, did notice and moved to another bench, with Ellen following me.

"A few weeks ago, I kind of met this cute guy here, and today he bought me juice," I exclaimed.

"Sounds like a date." She playfully seized on my discomfort.

"It was not a date."

I started to stand up, and Ellen pulled me back down. "I'm kidding. So, you've been talking to some guy that bought you juice. It's not like you had sex with him." After a beat, she added, "Did you have sex with him?"

"I'm glad I'm amusing you." I rifled in my purse for my keys. "I haven't had a conversation with a cute guy that wasn't my husband in years, and I really liked it. Is that wrong?"

"Yes, it's wrong. It's wrong that you haven't talked to a cute guy in that long. Flirting's fun. You should be doing it all the time," she said as if I was a four-year-old who had to be assured that it was okay to take an extra cookie from the cookie jar.

"Everyone flirts. When you're married, what else do you have to look forward to?" she said, smirking at me.

Was my life so boring that I was placing too much significance on a couple of short conversations with a man who wasn't my husband? I was being an idiot. "You're right, thanks. I'll call you later." I picked up my gym bag and crossed to the locker room door.

"Wait, you're not going anywhere until you show me who this guy is," Ellen said, stopping me from leaving.

"What are we, back in high school?"

She pushed the door open that led to the gym. "Point him out."

It was the only way she was going to ever let me leave. Besides, I wanted her to see how hot he was. "He's over there," I said, pointing. "In the *Breaking Bad* baseball cap."

Ellen stared at him. "Ooh, cute. And young. You sure know how to pick a guy to have juice with."

CHAPTER 8

A few weeks later, I walked into Brooklawn. I had been coming more often, not just Tuesdays anymore, because Dad had been getting increasingly worse, although he still had good days too. Every time I came in, I prayed for one of those good days.

I walked through the lobby and was heading to the elevator when Julia called me over. She put her arm around me and asked how I was doing. I said okay, but she knew I wasn't. Julia had worked at the facility for a long time, so she was familiar with a great deal of sadness from both the residents and their relatives. She often had to comfort grieving families, and I had a feeling that her incredible warmth today was her way of telling me something I didn't want to hear.

She led me to the dining room, saying she hated to drink her morning cup of coffee alone. I thought about admitting my feelings to her about my dad's condition but saying them out loud would mean I'd have to deal with them. I needed to stay positive or I'd lose my mind. I'd seen the changes in him, and what I hadn't seen for myself, Mom and Jerry had told me in detail, hence my trying to avoid the two of them.

Julia informed me that over the last three days, Dad had gotten even more agitated, and at times they were having trouble calming him. They would call my mom even if it was late, and she'd talk to him, and he'd settle down and go to sleep. This didn't happen a lot, but even twice a week was draining on my mom. The on-call doctor had prescribed anti-anxiety medication for Dad, which was helping a little, but the side effect was he slept even more.

In the past, I had confided to Julia that my mother and I didn't have the best relationship, so she made sure to tell me that my mother had come in early today and was with my father now. I would much rather have had him to myself. I could've lingered longer over the coffee, but I knew I couldn't avoid her if I wanted to spend time with my father.

When I opened the door to Dad's room, I heard a mix of my parents' laughter. I didn't see either of them right away, so I went farther into the room. I could see the bathroom door was open, and Dad was in his wheelchair in front of the mirror. Mom was running a disposable razor under the water. I could see their reflections. Dad's face was covered with shaving cream, and Mom had bags under her eyes, and there was a gray pallor to her face. Mom gently held his face still with one hand while the other hand went over his beard lightly with the razor. Dad was watching her in the mirror, a look of adoration on his face.

"Be careful," he said. "I still need my nose."

"I would never do anything to scar that beautiful face of yours," she said.

He reached up and touched her hand. "I love you," he said.

"I love you too," she said.

They didn't notice me, so I stood quietly, feeling uncomfortable with their intimacy. It was as though I'd walked in on them fooling around. I could have easily left without them knowing I was there, but instead I stomped my foot, and they both looked in the mirror and saw me.

"Hi," I said.

Mom wiped Dad's face off with a wet washcloth and then wheeled him out of the bathroom. "Hi, honey," Dad said. "Your mom was shaving me so I'll look my best when I come home tomorrow."

"You're not going home," I said reflexively. I didn't have a chance to think about why it would've been better to keep my mouth shut. Mom was shaking her head at me.

"Yes, I am, and I can't wait to have your mom's meatloaf again. The food on this ship is not the five-star rating that I was promised, although I do love sitting at the captain's table."

"Dad, you know where you are, right?" I said gently.

"Of course. It was a joke." I was relieved to see my dad back to his old self, silly jokes and all. He reached out and touched my neck. I was wearing the turquoise ring on a chain, the one he got me when I was five. "I can't believe you still have that," he said.

"I would never get rid of it. I love it." My mother gave me one of her looks. I knew she hated this ring.

Dad pushed down on the sides of his wheelchair and tried to stand up. "Wait, I'll call a nurse," Mom said. I would've helped him, but he was heavy, and I was afraid I'd drop him.

His tone changed. "There's no damn nurses here. They're all on strike." I'd never seen him this angry, let alone curse in any way.

"They're not on strike. They're right down the hall," I said.

"No, they aren't. I saw them picketing outside the window. Go look." He pointed to the window.

Mom and I looked at each other. I thought it was another one of his jokes, but I could see by his scowl that it wasn't.

"I'm helping your dad until the nurses come back to work," Mom said, playing along. She got a glass of water and put it up to my father's lips. Then she asked me, "What're you doing here today?" She had a slight edge to her voice. "I thought your dad and I'd have some time alone this morning."

I wasn't surprised that she didn't want me there. "I could leave and come back another time."

Mom looked at Dad with hope in her eyes. "Of course you should stay," he said, the anger now gone. "Your mom and I'll have plenty of time later."

"Remember, Isaac, I have to go to Caroline's granddaughter's birthday party this afternoon," Mom said to Dad.

"We can all visit for a little while. I love having my two girls around."

I knew I should've left, but I was a rebellious teenager, and Dad was the prize. The three of us made small talk for the next half hour, until I could see Dad was getting groggy again.

"I'll get going and let you rest," I said. Dad didn't reply; he was already closing his eyes. I leaned down and kissed his cheek.

"I'll walk you out," my mother said. I could see Jerry looking through the glass on the door like a peeping Tom. He was wearing his signature suit: gray jacket, white shirt, gray slacks, and a black tie. Mom didn't notice him and almost pushed the door into his face. Teenage me wished she had. Jerry looked so much like our father, which I thought was ironic. He had stocky legs and a long torso. He was not athletic and loved junk food, so his man boobs were the size of an eleven-year-old girl's. Just enough to notice, but not enough to make a statement. He was clean-shaven, as usual; his facial hair was the color of the inside of a chestnut and rarely grew. Unlike the hair on my arms and legs, which was in a constant state of fuzzy.

"You could've come in and seen Dad," I said to Jerry as we closed the door behind us.

"I saw him a few days ago," he said. Mom and Jerry and I huddled in the hall. "Did you tell her about the tests?" Jerry asked Mom but was looking at me.

"I was about to," she said.

"What tests?" I asked, my voice echoing down the hall.

"Your dad's doctor got back this morning, and he's going to run a series of tests. Blood work, then brain imaging, and then a neuropsychologist will test him for cognitive deficits," Mom said.

That many tests meant the doctor was thinking he'd find something. How was I going to keep convincing myself that Dad was just getting old or was taking some medication that had side effects? I wanted to stay in the dark. *Please let them keep me in the dark.*

"Maybe he has Alzheimer's," Jerry said. His tone made me wonder if there was a piece of him that almost enjoyed giving me bad news. I wondered if it would be immature to put my hands over my ears and hum loudly to drown him out.

"It's not Alzheimer's," I said emphatically.

"Whatever it is, we need answers," Mom said and went back in Dad's room, leaving me alone with Jerry.

Jerry straightened up to his full five-foot-ten-inch height, towering over me. "Mom's going to need us with Dad going downhill," he said.

"You don't have to be so negative. We don't know anything yet."

"I'm being realistic. You never could deal with stuff," he said, turning and walking away.

"I'm dealing with this," I called after him. "I'm dealing with it every day." Why was he being so mean? As I watched him leave, all I could think was that I wished I had a prescription for Xanax.

I walked into the house in a daze, forgetting to close the front door.

"Maggie, the dog's going to get out." Jim shut the door. I didn't say a word. "What's going on?" he asked.

"Nothing." I sat down on the couch and clutched a throw pillow to my chest.

He sat down next to me. "Obviously it's not nothing."

I filled him in on how the doctor was back, and now he was going to run tests on my dad. I also told him about Dad's hallucination and how horrible it was. I just wanted him to listen while I vented, and not try to give me a pep talk.

"I know it's scary, but maybe it won't be as bad as you think," he said. "It could be his medication like you said."

There's that pep talk. "What if it isn't?"

"Just this once, can you wait until you know something definitive before you start freaking out?"

"Just this once, can you not pretend everything's going to be fine? You're dismissing my feelings." I was beginning to wish I hadn't said anything.

"I'm not dismissing anything. I'm just saying—" Before he could finish, Gia came into the room.

"Can one of you help me find the poster board?" she asked.

"There's some in the garage," Jim said. Before he followed her out, he said, "I'll hope that you'll have worried for nothing."

I took the pillow I was holding, put it under my head, and curled up on the couch in a fetal position. I turned the television on and the channel to some mind-numbing sitcom. As the opening credits rolled, I dozed off. I didn't know how long I'd been asleep before I heard a knock on the front door. I didn't want to see anyone right now, so I tiptoed to the door and looked through the peephole. I recognized him immediately even though we'd never met. It was Jason, looking nothing like the confident kid I'd seen with Gia in our driveway. I looked terrible for our first meeting, but when I opened the door, he looked worse than I did.

"Hello," I said. "You must be Jason."

"Uh, yeah. Is Gia home?"

"Come in, I'll see where she is." While Jason stood uncomfortably in our entry hall, I went upstairs and knocked on Gia's door. "Jason's downstairs," I called out, because she didn't say I should come in.

"Why did you let him in?" she called through her closed door.

I opened it. I wasn't going to have this conversation out in the hall. She was sitting on her bed staring at her computer. "Was I supposed to leave him standing on the doorstep?"

"Yes," she said. "Tell him I'm not here."

"I already told him you were. I thought you were dating him?" She ignored the question. "Tell him I went to bed."

"It's five forty-five."

"Then say I'm studying, and I'll talk to him tomorrow." She was watching a YouTube video of some teenager giving contouring and highlighting makeup tips.

"Fine." I walked into the living room, trying to keep my expression neutral. "I'm sorry, Jason, she's studying for some big test. She'll call you later."

"She doesn't want to talk to me, does she?" Jason asked. Had my stupid face ratted me out? "Thanks for trying," he said, and I closed the door behind him. I went back upstairs to Gia's room. She'd moved on from YouTube to funny memes.

"What's going on with you two?" I asked.

"We got in an argument." She lowered the screen on her computer.

"He seems miserable."

"I'm miserable."

I sat down next to her on the bed. "Can I ask what the argument was over?"

"Sex."

Okay, be cool. "What about sex?"

"He thinks we should do it, and I don't want to." She leaned back against her headboard, crushing her stuffed zebra.

"Then don't."

"He says I'm the only seventeen-year-old that hasn't had sex."

"That's not true."

"Maybe I should just get it over with before I go to college." She pulled the stuffed zebra out from behind her and held it close to her chest.

"That's not the reason to do it."

"You've been married for a million years. What could you know about sex?"

"You're right. Now, how did you get here again?"

"You know what I mean," she said.

"I think it's smart to wait. When you have sex, you're putting a lot of trust in that person, and I don't want to see you get hurt. When I was your age, my boyfriend—"

"Stop!" She put her hands over her ears. "I don't want to hear anything about your sex life."

"I was just going to tell you about how my high school boyfriend broke my heart."

"Don't want to know." She took her hands off her ears.

"I'm only trying to help."

"I don't need your help. I already decided I'm not going to have sex now."

"Good. Then you won't make the same mistakes with boys that I made."

"I wouldn't anyway. I'm more mature than you were," she said callously. She squeezed her zebra one more time, then dropped it on the floor. "And I stand up for myself with men." *Ouch*. "Can you go now? I'm really busy," she said, dismissing me. Then she grabbed her headphones and went back on her computer. What happened to my sweet, respectful kid who hung on my every word? Female mice are smart. Sometimes they eat their babies right after they're born.

JIM

———◆———

When I get to my office, I discover the door was left unlocked. I hope nothing was taken. I have been doing everything wrong lately. I haven't been there for Maggie or my patients. I'm failing at everything.

When I open the door to the waiting room, I find a woman in her mid-fifties reading a magazine. She's one of my new patients. Cheryl apologizes for being early, but as she's new to therapy, she didn't know if I had paperwork for her to fill out. I introduce myself and tell her it's fine, and I'll be with her in a few minutes.

After I'm in my office with the door closed, I lay my briefcase down under my desk and sit down. I take a few deep breaths into my lungs and blow them out through my mouth. I feel confined, like an animal in a trap waiting either to be freed or die. I wonder how much longer I can keep this up. The voicemail light on my phone is blinking quickly, rhythmically, screaming for me to check it, but I don't.

After ten minutes, I open the door and usher Cheryl in. She's wearing Ugg slippers, flannel pants that could be pajamas, and a sweatshirt. Her face is perfectly made up, almost as if she just left the makeup counter at the mall. The scent of Ralph Lauren's Romance permeates the waiting room. Maggie's worn the same scent for years. Cheryl looks around, not sure where to sit. I motion for her to take a seat on the couch, thereby taking that big decision away from her. She's grateful. Before she sits down, she picks up all the throw pillows and moves them into the opposite corner. Then she fluffs up the bottom cushion and sits down. She leans heavily on the arm of the couch, bringing her legs up under her. She takes four tissues out of the box on the side table and crumples them up in her left hand. A small puddle is forming in the lower part of her eyes. I can see she's ready for her emotions to come flying out.

"So, what brings you in today?" I ask in as reassuring a voice as I can muster.

"I don't know where to begin. . . ." she says, but then immediately lunges into a story as if it's been bottled up for weeks. Like a popped cork that is letting the bubbles of the champagne escape into the atmosphere. I know it's wrong, yet as she's going on and on, I tune out. When I tune back in, she's saying, "And he's never home. If I knew marrying a heart surgeon was going to be like this, I might not have married him." She grabs another handful of tissues. At this rate I may have to get a new box. She continues, "I like my job, but I'm home by five, and our daughters are in college, so I sit home and wait for my husband to get back, and I never know when that will be. Sometimes he doesn't come home until the next morning, and he forgets to call." She blows her nose in one of the tissues and stuffs it in her purse even though there's a trash can nearby.

"I'm sure he wants to get off by five and come home and relax with you, but he can't because he's trapped in the job, and everyone needs him," I say.

"Yes, but not—" Cheryl starts to say, but I interrupt.

"Your husband has to be dealing with a lot of stress, and everyone wants him to be a certain way. He can't be everything to everyone, and he feels like no one takes his feelings into account. People get burned out, and then functioning becomes really hard, and you fight through it, but you feel like you're letting everyone down, and that makes things even worse," I say.

When I finish, she's staring at me and has peeled the polish off two of her nails. "So, you think I'm not understanding enough? I didn't expect you to take his side. You don't even know him."

"I'm not taking sides."

"So, when he started stealing drugs from the hospital and having affairs with the nurses, it was because I wasn't understanding enough?"

"Of course none of that is your fault. Forget what I said, but next time maybe lead with the drugs and cheating stuff."

I spent the next thirty minutes convincing her that I was wrong and shouldn't have jumped to conclusions. By the time she stood up to leave, she was more upset than when she came in. So, her first stab at therapy had been a rousing success.

CHAPTER 9

"How come we never go away for the weekend, where we drink margaritas and you give me foot massages?" I asked Jim while I scrolled through the pages of Facebook on my computer.

"Because we have a kid and I have to work?"

"So does my friend Jenny. She has three kids, but somehow she and her husband are always leaving town."

"Maybe their children hate them," he said, putting down the mystery novel he was reading.

"Why couldn't we be that lucky?"

Jim leaned over me, looking at the computer. His chest against my back set off a familiar reaction, making it feel more intimate than it was. "For all you know, Jenny's husband cheats all week long, so he takes her on romantic weekends so she won't figure it out." He stood up, and I instantly missed the feeling of him on me.

"You could cheat on me if you took me on weekends like that," I said.

"I'll keep that in mind." He picked up three files that were sitting on the counter. "Have you noticed that every time you go on Facebook, we end up in a discussion about why our lives are so boring?" he said.

"That's because all my friends from high school have more fun than we do. We just sit home and do nothing."

"I'm sorry, I wish I was more entertaining," he said with a heavy sigh. Then he picked up his jacket off the back of the couch. "Have a good day." He left through the back door into the garage.

I signed off Facebook feeling even more depressed than when I went on. The computer was not my friend. The vacuum was never my friend, but I decided to use it anyway.

I was getting the vacuum out of the hall closet when my phone vibrated. It was my mom asking if I could talk. I told her I was at the doctor and I'd call her later. As soon as I hung up, a text came in from Gia; she'd left her lunch at home. *Yay! I get to drive to her school. Won't my Facebook friends be jealous?*

By the time I got dressed and pulled up to the school, the lunch bell was ringing. I rolled my window down and waited a few minutes until Gia ran up to my car.

"What took you so long? I was about to die from starvation," she said, as if she hadn't eaten in a year.

She grabbed her lunch through the window. "Didn't you forget something?" I asked sarcastically.

"Oh, yeah, can I get three dollars to buy snacks out of the vending machine?"

"I meant a thank-you," I said as I reached for my wallet.

"Thanks, Mom," she said and turned to go.

"Maybe tonight we should talk about what you want to do for your eighteenth birthday."

"I already planned something."

"What do you mean you already planned something? It's a few months away. We need to do something big."

"I don't want anything big. I just want to take a bunch of friends to dinner and a movie. We can all drive ourselves, so you don't have to do anything. See you later." She ran off. I hated planning parties, but I had been doing it for seventeen years, and this would be the most important one of them all. How could she take that away from me? What was next, she wouldn't let me plan her wedding?

After I left her, I headed for the gym. It was making me crazy waiting for the results of my dad's tests, so exercise would get my mind off it. I could've taken Theo for a walk, but running into Michael would be a better mood booster.

As I crossed the parking lot of the gym, I stopped for a second to tie my shoe. "Hey," Michael said as he almost tripped over me.

"Oh, hi," I said. I was getting better at acting surprised when I ran into him. I didn't let on that I knew he was usually here at this time, because I wouldn't want him to think I was stalking him, even if that's what I was doing. I stood up. "Are you coming or going?"

"Going. I had to come earlier today because I have a meeting," he said.

I was disappointed we weren't going to work out together. "I was just leaving also," I lied. Could he tell I wasn't even sweaty?

"Strange I didn't see you in there," he said.

"I know, I didn't see you either." A text popped up on my phone. I couldn't hide my unhappiness with what I read.

"Everything okay?" he asked, putting his gym bag down on the concrete.

"It's my daughter. She isn't coming home after school, because she's going out with her boyfriend."

"And that's bad?"

"Sort of. They had a fight the other day, and I was hoping they wouldn't make up."

"You don't like him?" I shrugged my shoulders and nodded at the same time. "When I was seventeen, I was that boy parents didn't like," he said.

"Why didn't they like you?"

"I don't know. Probably my rugged good looks."

"Nah, that couldn't be it," I said with flirtatious sarcasm. I was becoming quite the charmer.

"I love that you're giving me shit."

"Something else I'm good at."

"I bet you're good at lots of things," he said, a grin creeping onto his face. He scanned the parking lot. "Now, if I could only remember where I left my car."

"You could hit the panic button." He did, and an alarm that was six cars away went off. It was so loud that a few people were looking around to see what idiot had set it off. Michael looked around too, so no one knew it was him. Then we started laughing, and he put his keys against his side and shut the alarm off.

"How's your writing going?" I asked.

"Good. Tomorrow I'm going to the Central Park Zoo to interview a primatologist about the tamarin monkey. They're endangered."

"I love monkeys. They crack me up. Will you get to hold one?"

"I hope so. They're supposed to be very gentle."

"That's cool that you get to do things like that."

"You want to come with me?"

Yes. Yes, I do. "Oh, I couldn't, but thanks for asking."

"Too bad. We would've had a lot of fun." He pressed the remote on his keys, and I heard the beep of his car opening. "I need to shower before my meeting. Hopefully I'll see you soon," he said.

"Have a good day," I said, and he went to his car. Why didn't I say I'd go with him to the zoo? What else did I have to do?

Then again, I barely knew the guy. What if he was a serial killer? What if he wasn't? He was hot. I watched him drive away. Darn dignity, it was the only thing keeping me from chasing after him. That and I looked stupid when I ran.

DAD

———— ✦ ————

"Are you comfortable, Mr. Rubin?" Dr. Myers asks, and I nod. She's a neuropsychologist who's going to administer some tests, at least that's what Dorothy told me. I got good grades in school, but I haven't taken a test in many decades. I'm anxious I'll fail. If I do, will she let me take a make-up test? My eighth-grade math teacher, Mrs. Stoneman, always gave us a pep talk before every test. Why can I remember that, and I can't remember who drove me here?

The doctor moves a chair from in front of her desk and wheels me over. Her office is warm and has cozy, comfortable-looking chairs, yet I'm not sitting in one. There's a framed diploma from UC Berkeley and a lot of books about various mental illnesses and syndromes. I wonder if what I have is in one of them. Lately I've been imagining strange things, and if I told anyone they might think I was crazy. Like the snakes in Dr. Myers' potted plants. I know they're not real, but still I see them slithering around.

She opens a drawer and pulls out a binder, along with a timer. "We'll be starting in just a minute," she says.

I start to sweat. She talks to me in a soft, kind voice, hoping I'll relax, which I won't be able to do until after this stupid thing is over. She says she's going to start by telling me three words, and in a little while, she'll ask me to repeat them back. My mind has more important things to concentrate on than remembering useless words. I tap my left fingers across my right knuckles as if I'm playing a piano; it relieves my nerves. When did I start doing that? I can't remember.

"Dog, apple, fork," she says very slowly.

"Dog, apple, fork," I say three times out loud, hoping they'll get stuck in my brain. Right after I say them, I feel the words begin to evaporate.

Next, she asks me who the president is, what year it is, and why I think I'm in her office. I'm pretty sure I got the president and the year right, and I tell her that I'm in her office because my family thinks I'm losing my marbles. I laugh, but she doesn't, and she doesn't deny it either. I know we're just getting started, but I'm already tired.

"You're doing very well, Mr. Rubin," she says, as if I'm a second grader working on a science project. I complete a bunch of other tests, and then she asks me to draw a clock. Of course, I know how to draw a clock. Even a child can draw a clock. She turns over an hourglass timer. The sand seems to be moving so quickly, it makes me edgier. I draw a circle, but then I get stuck. I keep staring at the circle, or is that a square? No, I think it's a circle. My vision blurs as I look at the paper. I write the number twelve at the bottom, or is that where the six goes? If she wasn't watching me, I'd have finished in two seconds. The sand finishes going through the hourglass.

Get me out of here. I'm tired of MRIs and CT Scans and whatever else they've made me do. I know there's something wrong, but can it be fixed? And if it can't, do I really need to know what it is? The last thing Dr. Myers asks me is to repeat those three words she told me before. Dammit, what were they? I think one of them was a type of fruit, but I can't remember the others.

"Banana, chair, balloon," I say, because those are the first words that come into my head, and I don't care if they're right. Dr. Myers writes something down and then calls Dorothy in.

"Goodbye, Mr. Rubin. It was a pleasure meeting you," Dr. Myers says. Not sure if I'd say the same about her.

CHAPTER 10

On the first day of every month, I would fill in our dry-erase calendar with doctor's appointments, after-school activities, and family birthdays. When I got to the twenty-fourth of the month, I realized that it was Jim's and my twentieth wedding anniversary, and neither of us had mentioned it. It was a glaring red light on how disconnected we were from each other. In the past, Jim loved celebrating our anniversary; he'd start planning a month in advance, and on the day, he'd give me a sappy card with a poem he'd written and a traditional gift that fit that year. On our second anniversary, which was cotton, he gave me fishnet stockings. I never quite believed they were made of cotton, but he said he'd done research. That night I put them on with nothing but my "anniversary suit," and he couldn't have been happier.

On our fifth anniversary, the year of wood, he waltzed into the house with a box wrapped in silver paper with a black ribbon. Inside was a beautiful cherrywood music box, and on the top was a painting of two perfect roses. He said they represented the flowers in his life, Gia and me. It was corny, but I loved it. When I lifted the lid, the song "The Hills Are Alive" from *The Sound of*

Music wafted through the living room. I'd told him how much I loved that song on our first date, and I was blown away that he'd remembered. The music box was still on my dresser, but the lid was broken at the hinges, and the picture of the roses had faded. Was that a metaphor for our marriage?

"Did you realize our anniversary is in two weeks?" I asked Jim as he brushed his teeth.

"Of course," he said, spitting blobs of toothpaste into the sink. He hadn't remembered either.

"I can ask my mom to stay with Gia if you want to go away, just the two of us." Gia wouldn't want anyone staying with her, but I wasn't going to leave her home alone with Jason in the picture.

"Sure," he said.

"We could go to that bed and breakfast in Norfolk that we used to love." We needed something to get our marriage back on track.

"Which one?" he asked.

We had only been to one. "The one with that cobblestone fireplace and the view of the forest?" I could see the wheels turning in his head, and he was coming up with nothing. "You know, the place where we barely left the room except to go buy another bottle of champagne."

"Oh yeah," he said with no conviction.

How could he not remember the most romantic weekend we'd ever spent together? "I'll call and see if they have a room available."

"Sounds good."

When he started flossing and spitting out little particles all over the place, I went downstairs. Instead of immediately making reservations, I picked up my gym bag and headed to my car. After changing, I went straight to the treadmills, hoping to find Michael. Being with him had become my escape. After thirty minutes when he still hadn't shown up, I became frustrated. Where was he? The extent of my disappointment surprised me. I looked everywhere except the men's locker room, and just as I was about to give up, I spotted him in a corner on one of the weight machines. He had been hidden behind a burly gentleman who was taking a break on the machine next to him. Michael had headphones on and was moving to his music and quietly singing. I loved that he was unaware of how dorky he looked. Then I caught a glimpse of myself in the mirror; he wasn't the only one who looked foolish. My skin was blotchy, and my bangs were curling upward. I couldn't let him see me like that.

I ducked back into the locker room and applied some tinted moisturizer. Not enough to look as if I had makeup on, but enough to look better than I had a few minutes ago. I brushed my bangs back in place and walked out of the locker room. I thought it would be less obvious that I needed to see him if I could get him to notice me first. I found a weight machine a little distance from him and hoped he'd see me. The machine I chose was for tightening your abs. I got on the incline bench and tucked my feet under the rollers. Then I laid back, put my hands behind my ears, and squeezed my stomach muscles as tight as I could and pulled myself up. I continued until my abs began screaming, but Michael still hadn't seen me. I surreptitiously glanced his way, but he was engrossed in his routine. I moved a little closer to him, this time getting on the pull-down machine. After I'd killed myself there, and he still hadn't looked my way, I decided to try one more machine before giving up and going over to him.

I picked an inner thigh machine because it was as close to him as I could get without being on top of him. The problem was my inner thighs hated working out. They were happy to stay mushy. I placed my legs in a contraption that reminded me of the gynecologist's office yet not as fun. I bore down and concentrated and pushed my thighs together. I put more weight on the machine than I had ever used in the past; in fact, it was more weight than anyone my size would have ever been able to squeeze. I was not going to give up, so I tried even harder, but I couldn't get the machine to move even an inch. I was now sweating profusely, and my thighs felt as if they were going to shoot off my body. I was grimacing when he finally noticed me. I couldn't tell by his expression if he was amused or impressed.

"You need to lower your weight on this machine. Seventy-five pounds is too much, you could hurt yourself," he said, pausing his own workout.

"That would explain why my thighs have been screaming at me."

Michael lightened the weight for me and sat down on the outer thigh machine next to me. He put three-hundred pounds of weight on and then pushed his thighs apart as effortlessly as a butterfly flapping its wings. "I'm so glad I ran into you," he said. Really, *he* wanted to run into *me*? *Please don't let my eyes light up.* "I wanted to get the name of that assisted living facility that your dad's in," he added.

Okay, not exactly what I was hoping he'd say. "It's Brooklawn Senior Center on Muldover Street."

"I'm not sure my mom will consider it, but I'm hoping she'll at least come with me to check it out."

"It's a nice place, as those places go."

"That's good. My mom needs more help, and she's lonely, so maybe it would also force her to be more social. I worry about her." He was sensitive and cute. He picked up his water bottle and took a drink. "Thanks for the info." He added weight to his machine and went back to his workout.

"So, no treadmill today?" I asked.

"I didn't want to risk my life," he said.

"And you shouldn't. Your life's too important to waste." A flush erupted on my cheeks, and a sensation of heat was on my back. Flirting made me warm, or was it perimenopause? We finished the thigh machines at the same time—or rather as soon as he stopped, I happily quit too. We switched machines, so now I was working my outer thighs and he was working his inner thighs, although his thighs were already perfect, not that I was looking. We were working out in unison, which seemed rather romantic in a sweaty way.

After we finished, we crossed to the free weights. He picked up a fifty-pound dumbbell in each hand and began doing bicep curls. I was entranced by the tightening and untightening of his arms and the way his tattoo brightened up under the overhead lights. I scanned the various weights on the rack.

"You should start with eights or tens if you've never lifted," he said.

"Oh, I lift all the time. I struggled to get the twenty-pound dumbbells off the stack. As soon as I tried to lift them, I realized I was in trouble. As coolly as I could, I put them back on the rack and picked up eights. "So, what were the tamarin monkeys like?" I asked.

"Amazing. They let me hold one of the babies."

"Wow, that's so cool." After ten curls, I put the eights back on the stack. Michael continued lifting.

"How's your daughter?" he asked.

"Speaking of monkeys?" I said, and he laughed. We kept up a steady conversation while he continued to lift. I felt weird standing and watching him work out, so I started stretching. I was acutely aware of my body and how I was moving it. I had to make sure nothing creaked or snapped or screamed out my age. He said it was great that I worked out so often. I told him it kept me sane, which he related to. "I have to work out in the morning or at lunchtime because the end of my day is taken up by homework and listening to my daughter's drama," I said.

"Let me guess. Who has a crush on who, who's mean, who says she's a vegan but eats chicken for lunch."

"I thought you didn't have kids."

"I don't. I date younger women. After my last girlfriend, I swore I'd only date women my own age."

"How old was your last girlfriend?" I asked.

"Twenty-two."

"Twenty-two?" I exclaimed, putting more emphasis on the twenty than I intended.

"You think I'm some dirty old man, don't you?"

"If you learned your lesson, I'll pretend you aren't creepy."

"Much appreciated."

"Why'd you and the twenty-two-year-old break up?" I couldn't stop bringing up that number.

"Every time I had a writing deadline, she'd say I was too busy for her. I told her I had to work to pay my bills, unlike her, whose parents still paid for everything. She kept saying that I wasn't any fun."

"My husband and I've had a similar conversation. I'm the one saying marriage should be more fun." Maybe I shouldn't be telling Michael this.

"I don't know if I could ever get married again," he said, putting the fifty-pound dumbbells back on the stack and picking up slightly heavier weights. He lay down on the bench and did chest presses. I was bored with stretching, so I got on the bench next to him and copied what he was doing but with ten-pound weights. Before I knew it, an hour had gone by, and I had gotten a good workout and was having an enjoyable time doing it. I didn't want to leave, but I needed to get some errands done before Gia came home. I also knew tomorrow I was going to be so sore I might not be able to walk or brush my hair.

"I promised my daughter I'd pick up supplies for her science project before she gets home today." When I stood up, he did also.

"It was nice having someone to work out with," he said.

"It was. Then again, you could always work out with one of your young girlfriends."

"They don't have their driver's licenses yet."

"Ha. Good one."

Michael picked up my towel and handed it to me. "See you soon, I hope."

I turned toward the mirror in front of me and saw that my hair was hanging out of my ponytail, my mascara was smeared, and there were sweat stains down the front of my tank top. I dreaded to think there might be sweat on my butt too. I couldn't wait to see him again, which when you're married, is not a good sign.

CHAPTER 11

———⚬———

On Monday, Michael wasn't at the gym. Tuesday, Wednesday, and Thursday, no sign of him either. I went in the morning. I went at lunchtime. I even asked the receptionist if he'd been there, and she hadn't seen him. I was not motivated to work out without him, so not only was I obsessing about him disappearing, but I was obsessing about the extra pounds I was gaining.

The more I thought about how much I missed him, the more anxious I got, yet I couldn't get him off my mind. I knew deep down that he shouldn't be this important to me. Jim noticed I hadn't been in a good mood, but I told him it was anxiety over my father. I'd never lied to him, and now I was becoming pretty good at it.

By the end of the week, I was beside myself not knowing what happened to Michael. On Saturday I showed up at the gym twice, but no Michael. I did run into Gia's friend Taylor though. I hadn't seen her since she went to college, and I almost didn't recognize her. When she graduated from high school last year, she had frizzy brown hair, a unibrow, and an ample midsection. The girl standing in front of me had blond straight hair, perfectly plucked eyebrows, and was wearing a cropped sports bra and tight running shorts. Her abs were giving my abs a heart attack.

I made an excuse and left quickly because her young, beautiful body was depressing.

Later that afternoon my flabby belly and I were standing in front of the Lacy Dream boutique. I was there to buy lingerie for my anniversary trip. I hoped it would make me feel sexy, so I could get my mind back on Jim. I also wondered if it would help his lack of a sex drive. Or would I need to resort to using handcuffs, a blindfold, and a leather flogger? That's something he wouldn't expect. I'd read *Fifty Shades of Gray*; I'd learned how to use that stuff. I looked at my reflection in the boutique window and imagined myself as a dominatrix. My reflection blushed and said, *No way. He needs to marry his second wife for that.*

I hated lingerie shopping, not because I didn't like pretty things but because trying them on in a dressing room under florescent lights and in front of a three-way mirror was worse than getting my varicose veins stripped.

The mannequin in the window was dressed in a white, lacy chemise. I envied her perfect body curves, except for that part where her two halves were bolted together. Would Michael think I looked sexy in that chemise? Wait, I meant Jim, Jim, my husband, Jim. As I berated myself for confusing them, I saw Ellen getting out of her car. She'd volunteered to come with me today to talk me through my insecurities. She was also a good buffer between me and some sales lady who'd try to convince me that a negligee with a weird cutout where my butt hung out would look fabulous on me.

Ellen was on her cell phone, gesturing wildly, which could only mean she was talking to her mother-in-law. We still hadn't figured out how to get off the phone with our mothers-in-law. With our own mothers, we would say goodbye, and if we "accidentally" hung up on them, oh well. Mothers-in-law were a different beast.

"Sure, yes, we'll try to be there for Thanksgiving this year," Ellen said and gave me her look for *Help me!* "No, no, you're right, we'll more than try." She mimed a gun to her head.

I put on my old lady voice and called out, "Ma'am, can you please help me? I can't get up these steps by myself."

Ellen smiled. "I gotta go. There's a senior citizen who's going to fall if I don't help her. . . . Yes, your son did marry a nice woman." She hung up and sighed. "Thanks, you always did make an excellent elderly woman."

"All that practicing has paid off," I said.

We opened the door to the boutique and went inside. There was a crystal chandelier hanging overhead, making the store look elegant, not trashy. There were racks with all different types of bras and chemises and tables with panties lined up in rows. "You look like you're about to get a tooth pulled," Ellen said. "Why are we doing this?"

I held up a pair of thong panties. "I need something for Jim."

"Wouldn't he be more comfortable in boxers?"

"Ha ha. I meant I need to do something to revitalize my marriage."

The lingerie was separated by colors. It was a rainbow of white, black, red, gray, and purple. Ellen walked over to one of the racks. "Okay, what color do you think will make Jim's eyes bulge out?" she asked.

"Whichever one takes ten pounds off me."

Ellen began collecting a wide variety of camisoles, bras, chemises, and thongs in black, red, and purple. "Hey, did you get the tests back for your dad?"

"Not yet. And between the waiting and whatever's going on with Jim and the thing with Michael, I've been a wreck."

She stopped pulling items and looked at me. "What kind of *thing* with Michael?"

"I just meant we've been working out together pretty often now. That is, until a week ago when he disappeared, and I realized how much I missed him."

"Tell me you're not having an affair."

"No, of course I'm not," I said emphatically. "We're just friends."

"You sound pretty invested for just friends."

"It's not a big deal," I said, trying to convince myself as much as her. "I just like the way I feel when I'm with him."

"Yeah, right. I saw the man in shorts." A saleswoman walked over to us, and Ellen waved her off, telling her she had things under control. The saleswoman gave her a dirty look.

"It's not just about his looks. When I'm with him I'm different than I am at home. I'm silly and funny and . . . sweet. Jim wouldn't say that about me anymore."

"That's because Jim sees you sick, bitchy, and yelling at a teenager."

"Do you think that's why he's distant and doesn't want to have sex? I'm a pain in the ass?"

A different saleswoman tried to help us, but Ellen let her know she was interrupting a private conversation. This saleswoman was not pleased either.

"I get it," Ellen said. "Michael's fun, and you don't have any responsibilities when you're with him. It's okay to have a crush, but just make sure you don't cross the line." I assured her it wasn't going in that direction. She told me how she once had a thing for a teller at the bank. She said it got so bad that she'd go in one day and take money out, only to go back the next day and put it back in. She finally stopped when Sam saw their bank statements and asked what the hell she was doing.

"Did you have to change banks?" I asked.

"No, I just went to a different teller. Eventually my crush left to go pursue his dream of being a figure skater." I rolled my eyes at her. "Go try these on," she said, dropping the large pile of lingerie she'd been collecting into my arms. I handed her all the items back except three chemises and one silk robe. If I tried on too many, I would get overwhelmed and leave with nothing.

I went into the dressing room, and Ellen sat outside it on a plush ottoman. "I think this anniversary trip will be good for you and Jim," she called through the door.

I wished I could say I was looking forward to leaving town for an entire weekend alone with him, but I was worried. Over the years we'd told each other everything about our pasts and all our funny stories, so what were we going to talk about? On this trip I wanted to avoid talking about Gia or my father or Jim's job, because that wasn't romantic. But what was left to talk about? I better start thinking of topics now.

I stripped off my clothes and examined my body. Since I'd been working out more, it was looking tighter. I moved the three-way mirror so I could see my butt and imagined it without cellulite. I wondered if Michael thought about me sexually.

"Are you ever going to come out and show me something?" Ellen called out impatiently. I grabbed the first thing I saw and put it on. It was the red chemise, and I knew right away that this was the one. I wrapped the silk robe over it and came out of the dressing room. Ellen motioned for me to open the robe. "You look so pretty. Michael—I mean Jim—will love it." I smacked her lightly on the arm.

After I'd paid a lot for a small amount of material, Ellen and I hugged goodbye, and I headed to the market for the fifteenth time that week. I wasn't in the mood, but if I ever let that stop me, we would've all starved. I wouldn't be there long, because I had a system. I'd start at the produce aisle, then work my way to the meat department. I was making good time until I got to the section with crackers and cookies. I got stuck behind some guy with his back to me who was blocking the aisle, staring at the Chips Ahoy cookies. There were a hundred types: chewy, chunky, Reese's, Heath bar, gooey, thins. It seemed as if they took up the whole aisle, and he was looking at all of them. I needed cookies too, which left me with nothing to do but stand behind him and wait. I couldn't help but notice his broad shoulders and tight butt. Ever since Michael, I was checking out any strange man in front of me. I got frustrated with waiting, and just as I was about to say excuse me, he turned slightly. It *was* Michael. No wonder I was admiring his body. His six feet to my five-two meant I had to reach my arm up to tap him on the shoulder.

"You come here often?" I asked. That sounded better in my head.

He turned and broke into a grin, "If it isn't my workout buddy. What're you doing here?"

"They have food here, don't they?" I said, trying for humor. "I thought I should get some before we all faded away."

"Funny," he said.

"I didn't know you shopped here. Do you live in the neighborhood?" I asked.

"No, I've never been to this market. I usually just buy food at Seven-Eleven." He pulled two boxes of crackers off the shelf. Did he notice that I looked good today, no workout clothes? I had on a scoop-neck T-shirt, a short skirt, tights, boots, and makeup that wasn't smeared.

"Have you been to the gym this week? I've barely had time to get there." I hoped he couldn't tell I was lying.

"No," he said. "My mom fell last weekend and hurt her hip, so I've been staying with her. Today's the first day I could get away."

"Oh no, I'm sorry."

"Thanks. I haven't worked out at all. Can't you tell from my bloated stomach?" he said, pulling his shirt up a little and patting his perfectly chiseled abs.

I wanted to reach out and touch them, but that would've been weird. I told him that when my dad started falling a lot was when we had to move him to assisted living. I grabbed the Oreos and then realized I needed oyster crackers also, but since they were directly behind him, I was worried that I'd graze his waist if I went for them. I couldn't get my mind off touching some part of him, which made me flustered. Finally, I struggled to reach the oyster crackers.

"Here, let me get those," he said. He looked inside my cart. "That's a lot of food."

I had only about half of what I came in for. I was embarrassed that there were only three of us at home. How did we eat so much? When Gia left, I'd never have to go to the market; I got sad just thinking about it. Then again, not having to cook every night would be a bright spot. "I'm almost done," I said, not copping to how much was still on my list.

We continued down the aisle, me pushing my cart, him holding his basket. "I need peanut butter and tomato sauce," he said.

"Peanut butter is on aisle four and tomato sauce on aisle six."

"You're a regular directory. Do you mind if I tag along with you?"

Did I mind? I became Cinderella, and he had asked me to the ball. "Of course not," I said. He held eye contact with me so long that I averted my gaze and wondered what he was thinking.

We moved to the next aisle. Oh God, tampons were next on my list. There was no way I was buying them with Michael here. Jim had witnessed an eight-pound baby come out of me, and I still didn't like buying them in front of him. Great, now I was going to have to make an extra stop at the drug store. I walked through the feminine hygiene section and turned the corner to where the peanut butter was. Michael assessed every brand on the shelf. "Seven-Eleven doesn't have this many choices," he said.

I rifled through my purse and pulled out a two-for-one coupon. "Will this help?" I asked.

He looked at me as if I'd given him a Ferrari. "Cool. I can give one to my mom." He dropped two peanut butters in his basket. "You sure you don't need this?" He held out the coupon.

"No, I'm good."

As we started down the aisle, he stopped to let a woman and her young son pass. We turned the corner into the frozen foods, and he looked at all the choices for frozen spinach. I handed him another coupon. Jim and Gia hated spinach, so I wasn't going to use it anyway.

"You don't need your coupons. It must be nice to be rich," he said as he opened the door of the freezer section to get the spinach.

I couldn't tell if he was being facetious, but I was still offended. "I'm not rich," I said.

"You volunteer. Obviously you can live on one salary."

"The only reason I don't work outside the house anymore is I'm taking care of my daughter."

"I didn't mean to insult you," he said, taken aback.

"Then how did you mean it?" I was more upset than I should've been. I worked hard; it shouldn't matter if I got paid for all the stuff I did. I considered taking back my coupons. "I hate when someone comments on my life when they don't know anything about it," I said.

"Hey, I'm sorry. I didn't mean to do that. People do that to me all the time when they hear I work freelance." He was contrite.

"No, I'm sorry," I said. "When someone brings up my not working, it pushes my buttons. I feel guilty that I haven't gone back to work since Gia got older, and when I told my husband that I might consider it, he was kind of negative."

"I really stepped in it, didn't I?"

"You couldn't have known."

"Well, for the record, I think you should do whatever would make me happy. Was this our first fight?" he asked playfully.

"Let's make it our last," I said, and he fist-bumped me.

We approached the deli counter. "I'm going to get something for lunch," he said. "Do you want anything? I owe you an apology sandwich."

"No, you don't. I'm good."

He pulled the number fifty-five from the dispenser, but the board said they were only up to forty-eight. "Do you want to go on? I may be here a while," he said.

"It's fine. I'll wait with you." A three-year-old boy stood up inside his cart. His mother had parked him next to a case of different kinds of cheese as she was waiting for her number to be called at the deli counter. The boy began grabbing cheeses and piling them on top of himself. Michael walked over and handed the boy more and more cheese until he was covered in Cheddar, Brie, Havarti, and Gouda. Michael quietly slipped back next to me. The boy began giggling loud enough that his harried mother turned around. She was still putting cheese away when they called her number at the deli counter.

"You're so mean," I whispered to Michael.

"But kids love me," he whispered back.

I laughed and then heard someone call out my name. It was the mother of one of Gia's newer friends. She was in her late forties and had blond hair down to the top of her butt. She wore a belly shirt with leggings and over-the-knee boots. We'd only met once at the mother-daughter tea, and now I was at a loss for her name. All I could remember was that her husband had left her for a drag queen. I waved in a way that said, *I know you, but I don't want to talk to you, and I hope you don't come over.* That hope was quashed as she excitedly rushed over as if we were best friends.

"Hi, Maggie, so good to see you." Ms. What's-Her-Name scanned Michael from chest to legs before introducing herself. "Hi, I'm Jessica, and your daughter Gia is friends with my daughter, Samantha."

I was flustered; this woman thought Michael was my husband. I wondered if it was terrible of me to be happy that she thought I could get a guy this young and this hot to marry me. But if she thought he was my husband, why was she looking at him as if she wanted to have him for lunch? I couldn't believe how rude that was. Wait a minute, he wasn't my husband.

"He's not my husband," I said. "My husband's at work. We're not together. This is my friend Michael. That I ran into here." I knew I was blabbering on with information she didn't need, but my guilt that Michael and I were together was overwhelming.

Jessica seemed relieved that Michael was only a friend and not my husband. She reached her hand out and shook Michael's hand. "Nice to meet you."

"Nice to meet you too," Michael said. Jessica didn't let go of his hand, and the look in her eye made me wonder if she would've had sex with him right here. Michael casually dropped her hand.

I wanted to say, *Goodbye, crazy lady,* but because Gia liked her daughter, instead I said, "Bye. Nice to see you."

Jessica turned her whole body toward Michael, cutting me out of the conversation. "Shelton is such a small town. I can't believe we've never met before," she said.

"Yeah, strange," he said.

The woman at the counter called Michael's number. "That's me. Bye," he said and walked over to the counter.

Jessica watched him for a moment and finally left, not too happily, I might add. I joined Michael at the counter as the man helping him asked what he wanted to order. Michael asked if he could taste one of the salads. After he sampled that one, he went on to taste three more. The man helping him was getting frustrated. Michael said he liked to try everything that life had to offer, even if it was just salads. I liked his attitude, as I was always worried about what other people thought. In the end, he ordered two of the salads and a sandwich.

As we left the deli counter, I purposely walked ahead of him. In case Jessica saw us again, I wanted it to look as though we weren't together. And then it hit me: What if at the next school function, she told Jim she saw me with Michael? Or what if she told her daughter, and her daughter told Gia? Now I was going to have to convince Gia that Jessica's daughter had a bad reputation or that she had a drug problem and she should stay away from her. That would be a new low; I couldn't malign a girl I didn't know. Besides, what could Jessica have seen anyway? It wasn't as if she saw Michael and me kissing.

Michael caught up to me in the meat department. "You don't like that woman, do you?"

"Was it that obvious?"

"Probably not to her. She seemed more intent on meeting your husband." He indicated himself and laughed.

"I think she was hoping you'd ask her out," I said.

"She's not my type. I like women with coupons." I did a coupon happy dance in my head. Michael picked up a package of chicken breasts and a package of ground turkey and looked at the nine things in his basket. "I'm done," he announced.

"Me too," I lied. I still needed at least a half dozen more items. I resigned myself to knowing I'd be back again tomorrow.

Michael waited for me to pay and then carried my groceries to the trunk of my car. "Why don't you give me your phone, and I'll put my number in. Then you can text me the next time you're going to work out, and we can meet," he said.

What was I supposed to do? I handed him my phone. "I'll give you my number too," I said. It would've been rude not to offer. We exchanged contact information, and then he snapped a picture of me, so when I called, my picture would come up on his phone. For obvious reasons, I didn't take a picture of him.

After getting in my car, I wondered two things. First, if I should tell Jim about Michael in case he saw my contacts. Then again, what would I say? *Hi, honey, how was your day? Oh, by the way, this hot guy I've been hanging with at the gym and hiding from you gave me his number.* And second, how did I go to the market today and still have nothing for dinner? The way our relationship had been lately, I wondered which would bother him more.

CHAPTER 12

———⋄———

"Look what you made me do," Gia said. She had dropped her backpack on the back of the couch, but it fell off, and its contents spilled on the floor. I wasn't the one who didn't zip up my backpack. She shoved a jumble of papers, pencils, and pens back inside. Before I could say she was going to lose points for a crumpled history essay, she let out a low growl of frustration. I couldn't keep up with her moods. Perimenopause and teenage angst had a lot in common.

"Do you want to talk about it?" I asked.

"No."

I wanted my little girl back. The one who told me everything. Her friends' moms were always commenting on how polite she was. I wondered if she had an identical twin who went out in public, and the yucky one sometimes came home and lived in her room. "Obviously something happened today," I said.

"I said I don't want to talk about it."

"Okay. I'm going to see your grandfather, but I could get you a snack before I go." She was seventeen, but I'd been doing the snack thing her whole life. I'd stop next year when she was gone.

"Not hungry." She ran up to her room, leaving her backpack on the floor still not zipped. It was a safe assumption that she hadn't made up with Jason, which I wasn't broken up over. She didn't need a boyfriend right now, with her close to graduation anyway.

Twenty minutes later I was walking down the hall to Dad's room when I saw Jerry coming out of one of the administrative offices. To avoid him, I slipped quietly into one of the resident's rooms, shut the door, and peeked out the little glass window at the top of the door.

"Who are you hiding from?" A heavily Russian-accented voice startled me. I turned to see Mr. Zlotnik, an eighty-five-year-old man.

"My brother's out there." I was being ridiculous, but I didn't want to listen to my little brother's judgments about me again.

"Say no more. My brother turned me in to KGB. You stay here as long as you like," Mr. Zlotnik said.

"Thanks," I said.

Mr. Zlotnik was sitting in a folding chair playing solitaire on a TV table. Several of the cards had fallen on the floor, but he hadn't seemed to notice. He smiled sweetly. "You remind me of my youngest girl."

I opened the door a crack and looked down the hall. Jerry was walking toward the dining room. My five-year-old self had the urge to stick out my tongue at his back. Since the coast was clear, I said goodbye to Mr. Zlotnik and thanked him for his hospitality. As I closed the door, he called out in his Russian lilt, "Come back soon. I like having young sexy thing in my room." I would not be going anywhere near Room 125 ever again.

As I escaped in the opposite direction of the dining room, I saw Michael at the front desk. He was in his usual uniform of sweatpants and a T-shirt. I didn't think I'd ever seen him in anything else. Next to him was an elegant gray-haired woman bent into a C over a walker. She was wearing a black pleated skirt, a black blazer, and black low-heeled pumps. She looked as if she was going to a funeral. She and Michael shared the same strong pointed chin, but Michael had a tiny dimple in his.

"Maggie's over there," Helen said, pointing at me. Helen was the head of admissions of Brooklawn. At sixty, with her bob haircut, cardigan collection, and calm demeanor, you'd never know she was a black belt in Taekwondo. "I'll join you in just a minute," she said and picked up the phone.

Michael waved, and I walked over to him and his mother. "Hey, it seems like forever since I've seen you," he said. It had been four days; had he missed me? "This is my mother, Charlotte Dewy. Mom, this is Maggie, the woman I told you about."

He told her about me? What did he tell her? "It's nice to meet you, Mrs. Dewy," I said.

She steadied herself on the walker and reached her hand out to shake mine. "It's nice to meet you, Maggie." She turned toward Michael. "I don't know why we're here. I had one fall, and then Michael insisted we take a look at this place."

"It wasn't just one fall," Michael said. He looked exhausted, as if he had fought a bear.

"It was hard for my dad to make the move too," I said.

"I've been fine on my own for the last fifteen years, and I'll be fine on my own for fifteen more," she stated emphatically.

Michael raised his eyebrows toward me to indicate what he had to deal with. Charlotte caught him and then took her cane and playfully swatted him. As she did, she almost lost her balance, but Michael grabbed her before she fell.

"Thanks for proving my point," he said.

"I wasn't even close to falling," she said and turned to me. "Michael thinks he knows what's best for me."

"One of us has to be the grown-up around here," he said. How did I suddenly get in the middle?

She looked down at his sweatpants. "This from a man who can't put on a proper pair of pants or keep a woman long-term."

Michael glared at her as Helen came over. "I'm so sorry, but it's going to be a few more minutes before I'll be free to give you a tour," she said. "I hope you don't mind waiting."

"No, we can wait," Michael said.

"Or we can come back another time," Charlotte said cheerfully.

"I can give them a tour if you want," I said to Helen. Even though I was there to see my dad, I wanted to be able to help Michael.

"That would be wonderful, Maggie," Helen said. "Charlotte, when you're done, come back here, and I'll answer any questions you have." Helen leaned into me and quietly said, "Thank you. I have to impress upon Miss Murdock that she can't keep smoking pot in the ceramics room." I nodded, and Helen hurried away.

"I'll show you my favorite parts of Brooklawn first," I said to Charlotte. As we headed down the hall, I kept the same pace as Charlotte and her walker. Michael stayed a step behind us.

When Charlotte stopped for a moment to catch her breath, he whispered in my ear, "I owe you for this." His minty breath made my neck hairs tingle.

"There are so many things to do here," I said to Charlotte. "It's like summer camp for adults."

"I hated summer camp. Too many bugs," Charlotte said. Michael crossed his hands tightly across his chest.

"Well, this is a bug-free environment," I said. I took them to the activity room, where residents were playing bridge and bingo and board games. "My dad loves this room. There's always someone to play cards with."

Charlotte turned away as if she'd seen something distasteful. Next, we went into the television room. "Those couches look comfortable, don't they, Mom?" Michael asked.

"I don't like sharing a television with a lot of people. I don't want to fight over the remote when my favorite shows are on."

"You can have your own television in your room. This one's for residents who enjoy watching together," I said. "They also have movie night." When I showed her the workout room, she said they didn't make cute workout pants for the elderly. When I showed her the dining room, she didn't like the blue dishes they used. I talked about Brooklawn as if it were a Four Seasons resort, but I understood it wasn't anyone's dream to wait out the rest of their life in an assisted living facility. I tried to look at this place from the perspective of the residents. Some looked happy, others looked lost. Getting old scared the hell out of me. Would Gia someday drag me to a place like this and tell me I had to move in? Would Jim notice I was gone?

We made our way back to the main desk, where Helen was waiting for us. "Why don't we go in my office so we can get to know each other?" she said to Charlotte, who followed her as if she were being led to a room that she'd never come out of.

Michael collapsed into a chair along the wall, I sat down next to him. He was radiating stress. "My mom would find something to complain about at the Sistine Chapel. Thanks for trying to help me."

"Asking your parent to give up their independence is huge. You have to be patient with her," I said.

"You're right. If someone wanted me to move here, I'd be more resistant than she is. I'm glad I ran into you. I hope I can take you out for a drink soon to thank you."

A few days ago, he'd given me his phone number; now he wanted to go for a drink. *Is a drink another way of saying sex?*

I knew I should pull back, but he was keeping me sane and happy, so what was the harm? It wasn't as if we were getting physical. As I was willing my cheeks to stop blushing, one of the nurses wheeled my dad toward us. He looked sharp in a white polo shirt and brown slacks.

"There's my beautiful girl," he said. I stood up and kissed him on the cheek. Dad looked at Michael. "Is your husband . . . uh, uh. . . ?" I knew he was struggling to remember Jim's name, but with Michael there, I pretended not to know what he was talking about.

"Dad, this is Michael. His mom's thinking about moving to Brooklawn."

Michael jumped up from the chair and shook Dad's hand. "Nice to meet you, sir," Michael said.

"So nice to meet a friend of my daughter's," Dad said. Did I say he was a friend? I purposely didn't say he was a friend.

"Maggie's told me so many wonderful things about you, Mr. Rubin," Michael said. Why did he say that? Was Dad going to wonder how friendly we were?

"You remind me of Maggie's husband," he said. "Jim's a big guy also. Isn't he, Maggie?" Terrific, now he remembers who Jim is.

"I guess so," I stammered.

"Mr. Rubin, we better get to the dining room. They're serving your favorite dessert," the nurse said as she released the brakes on his wheelchair.

"I'll come find you in a little while," I said, squeezing his hand. I hoped his confusion would kick in and he wouldn't remember meeting Michael today. Now I had another thing to worry about.

"Maggie, what's my favorite dessert?" Dad called as he disappeared around the corner.

"Cheesecake," I said under my breath as my heart split in two.

"He seems like a nice man. If my mom moves in here, maybe they can be friends." Right, just what I needed, my dad to be friends with my crush's mom. Maybe we could all go on a double date.

Michael and I sat back down. We continued talking quietly about what it was like to have aging parents. Twenty minutes later, Helen and Charlotte approached us. Michael and I had our heads close to each other. "I hope we're not interrupting you two," Charlotte said. "You look like you're in the middle of something important."

"No, we're not talking about anything," I said, feeling as if they'd caught us making plans to run away together.

Michael and I stood up, and Helen shook both Charlotte and Michael's hands. "It was nice meeting you both." Helen said. "Don't hesitate to contact me if you need anything."

Michael took his mother's arm. "Ready to go?" he asked.

"I was ready an hour ago," Charlotte said impatiently.

Michael said goodbye to me and led Charlotte away. After they were gone, I went to Dad's room to see if he was back. He was alone sitting in his club chair, staring off in the distance with a frown on his face.

His white polo was wrinkled, and there was a piece of cheese-cake hanging from a fold above his stomach. It took everything in my power not to grab the crumb and fling it in the trash, but I didn't want to embarrass him. When Dad was a prosecutor, criminals were afraid of him. He was a fast thinker and an even faster talker, and he put a lot of people away for a long time. Now he was doing nothing.

"Hi, honey. I wondered if you'd come by to see me today," he said.

If he didn't remember seeing me twenty-five minutes ago, there was no way he was going to remember meeting Michael. "I love seeing you. How are you doing?" I asked.

"I don't think I'm getting better. I'm afraid I'll never get to go home again. And I'm so lonely here. No one ever comes to visit me. I wish I could go to sleep and never wake up." Tears began to fall onto his cheeks, and he rounded his back and looked down toward his lap.

I'd never seen my dad cry before, and I wanted to scream, *Stop it!* I felt helpless and overwhelmed. "I'd be devastated if you didn't wake up."

"Why? You're never here. You don't care about me anymore. No one does," he said angrily through his tears.

"I love you. I promise I'll come much more often," I said, even though I'd been coming at least four times a week now. How could you argue with someone who didn't remember?

"I get why you don't want to. I sit here all day and do nothing. I never leave this room."

"You go to the dining room for meals, and you play cards with some of the residents."

"I don't like playing cards anymore because sometimes I don't remember how to play." He began to sob. I did everything in my power to hold back my own tears. "I shouldn't be telling you all this," he said in between sobs. "I'm sure you have enough in your life without me falling apart."

"It's okay," I said, my words falling flat. I sat there like an emotionless statue, not knowing what to say because I couldn't change anything. I handed him a tissue, and he pulled himself together. I was a horrible daughter, because all I could think about was that I had to get out of there. I hugged him hard. "I'm going to have to go," I said, feeling guilt as I'd never felt before. I would be a puddle if I stayed longer.

"I'm sorry I'm not any fun anymore," he said.

"You're always fun," I said, stumbling over my words. "I'll see you tomorrow." I hugged him again, then ran out of the room and out of the building. Before I made it to my car, I heard my mom calling out to me. She and Jerry were walking toward me, and they were the last people I wanted to see right now. Mom's hair was not brushed, and she was wearing only one earring.

Mom led me over to a wrought-iron bench outside the front entrance. The bench was cold under my legs. It was so uncomfortable that once I sat down, all I wanted to do was get up again, but my legs felt glued down. "Dad's tests came back," she said. "The doctor said your dad doesn't have Parkinson's at all. He has Lewy body dementia, which can look like Parkinson's." Mom said all of this without taking a breath.

"What is Lewy body dementia?" I asked.

"It's when your brain has problems processing the protein alpha-synuclein," Jerry said, jumping in. He loved knowing something that I didn't.

"Can't you just explain it like you're not trying to impress me?" I said.

Jerry spoke very slowly. "It's a type of dementia caused by abnormal deposits in the brain that are called Lewy bodies."

"That can't be right. Dad has Parkinson's, not some kind of dementia I've never heard of. The doctor can't change his mind like that," I said.

"Lewy body is hard to diagnose. It can look like Parkinson's," Mom said. "Your dad's confusion, his sleep issues, the way he can't pay attention, and the hallucinations are all associated with the disease." She kept talking, but all I could concentrate on was the fly that had landed on her hair that she wasn't swatting off.

"At some point, Dad may not be able to speak or know who

we are. They'll move him to the memory care unit when he gets really bad," Jerry said.

"I've seen the memory care unit. They lock the doors to keep the residents inside," I said. The thought of my dad being locked in anywhere made my skin crawl. I turned back to my mother. "Maybe we should get a second opinion."

"His doctor's a specialist in dementia. He went through all of your dad's scans and the cognitive testing. The doctor asked me all kinds of questions, and I realized your dad has been having symptoms for years. I just didn't know that's what they were."

"Does Dad know?" I asked.

"Not yet, and I'm worried how he's going to take it." She blinked repeatedly to avoid tears. Then she went to see my dad, leaving me with Jerry.

"This is not good," I said.

"Yeah, and the dementia has been progressing pretty quickly. The doctor said he's in the middle stages of the disease," Jerry said.

"I don't want to hear this right now," I said.

"You need to, because you and I are at a higher risk for getting it someday."

"Can you stop talking?" I asked.

"It would be just like you to hide your head in the sand."

"Why are you so mean to me?" I pushed Jerry and almost knocked him off the bench. He didn't even flinch. "It's not like they opened Dad's head and looked in his brain and saw these Lewy things," I said. "We don't even know for sure Dad has it. Doctors can be wrong." Jerry stood up, shook his head, and left.

I pulled my keys out of my purse and walked quickly to my car. I hit the unlock button, but nothing happened. I hit it again, but still nothing. What the hell was wrong with my car? And then I realized my trunk was open because I'd pushed the wrong button. I closed the trunk and got in the car. I was about to back out when I froze. My foot couldn't even push the pedal down. I put the car in park and turned it off. I took my hands off the wheel and started cracking my knuckles. It hurt, and the pain was poignant. If the doctor was right, my sharp, quick-witted father would forget his whole life. I didn't know how to wrap my head around that. I never wanted to lose him and certainly not this way. He'd be alive, but he wouldn't be living. He was going to be devastated when he heard his diagnosis.

I started the car again and tried to back out when a thought came into my head, and I slammed on the brakes. Could Jerry be right? Could we get dementia also? Last week, I forgot to turn the porch lights on at night, I forgot to return two library books, and I forgot to DVR *60 Minutes*. Had it already started?

I put my car in gear and drove to Jim's office. When I walked into the waiting room, I was thankful there wasn't anyone there. My shirt was rumpled, my makeup smeared, and except for my Michael Kors purse, I looked as if I could've been homeless. I pushed the red button in the waiting room that let Jim know his next client was there. I waited and waited, but he didn't open the door. Where was he? Didn't he know I was having a crisis out here? When he did finally come out, I shouted, "I think I have dementia."

He scanned the waiting room for any patients and, seeing it was empty, said, "Come in here." I followed him into his office. I wanted to pace, I needed to pace, but the room was small. I ended up walking in circles around the couch and chair. He sat down on the couch and watched me, sure this was just one of my rants.

"I have dementia, or at least I probably do. You're always saying I forget things, and you're right, I do. In fact, right now I can't remember what those things I forget even are."

"What are you talking about?"

"The doctor said my dad has Lewy body dementia."

"Oh no, that's terrible."

"Jerry said it could also be genetic."

He thought for a moment. "Let's take one step at a time. Even if your dad has it, that doesn't mean you'll get it too."

"But it doesn't mean I won't." I increased the speed I was pacing at.

"Can you sit down? You're making me dizzy," he said gently.

I couldn't sit, so I kept moving. "This whole thing freaks me out. And I'm terrified Gia could also get it."

"There's no reason to tell her anything. We don't want to scare her."

"Why would you think I'd want to scare her? What kind of mother would that make me?" The red light that told him his next patient was waiting lit up. We both looked at it. "I can't leave right now. I'm a mess," I said desperately.

"I know you're upset, and I'm really sorry. I promise we can talk about this for as long as you want when I get home." He used his soothing therapist voice. I hated that voice.

"I need you."

"And I feel awful that I can't be there for you right now, but my next client is here." He walked toward the door, expecting me to follow him.

It was unreasonable for me to expect him to cancel his client because I needed him, but I didn't care. "I'm not leaving." I raised my voice, so it was an octave below yelling.

Jim shushed me as if I were a child shouting during a bar mitzvah. "I really am sorry. I'll be home as soon as I can." He opened the door. In the waiting room was a woman in her early thirties, very pretty, and about to get my husband's undivided attention. As I walked through, I accidentally made eye contact with her. When I say accidentally, I mean that I purposely gave her a look that said, *Stay away from my husband.* As I closed the waiting room door, I heard Jim apologizing to her for keeping her waiting. Jim was probably happy to get rid of me. He got to be with some pretty young woman sitting across from him for an hour a week, getting his attention. Especially one who wasn't going to get dementia. I was likely putting my guilt on him for my relationship with Michael, but I was upset, and I didn't care.

When I got home, I tried making a cup of tea, but tea was overrated for calming nerves. I tried reading a book, but *Gone Girl* may not have been the best choice right now. My thoughts drifted to Michael. He'd understand what I was going through because he was dealing with his own mother's health issues. I would text him, if only I could find my phone. It wasn't in the kitchen, in my bedroom, or in the laundry room. Could not remembering where I put it be another sign of dementia? Finally, I saw the outline of it underneath a washcloth in the bathroom. How it got there, I'd never know.

Now, what should I text? If I told him how I fell apart at Jim's office, he could think I was crazy, and I didn't want him to see me that way. Would he think I was too forward being the first one to text? Was I overthinking this? I got sick of listening to my excuses, so I wrote:

Hey, it's Maggie. What're you don't? I hated autocorrect. I tried again. I typed, *What're you dong?* Great, now he thinks I'm a pervert. Finally, I carefully typed, *doing?*

It wasn't exactly original or charming, but the first text was out there. I put the phone down and washed the hairs from Jim's razor down the sink. When my phone vibrated, I pounced on it.

I'm at the dog park. How're you?

He was cute and he had a dog, what more could one ask for? I read his text again. How was I? I couldn't tell him the truth;

he'd think my life was a mess, and that could be a turnoff. Hmm, I needed to be casual and positive.

I thought for a minute, then texted. *Not great. I'm dealing with some stuff with my dad.*

I cursed my fingers for texting that. It was neither casual nor positive. After a full minute when he still hadn't answered, I was getting jumpy. I turned my WiFi on and off twice, but still nothing. I shouldn't have told him my problems. After another minute, I was certifiably crazy. Why wasn't he writing back? Was he ghosting me?

Finally, he texted. *Do you want to meet me here? We could talk.*

Which dog park are you at?

The one in Trumbull near the mall.

Okay, I can be there in fifteen minutes.

I thought about getting Theo's leash, but being a basset hound, he wasn't the kind of dog that liked the dog park. He didn't like anything other than eating and sleeping, which I could often relate to. I'd promised myself I'd exercise him more because his basset belly was almost touching the ground, but he was going to have to wait to get in shape.

At the park, Michael was sitting on a bench off to the side next to the jungle gym, where a couple of kids were being pushed on swings by their parents. The rest of the dogs and their owners were in the center of the park. It wasn't as cold today as it had been, so most of the people had on sweaters and scarves but no jackets. As I walked down the hill from the parking lot, a Pit bull running away from a tiny yapping Maltese almost knocked me over. No one rescued the pit bull; everyone was busy socializing, their canine children left to their own devices.

Michael was leaning down and petting a chocolate lab that looked to be about six months old. "Hey," I said and sat down next to him. "She's so cute. What's her name?"

"Jennifer Lopez. I like to name my dogs after celebrities. Unfortunately, Matt Damon passed away last year."

"Hey, sweetheart, you're such a pretty girl," I said as I reached down to pet her. She jumped up on the bench and started licking me all over my neck. I'd finally found something to calm my nerves.

"No, J. Lo." Michael pulled her back down. "Sorry, I'm still training her."

"It's fine. I love dogs, and she's adorable." A French bulldog hobbled by, as bulldogs are known to do, and J. Lo leapt completely over me and ran off to play with it.

"So, what's going on with your dad?" he asked.

"He was diagnosed with dementia."

"I thought he had Parkinson's."

"It's complicated." I wished J. Lo would come back, because petting her made me feel better.

"I had no idea things were so bad," he said.

"My dad's been so depressed lately. What's going to happen when he finds out he has dementia? My brother said at some point he's not going to recognize any of us. It's terrifying." My voice cracked. "I'm not handling it well. I don't know how I'll ever get over it."

"It's a lot to take in," he said.

I paused. "I'm sorry, I shouldn't be burdening you with all my stuff."

"I wish there was something I could do to help."

"Just talking to you helps." J. Lo bounded over to a woman near us and jumped up on her back. The woman laughed and turned around and started petting J. Lo. She had no clue that J. Lo had left a large brown mud stain on the back of her white pants. Michael didn't see it, and I looked away, pretending I didn't either. J. Lo ran back to us and started barking.

"That means she's ready to go, we've been here a while," he said. "But if you want, I can put her in the car, and we can talk longer."

"Thanks, but I should get home anyway."

Michael put the leash on J. Lo, and we walked to our cars. He put her in his back seat, attaching a special seat belt to her leash. "I feel bad leaving you like this." He moved toward me and enveloped me in a hug. A hug so caring, so empathetic. "Text me later and let me know how you're doing." His arms were so strong that even if I got dementia, I knew I'd remember this feeling.

DAD

—◦—

"Mr. Rubin, do you need anything?" the nurse asks when she comes in to check on me. I've been placed in a chair next to the window. Spring has come, the white blossoms of the flowering dogwoods are peeking out, and the Kentucky bluegrass has begun to turn from brown to green.

"Yes, an escape plan," I say.

"Aren't we treating you well?"

"I just miss my wife." I hate living without her, but she doesn't belong here. I wish I didn't belong here.

"I'm sure she'll be here soon. Do you want to go to the lounge and visit with people while you wait?"

"I'd rather stay here. Before you go, can you bring me . . . um . . . that?" I point, but I can't remember what it's called. "The . . . the . . ."

"The glass of water?" she asks. I nod. "Of course." She reaches over to the side table, picks up a glass, and holds the straw up to my lips.

I drink slowly and then take my lips off the straw so she knows I'm done. "Thank you. I keep drawing a blank. The other day, I forgot my granddaughter's name."

"We all forget things," she says, as if it happens to her all the time, but she hasn't been diagnosed with a disease? Will the dementia take over day by day, month by month? Will I notice as it's happening? I'm terrified that I will. This is not the way I thought my life would go. One minute I'm a young man, and the next I'm in an old age home where I can't do things for myself. I want my old life back.

"Hi, honey," Dorothy says as she walks in the room, carrying a few magazines. The nurse greets her and leaves us alone. I know how lucky I am to have a wife like Dorothy. She never complains and she gives up a lot to come see me every afternoon. She leans down and kisses me, and even though I feel as if I'm a hundred years old, my heart beats as fast as it did when we were dating.

"I'm relieved to see you," I say. She sits down on the edge of the bed.

"Is everything okay?" she asks in her worried tone.

I burst into tears. "I thought you got into an accident."

She looks perplexed. "Why would you think that?"

"When you weren't here already, I was sure something terrible happened." Ever since she told me about the dementia, the tears keep coming.

She gets up, comes over, and kneels next to my chair. Then she takes my hand and looks in my eyes. "I'm fine. Nothing's going to happen to me. I'll be here every day." She goes over to the table next to my bed and gets a tissue out of the box.

She waits quietly while I blow my nose and wipe my eyes. She stuffs the tissue in her pocket as her cell phone begins to ring. She fumbles in her purse and pulls out two receipts, a compact mirror, a granola bar, and a Sharpie before she finally finds her phone. She's so close to me that I can hear Jerry's voice coming through the speaker. He's asking questions about how I am, but she's being cryptic with her answers. I may be losing my mind, but I can still tell if someone's keeping things from me. Dorothy gets off the phone as quickly as she can.

"If Jerry wants to know how I am, he should come visit," I say.

"He will soon, but for now he sends his love," she says.

"Right," I say with as much sarcasm as I can muster. She hates when I point out that Jerry and I aren't close. It bothers me too, but it's too late to change it. I've apologized to Jerry, but I'm not sure he'll ever get over it. The things parents can do to mess up their children. "Do you think he'll notice when I die?" I ask.

"No one's dying," she says emphatically.

A rush of anger sweeps over me. "Didn't you stick me in this place so you could get rid of me until I die?" I'm swimming in my emotions, stuck at the bottom of a pool and unable to see the waterline.

"I would never do that."

"I didn't want to come here," I say.

"I'd much rather have you home with me too."

"Then let me come home."

"You need to be where there are people who can help you. I can't take care of you by myself anymore."

"Fine," I say. After a moment my anger subsides. Dorothy is relieved when the redness leaves my face, and I'm calm again.

She holds up a magazine, her way of changing the subject. She says she thought I'd like to read about the person on the cover because she knows how much I like him. When I tell her I have no idea who it is, she gets anxious. She tells me it's Stephen Colbert. Still I have no idea who that is, but to appease her, I pretend I do and thank her. She asks if I want to read it, but I tell her maybe later. Why would I want to read about someone I don't know?

I feel as if everything I once remembered is being taken over by the mud that's seeping into my brain. I remember all the lyrics from *If I Had A Hammer*, but I can't remember what I was doing five minutes ago.

Dorothy picks up her purse. "I'm going to run downstairs and get some coffee. I'll be right back," she says. Everything exhausts me lately, so when she comes back, I'll be asleep, and I probably won't remember she was here.

JIM

———⊹———

"Sir, I think you're done for the night," the bartender says.
"Done? Why would I be done?" I only had one vodka. Or
was it three? I've lost track, probably because I'm a little drunk.
Or a lot drunk. I've lost track of that too.

I have a fondness for this bar. The Tiki Hut is the place I
go to when I need to hide from the world. It's easy to pretend
I'm in the South Pacific, with all the bamboo hanging from
the ceiling, and the walls filled with masks of the gods of the
Hawaiian Islands.

I don't want to be anywhere but on this barstool getting
drunk. Hopefully I will forget how much I hate myself for not
being present for Maggie while she deals with her dad's illness.
What kind of selfish husband am I that all I can think about is
how much I hate my job?

"I'll take another vodka," I say. The bartender, who's dressed
in a grass skirt over shorts, ignores me. He pretends to wipe the
spots off the glasses. My phone rings again for the third time,
but I don't even look at it. "Bartender, why aren't you bringing
me another vodka?"

"Because you need to go home," Sam says as he sits down on the stool next to me.

"Where'd you come from?"

"I was born in Texas, but I've lived in Connecticut most of my life."

"Maggie called you, didn't she?" I ask.

"Yes. You didn't come home, and she couldn't reach you. I told her I had a feeling I knew where you were."

"I should've gone to a bar further from home. I need to find a place where nobody knows my name." I start laughing at the reference and almost fall off the stool. Sam helps me back up. "I'm fine, you can go." I push twenty bucks toward the bartender, and he pours another vodka.

"You haven't gotten drunk this often since we were in college," Sam says.

"Yeah, it's better than I remember."

"Won't be tomorrow."

The other patrons look as if they're having as much fun as I am. One man has his head on the bar. I think he's asleep—or dead; I'm not sure which. And the three women sitting in a corner are laughing uncontrollably.

"Hey," I yell to the bartender, "get my friend here a drink." The bartender looks at Sam, who shakes his head. "It's rude not to accept a drink from a friend." I pat him on the back.

"Fine, I'll have a Coke," Sam says to the bartender, then turns to me. "I gather you still haven't told Maggie that you're thinking of giving up your practice, have you?"

I down the vodka. "Her dad was just diagnosed with dementia, and now she thinks she's going to get it. I can't tell her I want to quit my job."

"She needs to understand why you've been weird."

"She already thinks I'm a horrible husband."

"And you think getting drunk's going to make that better?"

"I'm not drunk." I stand up quickly, get dizzy, and sit back down. "I'll be fine after I find the bathroom."

"It's in the back on your right," the bartender says, eavesdropping on our conversation. Then he walks away, his grass skirt sashaying as he goes.

I walk across the room, and instead of the bathroom, I end up in the kitchen. One of the busboys walks me to the bathroom. When I get back to the table, I tell Sam that I'm ready to go, and I take my keys out of my pocket.

"You could barely find your way to the bathroom. I'm not letting you drive home like this. We need to get you some food. Food and coffee." Sam practically picks me up and walks me out to his car. He drives around for what feels like an hour, although I'm drunk, so it could have been ten minutes. We go to a coffee shop, where he plies me with coffee and food until I stop talking nonsense. "I can't tell if you're sober, so I'll drive you home, and you can get your car in the morning," Sam says. I make him swear that he won't tell Ellen what I've told him.

We pull into the driveway, Maggie comes out, as if she's been standing at the window watching for me. Now I feel even worse than I already do. She looks wary, standing there in her pajamas with an unzipped parka over them. She thanks Sam, and he nods, gets back in his car, and drives away. Maggie and I are standing in the middle of the driveway. I see the disappointment in her eyes.

"You okay?" she asks.

"Yeah, but it's freezing out here." I realize I left my jacket in my car at the bar. As I walk toward the house, she stops me.

"We need to talk out here. I don't want to wake up Gia." I follow her to the doorstep, and we sit. "Are you getting drunk because of me? Because I was so upset about my father when I showed up at your office?" She puts her hands in the pockets of her parka.

"No. I wish I could've been there for you when you needed me."

"Me too, but I shouldn't have come to your office when you were working."

"You were upset, and I didn't handle it well. It's all over-whelming, your dad's illness, knowing Gia's leaving soon, my. . . ." I stop because I'm not sure I want to tell her, but I know if I don't, things will only get worse. A dog howls in the distance, which sets off a chain reaction of howling neighbor-hood dogs. If I howled with them, would she get distracted enough to forget that I was talking, or would she put me in a mental ward?

"Your what?" she asks.

I take a breath and confess. "My job. I don't know how much longer I can do it."

"What do you mean?"

"I'm going to lose it if I have to listen to one more person's problems."

"So when I came to you with mine, you must've wanted to run away."

"You're my wife, and I want to be there for you, but I also feel pressured to fix things."

"You can't fix anything. I just wanted you to listen." She stands up and pushes her sleeve over her hand and then wipes cobwebs off the sconce at the front door. "Do you want to quit?" she asks without looking at me.

"I want to take time off."

"But what about your patients? What would you tell them?" She finishes with the cobwebs and moves over to the dust on our front door.

"That I'm taking a sabbatical."

"What if you lose all of them?"

She wasn't making this easy. "I'd have to deal with that," I say.

"And what would you do on this sabbatical?"

"I don't know. I've been putting a bucket list together. Maybe I'd backpack through Europe, volunteer for Habitat for Humanity, or run a marathon in every state."

"You hate running," she says, which is true but not the point.

Then she bombards me with questions; Am I sorry that we got married and had Gia so young? Is this an excuse for me to leave her? What is she supposed to do while I'm out having these adventures? Her voice gets slightly higher in pitch with each question. She's panicking, and when I tell her I haven't thought things through, it only makes her question me more.

"Should I try to get a job? We're going to need the money," she says.

I wish I wasn't sobering up, because reality is setting in, and now *I'm* starting to panic. "Ignore me. I'm just tired and drunk and upset about your father. I'm not going to quit." I can't put her through this. She doesn't deserve my stress on top of hers. I stand up, open the front door, and put my arm around her shoulder. "Let's get some sleep," I say. She nods, then exhales loudly as if she's been holding her breath under water. By tomorrow she'll be telling Ellen she thinks I'm having a midlife crisis and she hopes I snap out of it. I follow her as she walks inside. I feel more trapped than before I told her.

CHAPTER 13

———— ✧ ————

Early the next morning, my brain began ruminating even before my eyes were open. How could Jim say he wanted to quit his job? I hoped it was the alcohol talking, since he'd never said he was unhappy at work before. I assured myself that it would all go away because I couldn't deal with anything else right now. Maybe if I got dementia, I'd forget it.

Gia came in my bedroom wearing pajamas and bright red lipstick. She asked what I thought of her new purchase. As long as she was living at home, I got to nix anything I thought was inappropriate, and ruby-red lips fell into that category. I cautiously asked her to get rid of the lipstick and braced for her reaction. She immediately took a tissue and wiped it off, then went back upstairs. That was not the reaction I expected. She must be up to something.

I pulled out my phone and texted: *Hi.*

While I waited for Michael to get back to me, I got the bag with my new red chemise and robe. I didn't have scissors in my closet, so I tore the tags off with my teeth. I remembered how Michael had bit off the string on his shirt the first time I met him. It was another thing we had in common, being opposed to scissors.

My phone dinged. *Hi.*

So I didn't look too eager, I counted thirty Mississippi's before I wrote back: *What're u up to?*

Writing an article.

Need a break? I might go to the gym.

He replied: *Can't. Stuck home waiting for a package.*

Darn it, I didn't like working out alone anymore, then he texted: *You want to come here?*

Yes, I wanted to come there, I wanted that badly, but should I go? The dog park was one thing—it was a public place—but his apartment? That seemed kind of intimate. What message would it send if I came over? Then again, Ellen and I hung out at her house all the time; this could be the same thing. It didn't have to mean anything if we were just friends, and we never touched each other.

Text me your address, I sent back.

I put on my most flattering jeans and a burgundy scoop-neck T-shirt over a black lace bra and panties. I could've kept my old bra and underwear on, but weren't you supposed to wear clean underwear in case you got in an accident?

I was startled when I found Jim in the kitchen eating a sleeve of graham crackers. He didn't seem to notice that there were now crumbs all over the counter. "I thought you left for work," I said, brushing them into my hand and then into the sink.

"I moved my clients to tomorrow and took today off."

"That's good. Then you can rest," I said. He grabbed another graham cracker square and headed to his home office. I was relieved that he didn't say anything more about quitting. Maybe a day off would do him good.

Gia came downstairs again, trailed by Taylor, who had spent the night. Taylor was wearing slinky pajama shorts that barely covered her butt and a tank top that left little to the imagination. I was glad Jim was in his office.

"I can't believe you broke up with Brandon. He really liked you," Gia said as she poured cereal into two bowls and added milk. Their conversation intrigued me, so I tried to blend into the sink as I quietly dried dishes.

"I know, but my new boyfriend is way hotter," Taylor said. "He's older, so he knows exactly how to treat a woman. And he loves teaching me things. Sometimes I pretend not to know what he's talking about because it turns him on to be the expert."

"You're an idiot, you know that, right?" Gia took two spoons out of the drawer, and they went back to her room. I was glad I wasn't Taylor's mother.

Fifteen minutes later I went to tell Jim I was going out but found his office door closed, which was good because I couldn't lie directly to his face. I could, however, lie to a closed door.

"I'm going to run some errands. I'll see you later," I called out and left before he could reply.

I turned on the car radio, and Queen's "Bohemian Rhapsody" was on. I sang "Is this the real life, is this just fantasy. . . ." at the top of my lungs, not caring that I was completely out of tune. I toned down my dance moves when a man in another car pulled up next to me and gave me a thumbs-up. The loud music didn't drown out the nervous gurgle coming from my stomach. I reminded myself again that Michael and I were just friends, and there was no reason to feel uncomfortable, but my intestines weren't getting the message. My GPS directed me fifteen minutes away into the next town. The houses turned from Cape Cods to nondescript apartments that resembled state college dorms. They weren't the nicest apartments, but weren't writers supposed to suffer for their craft? Michael's apartment was on a busy street and had one-hour parking. What could happen in an hour? A lot could happen in an hour, but that wasn't why I was there. I turned my engine off and wondered if I was making a mistake by coming here. While I sat and debated if I should text him an excuse and leave, I ran my fingers through my hair, trying to add more body. I would've washed it this morning if I'd known I was going to be seeing him. As I sat in my car, a woman walked by me with three dogs. She eyed me as if I were doing something wrong. Did she know I was a married woman going to another man's apartment? I got out of my car and smiled at her. A guilty woman wouldn't smile.

Michael's duplex was baby blue with a white staircase going up to the second floor. It reminded me of where my grand-parents used to live when I was a child. After my grandmother died, my grandfather was no longer happy to see me. When he heard our car, he'd open his front door and just stare. Then he'd grumble the whole time that I was messing up his stuff. I remembered how terrible I'd felt when I left imprints in his shag carpet.

My knees trembled as I climbed the stairs to Michael's apartment. I rang the bell, and I thought about how you were supposed to bring something the first time you visited someone's home, and I hadn't brought anything.

Michael opened the door holding a package of Top Ramen and wearing distressed skinny jeans and a tight V-neck white T-shirt. When Jim wore a V-neck, there was always hair peeking out, but there was no hair coming out of Michael's shirt. Did he shave his chest? Or wax? Or was he just naturally hairless?

"Hi. Come on in." I was disappointed to hear that his neigh-bor had taken J.Lo for a walk. His living room was small but homey and opened to an even smaller kitchen. Half-empty bottles of water were on the kitchen counter, and a painting of Superman giving the finger hung on the wall above the table. A laundry basket sat in the middle of the living room floor, and a pile of newspapers were stacked on the coffee table.

"Sorry about the mess," he said, pushing the laundry up against the wall.

"No worries." I liked his mess; it was liberating. It reminded me of my first apartment I shared with my best friend. That was before I became a neat freak. The television was tuned to a USC/UCLA football game.

"Do you want some soup?" he asked as he tore open the package of ramen and poured it into a saucepan. He added water and put it on the stove.

"No, thanks," I replied. I hadn't eaten Top Ramen since college.

"Do you mind if I eat? I'm starving."

"Of course not," I said.

He turned the burner on to simmer and then led me to the couch. "Do you want to get high?" He pulled a joint out of a drawer in the coffee table.

"No, thanks." I hadn't smoked since before Gia was born. He put the joint on top of the table, directly in front of me. Did he think I'd change my mind?

"I can't believe you're here," he said.

"I needed to get out of my house for a while."

"I get that." Since he didn't have a wife and kids to run away from, why would he ever need to leave?

He muted the television, and in the awkward silence I realized how totally alone we were. "Can I use your bathroom?" I asked. Whenever I got nervous, I needed to pee, which was always inconvenient when I went horseback riding.

He pointed. "It's next to my bedroom."

His bedroom. The place he goes to bed. The place he takes off his clothes and . . . I wanted to see his bedroom. As I walked toward the bathroom, Michael answered his phone, which gave me the opportunity to peek my head in, but I couldn't see much, so I walked in. A blue paisley comforter was pulled up to cover the whole bed, but parts of the white sheet stuck out from underneath in a haphazard way. There was a bottle of Calvin Klein cologne on his nightstand, next to a framed photograph of him at Disney World with a man and a toddler. On the dresser were a bunch of action hero figures. They were in various positions of combat, like Batman was fighting the Incredible Hulk.

I picked up Thor and was looking at him when I heard, "What do you think of my superheroes?" He said it as if it was perfectly normal to find me in his bedroom. I dropped Thor, knocking over Superman and causing Lex Luthor to launch into the air and nosedive under the bed.

"Sorry," I said and got down on my hands and knees to pick up Lex Luthor. I tried to stand them back up in their original positions, but they kept falling over. "These are cool. I noticed them on the way back from the bathroom." He knew I was lying because you couldn't see his dresser from the hallway, but he didn't say anything.

"My mom found them a week ago in her garage. If I'd known there was going to be a woman in my bedroom, maybe I would've left them in the box." As I continued to struggle to get them back in their original positions, Michael took Superman and Lex Luthor out of my hands and easily positioned them back down on the dresser so they were fighting each other. He moved closer to me. "You look really pretty today," he said.

"My hair's flat." I ran my fingers through it again.

"I like it. You look like a teenager." He brushed a strand out of my eyes, and it felt as if fireworks were exploding from my roots. Suddenly, I heard music playing—how cliché. Oh, wait, it was coming from his cell phone. Michael ran into the living room to grab it, and I followed.

"Hey, Kirk, I know you wanted the article yesterday, but I'm just about done," he said, then listened a beat. His mouth turned down. "I know you had a deadline, but I can get it to you in a couple of minutes." His shoulders drooped, and his lips were pressed tight. "Maybe you could use it at another time?" He rubbed his forehead. "No, no, I understand. Okay, bye." He dropped his phone down on the couch. Then he picked up the TV remote and threw it across the room. The batteries flew out and clanked as they hit the floor. I jumped. I'd never seen him angry. "I should've made the deadline. That article was going to pay my rent for the month." He picked the batteries up and tried putting them back into the remote, but the piece that held them in had broken off. He sat on the couch and put the remote back on the coffee table.

"I should go," I said.

"No, no, don't. I shouldn't have reacted that way."

I sat down next to him. "I'm sorry about your article."

"Me too. I'll try to sell it somewhere else."

"Wow, you're amazing. I wouldn't be able to get over the disappointment that quickly."

"Considering I just threw the remote, I would say I haven't. But in these situations, I remind myself that some stuff isn't worth it."

"I wish I could feel that way," I said. "I worry about everything. Right now, all I can think about is my dad and how bad I feel for him and whether I'm going to get the same disease someday."

"That's understandable."

"Yeah, but I wish I could be more optimistic."

"My mom has always said, 'Do not anticipate trouble, or worry about what may never happen. Keep in the sunlight.' She loves quoting Benjamin Franklin."

"My mom vibrates worry, which is why I have a hard time not seeing dark clouds everywhere. And right now, they aren't letting in any light."

"Years ago, I worried about everything too, but after my dad died so young, I thought I'd better live every moment like it's my last. As the Green Lantern says, 'No matter how bad things get, something good is out there, just over the horizon.'"

Had the universe put Michael in my life to teach me to stop focusing on all the things that were going wrong? The doctor could be wrong about my dad, or if he's right, Dad could stay stable for years. Doctors didn't know everything. If I stopped worrying all the time and loosened up and enjoyed myself, then in forty years if I lost my memory, I'd have no regrets. I was going to start doing some of the things on my bucket list. Maybe not heli-skiing, but I could at least share a bowl of Top Ramen with a cute guy. I'd add that to my bucket list later.

"You know what? I'd love some of that soup," I said.

Michael got two bowls out of the cabinet, filled them with ramen, and brought them to the card table that was in a nook between the kitchen and the living room. As I rested my arms on the table, it wobbled back and forth. Michael took a small piece of wood and pushed it under one of the legs. I blew on my soup and took a bite, the salty noodles slithering down my throat. He asked how Gia was doing, and I admitted I didn't really know.

"Lately it feels like there's a lot of secrets between us," I said. Sometimes her secrets, sometimes mine. I told him how Jim and I sometimes parented differently and how it could cause an argument, and then I realized I needed to keep my two worlds separate. I didn't want to talk about Jim with Michael.

Instead I told him about my childhood and how I had fought anxiety. I shared with him how I was afraid that when

Gia left for college, I wouldn't have a life anymore. I confessed that I had been looking for a job and didn't know that I would be able to get one. I even told him about Gia not wanting to have sex with Jason and how I worried about him dumping her.

He told me about how little money his parents had when he was growing up, how he'd been bullied in seventh grade, and how his grandfather had committed suicide when he was ten. He was such a good communicator and seemed genuinely interested in everything I said. It was the deepest conversation I'd had with anyone in a long time.

"When I was a teenager, I tried to sleep with as many girls as I could. I thought it made me cool," he said.

"I got really hurt by guys like you."

"Why do I feel like I owe you an apology?"

"You don't. It's hard being that age. I worry about Gia dating boys like that because they really messed up my self-confidence."

"I can't imagine you with low self-confidence. You're incredible," he said. I was touched, even if he was just saying it to be nice. "You're even more incredible than I am, and I'm a great catch," he said with an adorable smirk. I was eating up the flattery and was so enthralled that I didn't realize how long I'd been there. If I stayed any longer, I didn't know how I'd explain my absence to Jim, let alone the parking ticket I was going to get.

"I think I should go." I picked up my purse and headed to the door.

"Wait." He took an unopened bottle of wine off his counter. "I want you to have this wine. I think you'll like it."

"You don't need to give me anything."

"They had a two-for-one special, and I want to return your coupon favor."

"That's really thoughtful. Thank you."

He hugged me. His strong arms pulled me close, so close I couldn't feel any space between us. I wondered if I'd looked up at that moment, would we have kissed? My head was spinning. I wished he'd kissed me, and I was glad he didn't.

Jim greeted me as I walked in our front door. "Hey," he said.

I nonchalantly sniffed myself to see if I smelled like another man's apartment. "Hey." I put the wine down on the counter.

"What's with the red wine? You hate red wine."

"I thought it was time to try something new." He opened the bottle and poured both of us a glass. "Isn't it a little early for wine?" I said.

"Neither of us is going anywhere, so it's fine." I knew you weren't supposed to chug wine, but I did anyway. "This is really good. How did you hear about it?" he asked.

"The man in the store suggested it." Well, a man suggested it; he just was at his home, not in a store. When I thought about the things I could sweep under the rug, it blew me away.

"He has good taste. If you see him again, ask him for other recommendations."

"That shouldn't be a problem," I said.

He poured himself a little more and went back to his office. The wine was going to my head, which made me feel warm and cozy and not guilty at all.

CHAPTER 14

—◈—

I was naked in my closet, five bras and panties piled at my feet. I loved my closet. It wasn't large, but I could walk in, close the door, and hide from my family.

Jim and I were leaving on our anniversary trip today. I wanted to have a nice weekend and connect again, which wasn't going to happen if I slept in my usual sweatpants. Thus, the reason for all these bras and panties. I began to wonder if my banana yellow sweats were the reason that we never had sex. I wanted to have sex the way we did when we were first married, all passion and heat. The last few years the sex was satisfying, but predictable. Once or twice a week after the eleven o'clock news, we'd lie quietly in bed. The room would be completely dark, except for a blue light emanating from the DVR. One of us would reach out to the other, and then afterward, Jim would be snoring, and I'd be wide awake. It had been months since I was kept awake after good sex.

I picked up a pink bra and ran my fingers over the lace. It looked brand new because it was. I bought it two years ago but never wore it because the lace itched. It was pretty, so if it was uncomfortable, I could live with that. I slipped my arms in, then reached around my back and tried to hook it. I kept trying, but it wouldn't close. Finally, I turned the bra around to the front of my body, hooked it easily, then turned it back around and shoved my breasts inside. Then I picked up the matching panties and put my left leg in, but before I could get my right leg in, I lost my balance and ended up lying on the floor. I was alone in my closet, giggling. As I hadn't had a good laugh in a long time, I became almost hysterical.

When I stopped laughing, I picked myself up off the ground and pulled the panties the rest of the way up my legs. I gazed at myself in the full-length mirror on the wall. Were those wrinkles in my knees? What happened to my twenty-one-year-old knees? Those knees were killer. At least my butt was fairly tight. I struck a pose, putting on a pouty expression as if I were some sex kitten. As I changed from pose to pose, I wondered if Michael would like my pink bra and panties. Would he like taking them off me? Would he notice my knees? I knew it was totally natural to fantasize about other people while having sex. Except I wasn't having sex right now.

I was about to go away with my husband, so I had to stop thinking about Michael. Jim was the only man I should be thinking about. My phone rang, and I answered it, my voice echoing in the closet.

"I'm running a little late, I'll be home in about an hour," Jim said.

"We were supposed to be on the road in thirty minutes." My blood pressure was rising.

"It'll be fine. I only have to pack." He hung up.

As I got dressed, I took a deep breath and repeated a calming mantra in my head. *You will be having sex this weekend; you better be having sex this weekend.*

The doorbell rang, and I ran downstairs to answer it. "Am I late?" my mother asked as I opened the door.

"No, Mom, you're not late. You're never late." She came toward me for our obligatory hug. I counted to three in my head and let go.

"I'm so worried about your father." She walked into my kitchen, and I followed her. "Ever since I told him he has Lewy body dementia, it's as if he's given up and let the disease take over. I'm trying to be strong in front of him, but when I'm alone, I can't stop crying."

"I know. It's terrible."

"I'm thankful I have my granddaughter to distract me this weekend. Did you change the sheets for me?" I nodded. She went into the kitchen and opened my pantry cabinets and began rearranging my canned goods. I could have stopped her, but it was easier to just put everything back when I got home. My canned goods must've been a disaster, because she gave up on them and opened my silverware drawer. She took out the knives and put them where the forks were, then the spoons where the knives were. She was making me dizzy. "I thought I'd take Gia out to dinner one of the nights, and the other one, I'll cook," she said.

"You don't have to cook. I made Gia's favorite foods and put them in the fridge."

She closed the silverware drawer. "But I like to cook."

"With all you've been dealing with, I wanted to make things easier on you."

She softened. "That was thoughtful." I wasn't being thoughtful; I was protecting Gia from my mother's "famous" salmon patties. To this day, if I even smelled salmon, I got PTSD.

She moved my juice glasses to a different shelf. "I wrote a few things down for you," I said. I picked up a sheet of paper off the counter that had "Household Information" written at the top. I tried to hand it to her, but she wouldn't take it.

"Gia can tell me what to do," she said.

Poor Theo, he was never going to get fed. "I'll just leave the list on the counter," I said, relenting. "If you have any questions, you can always call me."

"I'll be fine, your house will be fine, everything will be fine," she said. Yeah, everything but my kitchen. "There is something important I want to talk to you about," she said.

Oh God, what could it be? It would be just like her to bring up something horrible right before I left for my anniversary trip. I began to sweat. "What is it?" I asked wearily.

"I think I should cut my hair off, like Scarlett Johansson's."

I was relieved that it wasn't something bad. Then I realized it was something bad. My elderly mother wanted to look like Scarlett Johansson. "I don't think most women look good with hair that short," I said. "Besides, I like your hair the way you've always had it." I hoped she would take the compliment and forget this ridiculous idea.

"Twenty years of the same haircut is too much. I should switch it up."

"No, you really shouldn't." I looked at the time. "Mom, I have some things I need to do before we leave. Gia's upstairs if you want to say hi." She ran up the stairs as fast as a seventy-five-year-old woman could run up stairs.

I spent the next half hour paying a few bills and putting away the laundry. As I folded the last of the shirts, Jim rushed through the door, cursing about the traffic. "I'll be ready soon," he said and grabbed two shirts out of the laundry basket I was holding. I should have packed for him. The last time we went away, he forgot socks.

While he was opening and closing drawers, I went to say goodbye to Gia. The door to her room was half-open. Gia was sitting on her bed, and my mom had her arms around her. A pang of jealousy rushed through me. I wished I had that kind of relationship with my mom. Had I been the first one to pull away or had she? The closest I'd felt to her in ages was when we were commiserating over my father.

Gia and Mom were looking at a website on Gia's iPad where you could download a picture of yourself and check out how different hairstyles would look on you. Gia held the iPad up and was trying to get her grandmother to sit still so she could take her picture. "Make sure you only shoot my left side. My right side makes me look older," Mom said. I was about to enter when I heard my mother ask Gia, "So, how's that boyfriend of yours?" I froze.

"Which one?" Gia asked, laughing.

"Good for you, Gia. Date them all."

Date them all? What the hell? I was so flustered that I accidentally smacked the door with my hand, and it flew open, banging into the wall. Mom and Gia jumped slightly.

"Hi," I said, casually leaning on the door frame. "Your dad and I are leaving in a couple of minutes."

"Oh, I thought you already left," Gia said.

"I'd never go without saying goodbye." As I leaned down and kissed her on the top of her head, my phone buzzed from my back pocket. It was a text from Michael. I loved seeing his name on my phone.

I hope you're having a good day. I texted a thumbs-up and a happy face emoji. I put the phone back in my pocket.

"Tell Dad to come say goodbye," Gia said.

"Have a great time and don't worry about a thing," Mom said. "Us girls will be fine." The two of them went back to their hairstyling adventure, as if I'd been dismissed from the room.

Jim and I were finally on the road. I regretted wearing a sexy, off-the-shoulder shirt for an hour and a half car ride. Even though it was only fifty degrees, I wanted to look good. I spent the first twenty minutes pulling it back down onto my shoulders because it kept hiking up around my ears. Jim didn't notice because he was busy changing radio stations every two minutes. We were listening to the weather report, then Jay-Z, then the Mets game, then Lionel Richie's "Dancing on the Ceiling." We were ill at ease with each other, which was not how I was hoping to start the weekend. I hoped the rest of the time wouldn't be filled with our nervous energy. I'd put a bottle of champagne in my luggage, just in case. If we were drunk, we'd either be less anxious or not care that we weren't.

We pulled up to the bed and breakfast, and it was just as I remembered. It was in the middle of acres of forest land and looked like a historical mansion, painted white with black shutters and a wraparound porch. Since it was still cold outside, there was a little bit of snow on the roof and smoke coming out of the chimney. There was no valet and no bellhop, but a young man greeted us and checked us in. I assumed they would have updated the rooms, but not much had changed. It still felt cozy though, and there was wood stacked neatly next to the fireplace. I sat down on the pure white comforter, and little particles of dust shot up around me. I wiped the dust off. I could have picked some luxurious five-star resort, but this inn represented a special time in our relationship, and I wanted to see if we could recapture that. When I saw that the staff had lit candles next to the bathtub, I knew I had made the right decision.

"I remember this place," Jim said as he walked around the room picking up little tchotchkes off the nightstand. I was happy he hadn't forgotten the crazy, lustful weekend we'd spent here. He fell back on the bed. "This is the bed you fell off our first night and got that huge bruise on your hip. And you weren't even drunk."

"No, that was just my graceful self. You should've dumped me right then and there," I said.

"Are you kidding? You were laughing so hard. It was adorable."

"I was so embarrassed and worried I'd pee."

"It made me love you more."

"You've never told me that." I bent down and gave him a slow, sensual kiss. "I was thinking it might be nice to take a shower," I said leaning my elbow against the wall and putting my hand on my hip in what I thought was a seductive pose.

"Okay," he said, rising off the bed. "Go ahead. I'll watch television." He picked up the remote.

Watching television wasn't the kind of fun *I* wanted to have. I trudged off to the bathroom to take my shower alone. My husband would rather watch Judge Judy than shower with me.

When I was fully pruned, I came out in my new lingerie and robe. The television was off, and Jim was sitting outside our room on the enclosed patio. It looked out at a beautiful field, and there wasn't a soul in sight. As I walked toward the french doors that led to the patio, my phone was vibrating in my purse. I should've ignored it, but I didn't.

Michael texted: *Going to the gym tomorrow at 9:00. Want to join me?*

Can't this weekend. Gia has a lot going on.

No problem. See u next week.

I put the phone facedown on the desk. I was trying to concentrate on my marriage, and that text wasn't helping. I opened the patio doors and saw Jim had the bottle of champagne on ice, and a plate of chocolate-covered strawberries he must've ordered while I was in the bathroom. I instantly forgave him for not showering with me.

"Wow, you look beautiful." Wait until he saw what I had on under my robe. He handed me a glass of champagne. "Here's to twenty more years. Happy anniversary," he said.

"Happy anniversary," I said as we clinked glasses. He picked up a strawberry and fed it to me, and thoughts of anyone except the man in front of me drifted away. He licked the chocolate off my fingers, causing my breath to quicken. Everything was right with the world.

He took our glasses and put them on the table. He began kissing my neck. He moved his lips from my neck up to my ear and then to my lips. We kissed slowly and tentatively at first, then more intensely. We had been kissing for so many years that it had become automatic, but this felt different. Almost new. I lost myself in that kiss. So lost that I didn't even notice when he untied my robe and slipped it from my shoulders. He picked me up and carried me inside to the bed. I always thought being picked up and carried in a moment of passion would be romantic, but when it was happening, I was worried about two things. One, he might realize I was heavier than I looked, and two, the lights were on, so he was going to see all of me. When he placed me down on the bed and began to peel away the chemise, those reservations evaporated. For the next half hour, we made love like we hadn't for a long time.

Afterward, he was on his back, and I snuggled next to him. "This is exactly what we needed," I said.

"Yep. And food. We need food. I'm starving," he said. "I'm going to take a quick shower, and then we can get dinner." When he stood up, my phone buzzed from the desk. "Sounds like you got a text," he said.

"I'll look at it later." My heart was racing because I was worried it was from Michael.

"You should check it," he insisted as he crossed toward my phone. "It could be Gia."

I jumped up and got to my phone before he did. That didn't look suspicious. Relief swept over me when I saw it was my mother looking for my cast-iron pot. She must've moved it in her great kitchen reorganization.

The rest of the weekend, we drank a little too much, made fun of other guests, and took long walks. I also beat him at a mean game of croquet. By the time we were pulling into our driveway, we were connecting on a level we hadn't been for a long time. Before we got out of the car, Jim leaned over and gave me a long, slow kiss. "I had a nice time this weekend," he said.

"Me too." I hadn't thought about Michael in the past few days, and I finally felt like we were a united front facing the world together. Jim took my hand, and we walked toward the house. Maybe everything would be all right with us, and it was, right until we crossed the threshold. As Gia ran up, Jim dropped my hand. She was talking nonstop, and Mom was bombarding me with questions about how our weekend was.

Jim looked at me, and I was about to smile at him as if to say, "Can you believe this?" when he said, "I'm going to go catch up on phone calls. Let me know when dinner's ready." He walked into his office, taking my good feelings with him.

CHAPTER 15

—————— ⊹ ——————

I was standing on our deck, a mug of hazelnut coffee going cold in my hands. The blades of grass in the backyard were growing taller and needed a good mowing. Jim hadn't been able to do it in a while because we'd been getting more rain than usual. As I stood there, a cool droplet fell on my shoulder, and I knew it was time to go back inside.

I filled my mug with fresh coffee and added my usual: one Stevia and one Sweet'n Low and one tablespoon of half and half. The doorbell rang. I opened the door with one hand, holding the mug in the other. Ellen charged through the door, and in one fluid movement she slipped her feet out of her shoes, dropped her purse on the floor, took my cup of coffee out of my hand, and melted into the couch. She took a swig, not bothering to see if it was hot. "Perfect, just the way I like it," she said.

"Don't you have to go to work?" I asked.

"When you're an editor, you don't have to make excuses. They think I'm at a doctor's appointment." I got myself another cup of coffee and sat across from her. "I want to hear about your trip," she said.

"It was really nice, but as soon as we walked through the door, Jim went back to hiding in his home office. The weekend didn't solve anything," I said, putting my mug on the coffee table.

"You guys are just going through a rough patch."

"This rough patch has been going on for a long time, what if it doesn't end?"

"Of course it will."

"I hope you're right, but for now Michael helps me feel less lonely."

"This Michael thing's giving me a bad feeling."

"We haven't crossed any lines."

"Are you sure about that?"

"Yes. When I'm around him I'm distracted from all the crappy stuff in my life."

"That's what your husband's for."

"My husband isn't emotionally available to me. And before our trip, he came home drunk and said he wanted to quit his job and do all kinds of things that didn't include me." I got up and poured more coffee into both our mugs.

"I'm sure he didn't mean it."

"I think he did."

"You said he was drunk."

"When you're drunk, you say what you've *really* been thinking. Our anniversary weekend was just a moment in time. What if he wants to move on without me?"

"I have known Jim for years, and he doesn't. And you getting closer to Michael is only going to make things worse. You need to stop seeing him."

"I don't want to." I blew on my coffee before taking a swig. "What if it's time for Jim and me to start over with someone new?" I was saying things out loud that I'd been thinking about in the middle of the night when I couldn't sleep. "Have you ever thought about what it would be like if you and Sam split up?" I asked.

"Of course. Then my divorced friends tell me their dating disaster stories, and I figure whatever we're going through isn't that bad."

"If Jim and I split up, he could go on all his adventures, and I could start over with someone who wanted to experience things with me." I was picking up steam and couldn't stop myself from moving forward.

"I know you don't mean that, but if you want to go down this road, I'll do it with you."

"You're going to leave Sam?"

"No, I'm not crazy," she said. "But you need a reality check." She got a pad of paper and a pen off my desk, then wrote at the top: "Things to consider if I leave Jim for Michael," and she underlined it twice. She drew two columns. On the top of one, she wrote "Pros," and at the top of the other, she wrote "Cons." "So if you and Jim split up, you'd have some big decisions to make. Like which one of you moves out of the house, how you'd divide up your finances, and who would Gia live with when she came home from college. You'd have to get a good job and therapy for Gia when she hates you."

"You're trying to scare me."

"I'm telling you like it is. Which one of you is Gia going to live with?"

"Me, of course."

"Is that a pro or a con?" she asked. I gave her a dirty look. "If Gia's living with you, she's not going to be happy that you're dating Michael."

"Then I won't date him."

"Isn't that the reason you'd leave Jim?" She liked watching me squirm. I took the blanket that was draped on the back of the couch, pulled it over myself, and tucked my feet under it. She went on. "Would you stay in the house or move out?"

"I'm not leaving my house."

"But if you got a new place, you could redecorate." She wrote in the pro column, "Redecorate new place."

I took the pen out of her hand and crossed it out. "I love my house. I'm not moving."

"Fine, then Jim would have to. Can you afford two house-holds? You might have to stop buying shoes and food."

"I get it. I'm not going to leave Jim."

"Good. Then promise you'll stay away from Michael."

"Fine." I wasn't sure if I meant it, but it got her off my case. She threw the list at the trash can under my desk. I stood up, and the blanket dropped to the floor.

"Talk to Jim and work this out." What did she think I'd been doing for the last six months? "I better go. I still have an errand to run before I go to the office," she said. "Then again, if I left Sam, I wouldn't have to pick up his prescriptions." She stood up and pulled me into a hug, but I wasn't in a hugging mood, so I just stood there, stiff.

After she was gone, I thought about what she said. If I had to give up Michael, I needed to find something else to keep me busy. I decided to get up the nerve to call Lorna, and officially ask for my old job back. After months of looking online and either not finding anything or never hearing back, I might as well try. I practiced what I wanted to say, and then I dialed a phone number I'd never forgotten.

"Lorna Danzig, please. Tell her it's Maggie Dolin. Yes, I'll hold." Even though the horn of the commuter train in the distance was faint, it vibrated through me and pierced the quiet in the woods outside the house.

"Maggie, how are you?" Lorna chirped a few moments later.

"I'm good. I wanted to talk to you about something. I've been thinking seriously about getting back in the work force and wanted to see if there was anything at Shier and Boggs." I held my breath, waiting for what seemed like an hour for her to answer.

"Oh . . . we aren't hiring. In fact, we just laid off a bunch of people. The publishing business isn't what it used to be. I wish I could help, you know how fond I am of you."

"No problem, just thought I'd throw it out there."

"If you need a reference, I'd be happy to write one. Now, promise you'll call me soon about that lunch."

"I will."

I hung up. I knew it had been a slim chance, but hearing her say no made it final. If someone who knew me wouldn't hire me, why would someone who didn't? I felt so defeated, and I needed to get out of the house before I began spiraling. Even running errands was better than sitting here. I went to the market, then to the bank, and on my way home, I was driving by the high school when I saw Gia walking into the parking lot with Jason. There wasn't anyone else around, and she was supposed to be in class. This day couldn't get any worse. The two of them got into Jason's car and drove away. I ducked so she wouldn't see me. When a loud honking from behind startled me, I realized I'd stopped in the middle of the street. I thought about following them, but I didn't see which direction they went.

As I pulled into my driveway, Michael called. He wanted to take me out for that drink for helping with his mother. I hesitated when I heard Ellen's voice in my head telling me to stay away from him. And maybe if I got my old job back, or my dad remembered my name, or my husband wanted more to do with me, I would've listened to her. But what did she know? I'd gone to his apartment and nothing happened, so why would one drink in a public place be an issue?

A little later, I found myself sitting in a sleazy bar. Well, I didn't find myself there; I put myself there. It was unlike me to be carefree and wild, and in a bar in the middle of the day. Then again, I was nursing a club soda, so how wild was I being?

Murphy's Pub was inside an old bowling alley in the next town over. It was a hole in the wall that hadn't been touched since 1975, and that was probably only to buy a new jukebox. None of my or Jim's friends bowled, and if they did, they'd go to the nicer alley near our house, so I wasn't worried I'd run in to anyone. There were three televisions on the walls, one with a football game, one with a surfing competition, and one on CNN. A half dozen men were milling around, and at a table near the bar were two women loudly scrutinizing them. They thought one was too fat, one was too hairy, and one looked like a serial killer. I thought the serial killer was kind of cute, but I avoided making eye contact because flirting with one man was my limit. When I drummed my fingers on the bar, one of the women gave me a dirty look, so I took out my phone and pretended to be doing something important. I was playing Words with Friends with an old classmate from high school whom I hadn't seen in twenty years. I threw down letters randomly and got twenty points for the word *otitis*, which I had no idea was a word.

Then my phone rang. Was Michael canceling on me? Being stood up in a nice restaurant would be bad, but being stood up in a dive bar would be tragic.

The caller turned out to be Ellen. "Hi, I left my umbrella at your house this morning. Can I run by in about fifteen minutes and get it?"

"No."

"Oh, you're not home?"

"I'm home. Why do you think I'm not at home? I'm sitting in my kitchen having iced tea."

"Then why can't I come by?"

"Because I'm at Murphy's Pub waiting for Michael." It was impossible for me to lie to her.

"Seriously? What happened between this morning and now?"

"Nothing. He asked me to meet him for a drink."

"You said this wasn't going to continue."

"It's just one drink."

"I think you're making a mistake."

"Then it's mine to make." Michael opened the door and walked into the dark room. The sunlight that surrounded him gave him an angelic aura. "Gotta go, talk to you later." I dropped my phone in my purse. Michael came up beside me. His hair was wet as if he'd just showered. He gave me a hug and sat down. Those picky women looked him over. Ha! There was nothing to criticize about this guy. I gave them a dismissive nod, and they turned around.

When Michael asked if I wanted a real drink, I ordered a glass of wine, and he got one of the beers on tap. The bartender was staring at my wedding ring and noticing that Michael wasn't wearing one. At least that's what I assumed when he was putting our drinks down. Michael reached for my glass of wine to hand it to me at the same time that I reached for it. Our hands touched. He let his fingers linger over mine before letting go.

A man in a cowboy hat walked toward the juke box. No one wore cowboy hats in Connecticut, although Murphy's Pub seemed like the appropriate place to wear one if you were going to. Suddenly, the sound of Mariah Carey's song "Love Takes Time" filled the room. *Love takes time to heal when you're hurting so much...*

"I played this song incessantly when I was fifteen and my boyfriend broke up with me," I said.

"That's depressing . . . and so unhip." He grinned.

"I was hip. I was also a Pearl Jam fan." I was a Barry Manilow fan, but I wasn't going to admit that.

"My ex-wife was into alternative rock also."

"If you don't mind me asking, why did you two break up?"

"I cheated on her. Sometimes I don't think before getting into situations that I shouldn't." He paused and looked me dead in the eyes. "Have you ever cheated on anyone?"

"No."

"How does your husband feel about us hanging out?"

"He's fine with it. I have a lot of male friends." I hadn't had a male friend since I stopped working.

"He must be really secure, having such a hot wife."

I felt my ears get hot and knew they were turning red. "He is." It bothered me that I lied to Michael about Jim, when I should've been bothered that I was lying to Jim about Michael. A woman wearing an extremely low-cut shirt with miles of cleavage asked if the seat next to Michael was taken. Michael didn't even give her the once-over, which gave me a secret thrill. "So, what did your mother think of Brooklawn?" I asked.

"First she said she hated it. The next morning, she said it was fine. That afternoon, she said if I was going to force her to live there, she might as well get used to it."

The bartender asked if we wanted another drink. I was feeling slightly buzzed, so I knew it wasn't a good idea. "I'll have another glass of wine," I said. As the bartender brought over the wine bottle, my good sense prevailed, and I put my hand over my glass before he could pour it. "I changed my mind. I have to drive home." The bartender nodded and walked away.

"I'd offer to drive you home, but I rode my bike here. My car's in the shop."

Over the next hour, we shared even more about our lives. I told him about my relationship with Jerry and how he resented me. He told me how his insecurities with his father affected his first marriage. I even told him about what happened with Lorna and my old job. He was empathetic and validated my feelings. I knew sharing my problems with him was going to bring us closer, but at that moment I didn't care.

In the past Jim had been my touchstone. He'd always been there for me, no matter how big or small the issue. When we'd been dating for three months, I got my jacket zipper stuck on my shirt. He spent almost a half hour trying to help me out of my coat. It was not only sweet but showed how patient he was. Granted, it was the first night we were planning on having sex, so no zipper was going to stop him, but the care he took not to rip my shirt made me like him even more. Lately, Jim wouldn't have noticed if I got my head stuck in a zipper.

I looked up at the TV, and CNN had announced the time. It had been two hours since I got here. "Oh no, I'm not going to be able to pick up the ice cream that Gia asked me to get," I said.

"She'll understand."

"You don't have a teenager."

He paid our bar tab and walked me to my car. "This has been fun," he said. "We should do it again soon." He opened the door for me, then leaned in and kissed me on the cheek. It felt so good and so wrong all at the same time.

"I hope you have a good afternoon," I squeaked out. On the drive home, I touched my cheek. I could feel his lips on me as if they were still there. I was playing with fire, but not knowing what would happen next was an adrenaline rush.

Two minutes after I walked in, Gia got home. Her keys jangled against the front door so loudly it was as if she was fighting with them to get in. She finally conquered the lock and entered, wearing earbuds. She put her backpack on the counter and breezed past me. Why couldn't she ever take that backpack with her? Before going up the stairs, she pulled out one of her earbuds.

"Did you get my strawberry ice cream?" she asked

"Hi, Mom," I said sarcastically.

"Hi."

"I didn't get to the market today."

"Seriously?" She pouted. "All I wanted was a little ice cream, and you're telling me we still don't have any?"

Did she think I worked for her? I was about to get upset, but instead I took a breath and said what any other mother would have said in this situation. "I'll go tomorrow." Okay, I said what any mother who felt guilty after spending the afternoon with a man who wasn't her husband would've said.

"By tomorrow I won't care," she snarled.

"Good, because now I'm not going."

She groaned, put her earbuds back in, and stomped as loud as she could on carpeted stairs up to her room.

I sat down at the kitchen table with *People* magazine. I read all about how some woman had been kidnapped from her house and turned up three weeks later, saying the kidnappers fed her steak and gave her a comfortable bed. Why couldn't I be kidnapped by those people? After reading through most of the magazine, skipping the article on home decorating tips from Snoop Dogg, my phone buzzed.

Was Gia mad that you didn't get her ice cream? Was Michael psychic too?

Yep, she was a snot. Now I'm glad I didn't get it.

Me too. We got to spend more time together. He sent me a yellow emoticon heart. Was a yellow heart for friendship? Yellow roses were. I wrote him back and made sure to send him the same yellow heart and no other emoticon so it wouldn't look as if I was upping the ante.

I was smiling when I looked up from my phone, and Gia was standing at the top of the stairs, staring at me. Okay, face, stop looking like you're a cheater. "Who are you texting?" Gia asked.

I put the phone back in my pocket. "Your grandmother."

She eyed me suspiciously. I was never a good liar, although I had become a better one since I'd met Michael. She came down the stairs and got her backpack from the kitchen. "You don't usually smile when you text Grandma. What did she say?" She sat down next to me.

Why was she grilling me? "It's a private joke."

"Well, maybe if you texted less, you would've had time to get my ice cream."

I brought my hand down on the table so hard the stinging in my fingers shot up through my arm. "This coming from the girl who left school in the middle of the day with her boyfriend," I blurted.

"You were spying on me?" She was stunned.

"I was driving by your school and saw you two get in the car. Where did you go?"

"To have sex."

"Ha, ha, very funny." She gave me a half-shrug and a slight smile. "You had sex?"

"Yes."

I started biting my lower lip, pulling the skin off in little bits. "You're not allowed to leave school in the middle of the day," I said. She had sex, and I was nagging her about leaving school. My brain could not process this right now.

"I'm a senior. What's the difference?"

"I don't care if you're a senior. Your grades still matter." I always thought I'd be one of those moms who could be supportive and listen to anything without judgment. But nope, I was judgmental. "I thought you wanted to wait to have sex until college," I said as calmly as I could muster.

"I changed my mind."

"I wish we could've talked first."

"You would've tried to talk me out of it."

"No, I wouldn't. Yes, I would've. I don't know." Oh my God, what should I say to her? This was a big moment. I put my arm around her and lowered my voice. "Did you use protection? Are you okay? Did he pressure you?"

"This is why I didn't tell you. I didn't want all the questions. When I told Dad, he didn't ask me anything."

"You told your father you were going to have sex?" I said, dropping my arm from around her shoulders. I felt as if I'd been slapped.

"I told him not to tell you."

"Well, clearly he didn't." I felt my toes clenching in my shoes. How could Jim not tell me something so important? Then again, Jim hadn't been telling me much of anything lately.

"I knew Dad would be calmer than you. He wasn't happy about it, but he at least listened without getting upset."

"I'm not upset," I said, clearly upset but trying to get it together.

"You should be happy. At least I'm dating someone my own age. Taylor sleeps with older guys."

"That's horrible, but I'm not Taylor's mother. I'm your mother, and I should know everything you do."

"Well, next year when I go to college, you won't know anything. Besides, you always said it was my body and I should make my own decisions about it."

"I said that when I thought you weren't going to have sex. I gave birth to you, so until you're eighteen, your body is mine." Okay, that sounded nuts.

"This is ridiculous. It's my life, and you need to stay out of it and get one of your own." She ran up the stairs and slammed her bedroom door. I stopped myself from hitting my hand down on the table again because it still hurt from before.

Gia didn't come out of her room for hours, and when I offered her dinner, she declined, which was good because I was afraid I'd poison her. At eight o'clock, Jim came home, and before he even put his keys on the hook, I said, "You told Gia it was a good idea to have sex with Jason?"

"What're you talking about? I never said that."

"She said you didn't try to talk her out of it."

"She didn't tell me she was going to. All she said was she was thinking about it, and I told her that it was a big decision and she couldn't go back once she did it." Okay, that was reasonable. "Are you saying she went through with it?" he asked.

"Yes."

"Oh God. What did you say to her?"

"When she told me, I was shocked. I don't think I handled it well. Hopefully I didn't shame her."

"There's nothing wrong with a little shame." He gave me a halfhearted smile. "Should I go talk to her?" he asked.

"I wouldn't. There'll be plenty of time to talk to her later, since I'm chaining her door closed." He kissed me on the cheek. The kiss wasn't as tender and warm as the one from Michael, but it was something. When Jim reached for a bottle of wine from the cabinet, I said, "Maybe we should start with whiskey."

CHAPTER 16

———— ✦ ————

I turned over in bed and was accosted by a furry lick going up and down my nose, pausing almost purposefully at my nostrils for a little too long. Theo had no manners when he was hungry. Couldn't he see it was Saturday morning, and I didn't have to be anywhere? He moved to the other side of the bed, jumped up, and put his front paws on the mattress, staring at me as if to say, "I only eat once every twelve hours. Have a heart." As I gazed at his droopy, mournful face, the phone rang. Like clockwork, it was my mother. Why couldn't she take the weekends off? I picked up because I knew if I avoided answering, she was only going to try to track me down. She gave me the daily update on my father, an update I especially tried to avoid on weekends. The home was moving him to the memory care unit this week. The more time that went on, the more helpless I felt, and hearing about it every day made things worse.

I got off the phone as quickly as I could. Jim was not on his side of the bed, or in the bathroom. He liked to sleep later than I did on weekends, so where was he? Then I heard the clanging of pots and pans. I was the only one who cooked, so who was touching my pots? Maybe I was being surprised with breakfast in bed? But it wasn't my birthday. . . or Mother's Day. As I thought about what it would be like to have someone serve me, Jim came into the room with a cup of coffee. I propped up the pillows behind my back and sat up, my pajamas askew from a good night's sleep.

He put the coffee on the side table. "You were completely unconscious when I woke up. I was worried you were dead."

"If you were so worried, why didn't you try to wake me?"

"I figured if you were already dead, there was no rush."

I threw my pillow at him. He picked up the cup of coffee. "Is that for me?" I asked expectantly.

"Uh, it can be. . . ."

My disappointment was palpable, but I tried to hide it. "That's okay."

"You sure?" he said as he took a sip from the cup. I could smell the aroma and wished I'd admitted I wanted it.

He took off his pajama bottoms and stood naked from the waist down. I was definitely sexually deprived, because every ounce of my anger at him took a vacation. Or at least it was about to take a vacation until after we had sex.

"So . . . what should we do this morning?" I asked in what I thought was my sexiest voice. I gave him a come-hither look, but since I hadn't done that look in a long time, it was possible I looked like a drunken sailor.

Jim, not picking up on my sexy vibe, or not turned on by a drunken sailor, rifled through his drawer for underwear and socks. "I don't know. What do you want to do?" He went into the bathroom and left the door open while he peed. My sexy feeling took a bow and left the stage. Through the sounds of the toilet flushing, he said, "Can you make your amazing waffles this morning? I already got the waffle iron out."

"Okay. Do we have bacon?" I asked.

"I don't know."

I don't know was code for if he knew the answer, I might ask him to cook it. "I'll be down in a minute," I said.

Before he went into his office to do whatever it was he did in there, he asked if I wanted to go out for a late lunch. I quickly agreed. I was happy that he wanted to spend time with me, which was also depressing since he was my husband. As I got out of bed, I caught sight of myself in our full-length mirror. I was wearing flowered flannel pajamas, with messy hair and crusty old mascara under my eyes. I wouldn't have wanted to have sex with me either. Then again, Jim peed with the door open, so how picky should he be?

I grabbed my clothes and headed to the shower. After cleaning the leftover makeup off my face and washing my hair, I was presentable. No more drunken sailor here. Jim was on the phone in the living room talking about some networking event that he wanted to attend.

When I went into the kitchen to pour myself coffee, I found the pot was empty. Jeez, how much coffee did he drink? Jim walked in and saw me looking at the empty coffee pot. He asked if I wanted him to make some more, but I told him I'd have tea. He put water in the kettle and turned on the stove, then put the empty coffee pot in the sink.

"Are you going to wash that?" I hated sounding like a nag.

"I will. Later," he said. I put on my purple latex gloves, turned on the water, and washed the coffee pot. Jim stared at me. "I told you I'd wash it later."

"My later is later. Your later is never."

Jim went back to his office while I made waffles and bacon. When everything was done, I called him and Gia in. Gia pulled a chair out from the kitchen table and made sure it scraped the floor as loudly as it could. She put a waffle on her plate, grabbed the syrup, and poured half the bottle on it. It took everything inside me not to say anything. Then she stuffed a huge piece of the waffle in her mouth. I was worried I'd have to Heimlich her, and I didn't remember how.

I asked her to get napkins for everyone. She didn't say anything but did get up so quietly that it made me nervous. It felt like when you're in a haunted house and you know that when you turn the corner, something's going to jump out at you.

"I'm sorry if I didn't handle the whole sex thing well. You threw me off when you blurted it out," I said. "All I wanted was to make sure you were all right."

"I know." She licked the syrup off her fingers. "I felt weird talking about it."

"I hope this was your decision and not because you felt pressured."

"If I didn't want to, I wouldn't have. I make my own decisions."

I was glad to hear she was stronger than I was when I was her age. When I was seventeen, I didn't think I had a right to say how I was feeling. I still didn't stand up for myself enough.

"Can I ask if you're okay and if you used protection?" I asked.

"Yes and yes. Now can we change the subject?"

I was not going to get more out of her. I pushed the plate of bacon toward her. "You want some? I made it extra crunchy for you."

She took a strip of bacon and went upstairs. I didn't know if she was still mad at me or having second thoughts about having sex. I hoped it was the latter.

Jim came in and sat down in the same spot where Gia had been sitting. Before I could tell him that she'd spilled syrup on the table, he put his arm down in it. He grumbled as he wet a paper towel and wiped off both the table and his arm. It was karma for his drinking all the coffee. After he finished cursing to himself, I told him that I'd talked to Gia. He was relieved she was okay and quickly changed the subject. While we ate, we discussed what to do about the broken thermostat in our bedroom and whether we needed to finally paint the exterior of our house. He polished off three waffles and five slices of bacon. Then he put his plate in the dishwasher and left. Another family breakfast over in breakneck speed. It had taken me twenty-five minutes to cook it and two minutes for everyone to scarf it down.

Just as I finished washing the dishes and wiping down the sticky table, Jim came back in and took his keys off the hook. "I'm going to go help Sam hang some shelves," he said. "When I get back, we can go to lunch. Where do you want to go?"

We did what we always did when faced with a decision as big as where to eat. "I don't want Mexican, Asian, Greek, or Thai," I said.

"I don't want French, Japanese, or Middle Eastern."

We stared at each other a moment, until I said, "You pick." He came back with La Cucina, which was our favorite place. I was happy because it was where I wanted to go and one of the few places we always agreed on.

La Cucina was a family-run restaurant that Jim and I had found by accident years ago. We'd been dating for four months when he asked me to take him to urgent care. He'd been opening a package with a knife, when the knife slipped and cut his hand open. I was honored that he'd chosen me to take care of him. When I got to his apartment, he had a dish towel carefully wrapped around his arm, but the blood was soaking through. After the doctor stitched him up, we were starving. Next door to the urgent care was a nondescript storefront flying an Italian flag. There was a banner that read "Grand Opening," but no one was inside. We'd stopped to look at the menu when Angelo, the owner, opened the door and greeted us warmly. It would've been embarrassing to walk away, so we went in and had the best Italian meal either of us had ever had. That day, we were the only customers, but over the years it had become very popular.

"I'll be back around one thirty," he said and left. A few minutes later, Taylor came to get Gia. I wasn't thrilled they were hanging out so much. I didn't think Taylor was the best influence on her. The house rattled as Gia slammed the front door behind her. I never got why teenagers slammed doors. Was it that they were so happy to be free of their parents that they wanted to make sure the whole neighborhood knew it?

When Jim and I got to La Cucina, it was two o'clock, which for our town was like having lunch in the middle of the night. There was one other couple sitting at the bar. Angelo greeted us with his big Italian grin. He wore a white apron stained with tomato sauce. "It's so good to see you both," he said and pulled us into a group hug.

"How's the family?" Jim asked.

Angelo replied with the same answer he'd had for twenty years. "Driving me crazy, but the loves of my life. Your favorite table is waiting for you."

Every table in the restaurant was lovely, but there was one we liked the best. It was in a corner by a window with a view of a duck pond, and it was the most private table in the restaurant. When Jim and I were dating, we would sit at that table for hours having intimate conversations and kissing without feeling self-conscious.

Our waitress, Marcia, was a sixty-eight-year-old mother of eight who'd been working there since it opened. As we'd grown older, she'd grown larger, and her plaid apron could no longer be tied around her, so she let the strings hang down her back. She put menus in front of us, but as we knew them by heart, there was no need to even open them. As the busboy poured water, Jim began staring out the window. There was a young father with his two boys feeding the ducks. The boys looked to be about three and five years old.

"They're cute, aren't they?" I said.

"Huh?"

"The kids." I pointed out the window.

"Yeah, cute."

"Are you worried about work again?" I asked.

"I have a lot of patients in crisis." He told me how one of his patients had parents who were about to be evicted from their house, one just told her husband after fifty-five years of marriage that she's gay, and another had a four-year-old who had been diagnosed with severe OCD.

"That's terrible and I feel for them, but I also need you to be there for me," I said.

"I'm sorry, you're right."

Every time he said I was right, I cringed. It didn't mean anything unless his behavior changed. We sat in silence a moment, and I saw how stressed he looked. I wondered if I was being selfish about my own needs. Did I need to be more understanding? I was about to apologize for not being more compassionate about what he was going through when I realized he was typing furiously on his phone.

"Have you still been thinking about quitting your job?" I asked nervously.

"No, I know it wasn't realistic, but if I can take most weekends off, that might help. I will try to be more connected to you."

Hearing that made me feel better, and I believed him until I started talking again and noticed he wasn't answering and again had his nose in his phone. Were things ever going to change?

"Sorry, I'll be just a sec." He continued typing, seeming to already have forgotten about being present in my life. Marcia brought over bread and olive oil. I was glad for the interruption because I was about to shove his phone up his nose.

I took a sip of water and almost spit it out when I noticed a couple entering the restaurant. It was Michael with a woman. What was he doing at Jim's and my restaurant? What was he doing with another woman? My brain was firing every neuron at once. Please let her be his sister, or a very pretty cousin. As Angelo led them to a table, Michael put his hand on the small of her back. Dammit, she wasn't his sister. He'd never mentioned he was dating anyone.

The woman sat down next to him on the same side of the booth. How romantic. I was crestfallen. They were both facing in my direction, and I couldn't take my eyes off her. She was petite and around thirty. At least he was with someone his own age. Oh God, Michael was on a date, a date with a pretty woman, a date that wasn't me. I felt as if I kept saying the word *date* over and over in my head until I hated the word. She had that shiny, long hair, the kind you only get with extensions. I had on a dorky denim headband. Why couldn't I have blow-dried my hair? There wasn't anything wrong with her. How could he do that to me? I should be the only pretty person in his life. I was obsessed with whatever relationship he had with her, and I was so jealous I wanted to throw up.

There were now two tables of customers between Michael and me, so if I was lucky, maybe he wouldn't notice me. Marcia came back and asked us what we wanted to order. Thank goodness, her girth was big enough for me to hide behind. I hunched my shoulders and cocked my head and got as small as I could without doing damage to my back. I must have looked like a contortionist. I ordered my usual, but I wouldn't be able to eat any of it. My stomach was doing flip-flops because I thought any minute Michael might see me. Would he come over when he did? Jim would want to know who he was.

When Marcia walked away, I no longer had my human shield. I looked up to see what was going on at their table, and Michael was looking at me. He smiled and looked at Jim, then back at me. I must've looked panicked because he made a subtle nod of his head and went back to his conversation. It was as if we were both part of the same secret club.

"I'm listening," Jim said.

Was I talking? I didn't think I was talking. What was he listening to? "I didn't say anything," I said, wondering if he could see the guilt on my face and realizing the irony of my not being present.

"I meant I'm here for you," Jim said.

"Thanks, I appreciate that, but if you have important texts to send, it's fine." I never thought that would come out of my mouth. I was afraid if Jim really looked up at me, he'd know something was wrong. Jim started typing another text.

Michael's date was leaning into him, smiling and laughing. She liked him. I wondered if she knew that he didn't have a lot of money. I wondered if she knew that he didn't have a stable career. I wondered if she would've cared.

How could I be so distressed? Michael and I weren't dating. Besides, I was with my husband. What I needed to do was get off my butt, walk over there, and say hi. *Here I go. I'm going to get up now. Yep, nothing's going to stop me.* But how would I introduce Jim to him? *"Jim, this is Michael, a man I've been seeing, I mean hanging out with, I mean, what I mean is . . . he's a man that I somehow forgot to mention to you."*

Jim had looked up from his phone and was talking again. "Hello . . . I'm talking to you."

Now he wanted to talk. "Sorry."

"Are you mad at me?"

"For what?" I asked, although there were several reasons that came to mind.

"Because I've been on my phone. We can talk about Gia and Jason now if you want."

"It's fine. We can talk about them later," I said.

Jim was finally willing to talk to me about something important, but right now I couldn't concentrate. I was too distracted by Michael's date to talk about Gia, or even know who Gia was for that matter.

CHAPTER 17

———— ⊰✦⊱ ————

Over the next few days, Michael texted me a few times, but I didn't text back. I wasn't sure how to act around him after seeing him on a date.

"Good morning, Dad," I said as I entered his room. Lately, I was hesitant every time I saw him because I never knew how he was going to be. And now that he was in the memory care unit, I had to have a nurse unlock the main door for me, so I couldn't just come and go easily. Dad was sitting in his wheelchair watching *Wheel of Fortune* on the television. I was comforted for a moment until he started banging on the remote control. The channel changed, and a nature special came on. He hated nature specials. He loved animals but used to joke that the animals in these shows were actors and weren't getting paid enough to have to deal with the bad writing. I wanted to connect with him on anything, so I pulled up a chair and sat down. If he wanted to watch a nature show, then that could be our new thing. "I didn't know you liked elephants, Dad." He didn't respond. He was watching so intently that his face had relaxed into a half-smile.

"That baby elephant is cute," I said. He blinked a few times, but still nothing. In the past we were never not talking about something, so watching in silence was painful.

"Do you have my pills?" he asked, startling me.

"No, Dad."

"Aren't you supposed to give them to me now, nurse?"

"Dad, it's me, Maggie."

He stared through me. "You're not Maggie." He started hitting the button over and over that called the nurse. I stood up, shocked.

A nurse came into the room. "Are you okay, Mr. Rubin? Oh, hi, Maggie," she said, noticing me.

"This isn't Maggie," Dad said, getting agitated. "This woman's an imposter. She looks like my daughter, but she's not her. I would know Maggie anywhere."

The nurse looked at me with such sympathy it made my anguish worse. I had no idea what to do. I pulled out my driver's license from my wallet and bent down next to him. I held my ID up to my head. "See, Margaret Dolin, and that's my name and address. Look, that's my picture."

Dad shook his head, refusing to look at it. "I don't care what it says. You aren't my daughter." I was dumbfounded. He had no idea who I was.

The nurse put Dad's pills in his mouth and helped him take a drink. She told him she'd come back soon to check on him again. She put her hand on my shoulder for a moment, then left.

"Dad, I love you."

"I'm not your dad. Why are you still here?" he said to me.

I was speechless. "I'll go find Maggie," I stammered and walked to the door hurriedly.

"Wait," he said, and I turned expectantly. "Can you ask a nurse to bring my medication? They keep forgetting about me."

"Okay," I said and got out of there. I collapsed against the wall outside his room and breathed in, trying to get my emotions in check. I could feel myself starting to grieve him, and he was still alive. If I let one tear escape, I'd be a mess, so I pushed down the sobs that had begun to rise in my throat. I ducked into the nearest bathroom and splashed water on my face. It didn't help. I looked in the mirror and relaxed my facial muscles into a smile. If I pretended to be happy, maybe my face would get the message, although I ended up looking like the Cheshire Cat.

I waited as long as I could, then asked a nurse to unlock the door of the memory ward for me. As I left, Jerry was walking in my direction. I didn't think my day could get any more painful. I had the worst luck when it came to running into him.

"What are you doing here?" I asked.

"I had a meeting with Dad's doctor."

"Why?"

"Mom gets confused by all the information, so she asked me to step in and then explain things to her."

"I could've done that. You don't care about Dad the way I do," I said.

"I care, even if we don't have a great relationship."

"Whose fault is that?"

"Both of ours."

"You're always angry at him."

He softened. "I am, but I wasn't always. By the time I was eight, I realized that he treated you differently. He brought you gifts from business trips. He took you bowling. He helped you with your Girl Scout badges."

He was right, but I felt disloyal to my dad agreeing with him. "He did stuff with you too," I said.

"Like what?"

I thought for a moment. "He went to all your soccer games."

"I played in one soccer game, then I quit. So yes, he came to my soccer game. Mostly he ignored me and doted on you."

I'd convinced myself that Jerry was cold and selfish, but maybe I was the selfish one. I liked having Dad to myself. I didn't want a sibling when I was six years old. "Do you blame me for that?" I asked.

"I blamed you both. I never thought he liked me, and I tried many times to win him over. I even went to law school because I was hoping that it would give us something to talk about, but instead he said he didn't like talking about work outside the courtroom."

"I'm sorry. It's not too late to fix things," I said.

"When Dad got what we thought was Parkinson's, I started coming to see him more. I hoped we could work through things, but he spent most of the time talking about you."

"That won't be an issue anymore, because now he's replaced me with a different Maggie."

"Is this one nicer?"

"Ha, ha." I saw my little brother in a way I'd never seen him. He was just as vulnerable as I was. "I wish we'd talked like this a long time ago," I said. "Maybe we could've been closer."

"Right. I was going to be closer to the person who tried to squish me under her trundle bed when I was three?"

"You and Mom are never going to let me live that down."

"Nope. That or when you told Mom and Dad that my friends and I drank half their vodka and filled the rest of the bottle with water." He smacked me lightly on the back of the head, and we laughed.

"What did the doctor tell you today about Dad's condition?" I asked.

"The disease is progressing faster than expected, and the average life expectancy after the onset of symptoms is five to eight years. Since Dad's been having undiagnosed symptoms for a few years, the doctor isn't overly optimistic."

I walked outside Brooklawn feeling even worse, if that were possible. The sky was a piercing blue with one ominous dark cloud. A grand elm tree stood in the middle of the lawn, its branches reaching out, offering me comfort beneath them. As I slid down its trunk to sit on the grass underneath, I didn't notice the leftover patch of snow. Feeling a small, wet spot against my skin caused my emotional dam to burst. I was a tearful woman loitering outside an old age home with a soggy butt.

When I stood up, I noticed Michael's faded red van, with one perfect dent in the rear passenger side, pulling into the circular driveway. He began taking suitcases and boxes out of the van. Charlotte was standing with her walker next to the suitcases. She looked like a scared child. Michael was distracted and hadn't noticed me, which was good because I didn't know what I was going to say to him. He'd texted me three times over the last week, and I hadn't texted him back. I was dealing with so much, and hearing him say he had a girlfriend was only going to make me feel worse.

Charlotte called out my name; she was relieved to see a familiar face. I walked toward them, holding my purse against my wet rear end.

"Hey," Michael said, giving me a now familiar hug. "I've been texting you."

"I know," I said.

He looked at me the way no one else had in a long time. He knew something was wrong. "You okay?" he whispered. I shook my head. I couldn't say anything because I thought my voice would betray my sorrow.

"Let me get my mom settled and then we can talk," he said.

He went back to unloading the van and I walked with Charlotte inside Brooklawn. We sat in her empty room, not saying much. She was overwhelmed with the move and was happy not to make small talk. Michael filled up the room with her belongings. He'd brought as many things as he could from home to help her feel more comfortable. He put a picture of her and Michael's father on the nightstand. Then he put a worn-out stuffed bear on her bed, and a quilt that had pictures of her parents and sisters appliquéd on it but had a small tear at the bottom. There were also three huge suitcases with more clothes in them than she could ever need.

Lila, a slightly younger but even more bent-over version of Charlotte, came into the room. She wanted to meet another newbie. We all exchanged hellos. Lila used to be an English teacher. She started talking and didn't stop the entire time Michael was arranging Charlotte's clothes in her closet. Charlotte seemed comforted by Lila's voice, but I wanted to smack her when she started to explain the difference between the word *homophobe* and *homophone*. When everything was unpacked, Lila convinced Charlotte to go with her to the activity room, leaving Michael and me on our own.

"Do you want to go across the street and grab some coffee?" he asked.

"Sure," I said.

"Let me move the van out of the driveway, and I'll meet you over there."

The Coffee Station used to be an old gas station with an am-pm mini mart. It had been turned into a bakery and coffee house about ten years ago. I was bringing my dad scones from there, but then he started leaving them on his table to feed the kangaroos he hallucinated.

As I entered the bakery, the scent of warm pastries permeated my nostrils. I couldn't just get coffee when there was a case of chocolate-and-almond croissants in front of me. I would numb my feelings with baked goods.

As I waited in line, my phone buzzed. Michael was having trouble finding a parking spot for the van and asked if I could get him a bagel and an espresso. Just as I had finished paying, he came in and helped me take the food and drinks to a table.

"Thanks for buying me breakfast," he said, devouring half of his bagel as if he hadn't eaten in two days. I took a bite of my croissant and wanted to enjoy the buttery warm feeling in my mouth, but instead the croissant got stuck in my throat. It took a moment to clear my airways.

Michael grimaced when he realized how hot the espresso was. "I've been worried about you. What's going on?"

"A lot of things, but mostly my father."

"Do you want to talk about it?"

"Not really."

"Got it," he said in between blowing on his drink.

He went back to munching on his bagel. We both got quiet. It was the first time we'd been together when we weren't saying anything. The silence was making me anxious, and I started fidgeting. I cracked my knuckles and twirled my ring until I blurted out, "So, how was your date the other night?" I hoped my voice didn't betray how distressed I was about seeing him with another woman. He'd think I was crazy and needy, which I was, but I didn't want him to know it.

"Good."

"The woman you were with seemed . . . nice." Realizing I hadn't even met her, I added, "I mean, she looked nice."

"My friend Eric fixed us up. Amanda's a lawyer at his firm."

Great, she's younger than me and more successful. Hit me where it hurts. "Cool" was all I could muster. I sounded like a teenager. I stuffed my mouth with croissant to stop from saying anything that would reveal how jealous I was.

"We've gone out a few times, but I'm not really into her," he said. "I would've rather been with you."

As upset as I was about my father, his words made me feel a little better. "I was thrown seeing you with a woman." I shouldn't have said that. I wasn't doing anything to stop our relationship from progressing further.

"I assume that was your husband you were with. Or you have a really old son," he said.

"Yes, I'm actually eighty."

"You hold up well for an old broad." He lifted the lid on his espresso and added two more sugar packets. "Your husband looked different than I'd imagined."

"Different how?"

"I don't know, just different."

"I could've introduced you, but it would've been awkward since I haven't told Jim about you."

"I got that from your expression at the restaurant." The look on his face surprised me. He was intrigued. "You said Jim was fine with us hanging out."

"I lied."

"Would he be mad if he knew?"

"I wouldn't be happy if he was hanging out with some woman."

"Then maybe you shouldn't tell him," Michael said pointedly.

My heart began to beat out of my chest. I didn't want to tell Jim. I wanted to keep Michael my little secret. I knocked over my chai tea. As it was trickling down toward my purse, Michael jumped up to get napkins, leaving his phone on the table. The phone vibrated, and I couldn't help looking at the caller ID. Well, I could have, considering the phone was not facing me. As it rang, a picture of the woman that he was with the other day was displayed. He already had her picture in his phone? He came back, and I motioned toward his phone.

"Your phone rang," I said. He took a quick look and then slipped it in his pocket. He wiped up the table. "Anything important?" I asked, trying not to sound like a jealous girlfriend.

"It was Amanda. I need to tell her what time I'm picking her up tonight."

"I thought you weren't that interested in her."

"I'm not, but she's sweet, and besides, the woman I'm most attracted to is married."

Did he mean me? What a dope—of course he meant me. He reached across the table and gently took my hand, and our eyes met. I knew I shouldn't be holding hands with another man in a public place. Well, anywhere for that matter. But I didn't let go. Staring into his eyes, I felt vulnerable and emotional.

"You said you didn't want to talk about your dad, but if you tell me what happened, maybe I can help," he said.

"Thanks, but there's nothing anyone can do. My dad's condition is bad, and I haven't had time to come to terms with it, not that I could anyway."

"I'm sorry you have to go through this. He seems like a nice man."

"He was . . . is." I let go of Michael's hand and wiped away tears that started forming. "What was your dad like?" I asked.

"Tough, and hard on me. He was a journalist and the reason I became a writer. He was also the reason I never thought I was good enough." He gave me a sad smile.

"Would I know him?"

"Rick Sanders."

"He wrote that book about the Clinton-Lewinsky scandal."

"Yeah."

"My mother's always been hard on me," I said.

"Is this a competition?" he asked, smirking. "If it is, I win."

"We'll see about that once you get to know me better."

"I'd like to get to know you better," he said, leering at me. "And I'd love to stay here with you all day, but I have to go back and check on my mom." We stood up. "Are you going to be okay?" he asked.

"What choice do I have?"

As we walked out, he held the door open for two elderly women who were slowly making their way in. They thanked him profusely.

When we got back to Brooklawn, we found my father and Charlotte in the dining room having tea. They were laughing like teenagers on a date. Michael was relieved to see his mom happy. I was horrified to see my father, who had never been a flirt, batting his eyes and leaning into her like a lovesick puppy.

"Hi," I said hesitantly, not sure if he would still think I was an imposter.

"Hi," he said. "This is my new friend Charlotte. We were just getting to know each other." I couldn't tell if he knew who I was.

"Isaac, this is my son, Michael," Charlotte said to my dad. Michael shook his hand, and no one commented that they'd met before.

A nurse came over to us. "Mr. Rubin, your wife called. She'll be here soon. Do you want to go back to your room?"

"You must be mistaken, young lady," he said to the nurse, who was in her fifties. "I'm not married."

I abruptly turned and walked out without saying anything. I couldn't stand here and listen to this. Michael said goodbye to his mother, told her he'd be back tomorrow, then went after me. I ran to my car. When Michael caught up, he motioned for me to roll down my window.

"He's been married to the love of his life for forty-eight years, and he has no memory of her," I said. "This damn disease has taken him away, and he's never coming back." I was enraged as much as I was sad, and I was embarrassed that I was spilling my feelings all over him.

"Come with me." He opened my door, took me by the arm, and helped me out of the car.

"I need to go home," I said.

"You need a distraction. We'll go to the lake. Three baby ducks were just born there."

"I can't."

"It's only three ducks. We'll be back in fifteen minutes." He led me to his van, and I got inside. It smelled of old french fries and Axe cologne. "I'm sorry about my mom," he said apologetically. "She hasn't had a man pay attention to her since my father died." Michael steered the van out of the parking lot and onto the open road.

"At least your mom's single." I was so messed up I couldn't see the irony of my dad flirting with another woman while he was married. When we stopped at a light, Michael wiped a tear off my face. It was the gentlest, most caring thing that had happened to me in a very long time. As we waited for the light to change, three girls crossed the street in front of us. Two of them were Gia's friends, Lily and Talia.

"Oh my God," I said.

"What?"

"Those girls, they're Gia's friends."

"And . . . ?"

"And I'm in the car with you. If they see me, they're going to ask Gia who you are." I ducked my head down. There was a lone french fry in the corner of the doormat. I tried not to think how long it had been there.

It seemed like forever before the light turned green, and he drove through the intersection and out of harm's way. Was I so lonely that I would take the chance of screwing up my marriage and my family just for attention and excitement? Ellen was right; I was putting too much on the line for a fun flirtation. I needed to stay away from him if I wanted to stay married. And I did want to stay married. After twenty years, I couldn't imagine my life differently. Michael dropped me back off in the parking lot at Brooklawn, and as I walked to my car, I felt as if I was doing the walk of shame.

DAD

———✦———

"Papa, I like your new room," Gia says. It's her first time seeing me in the memory care unit. This room is a little smaller, but Dorothy squeezed everything in that I had from my other room. She wanted to make me comfortable, but that isn't a feeling I'll ever have again. It makes me happy that Gia, Maggie, and Jim have all come today. It's not often they're all here at the same time, or at least I don't remember it happening.

"You seem better today, Dad," Maggie says cautiously.

"I haven't felt this good in a while." I put my hand on Gia's hand, and she looks up at me. "How are you doing, honey?"

"I'm good, Papa. I'll be leaving for college in six months. I'm going to miss you so much." Maggie and Jim look miserable, as if they're already living the day she leaves them.

"I'll miss you too." I begin to tremble, wondering what I will be like by then.

"I can't wait to live in a dorm and meet new friends and—" Gia continues, and I try to interrupt her, but the words catch in my throat, and I start coughing. Maggie gets me water.

"Dad, we don't want to wear you out. We can come back another day," Maggie says.

"No," I say with a little too much force. I drink one more sip and clear my throat. Then I try to straighten up as best I can, but without much strength, I don't accomplish a lot. "I love you all so much."

"We love you too," Maggie says. She's cracking her knuckles. Jim puts his hand on her shoulder, but she doesn't stop.

"Mom and Dad said that you weren't doing great, but you seem okay to me," Gia says.

"I'm having a good day, but I don't have a lot of them."

"But you'll still come to my graduation, won't you?" Gia's starting to get upset.

"Hopefully, we can make that happen," Maggie says, trying to comfort her. Maggie doesn't believe that any more than I do.

"We'll see, honey," Jim says to Gia.

"But you look fine," Gia says.

"But I'm not," I say sadly.

She gets what I'm trying to say but doesn't want to hear it. Hell, I don't want to hear it. Fear is etched on her face. "I don't want you to die, Papa." Gia puts her head on my shoulder.

"He's not dying," Maggie says emphatically.

Jim tries to comfort Gia, but she pulls away. Maggie tells her they'll take things as they come, and hopefully it will work out. I'm grateful for her outlook; I wish I had the same one, but I know this disease is eating me. I ask Jim to give Maggie and me a few minutes alone. Jim hugs me, and Gia leans down so I can kiss her on the cheek, and they go. Maggie quietly retreats inside herself.

After a moment of silence, she says, "I'm scared." She moves over to be closer to me.

"I'm scared too."

"I don't know how to lose you."

"I wish I could always be here for you, but we both know that's not possible."

She begins to cry.

"I need you to promise you won't visit all the time if I don't know who you are," I say. "I don't want you to have hope when there isn't any."

"I can't make that promise." She sniffles.

"Well, you need to. And keep reminding your mother how much I love her and how wonderful our life was together."

Maggie gets a tissue and blows her nose. "This is all too much for me, Dad," she says.

"You're strong, and when you're not, lean on Jim."

"What if I can't handle it?"

"You're not going to have a choice."

She wraps her arms around me, and I know I've said enough.

CHAPTER 18

―――――・◈・―――――

We didn't see another good day from Dad afterward. In fact, he stopped recognizing my mom entirely and knew me only once. The doctor told us that once he took this turn, we shouldn't expect many more lucid moments. I kept hearing my father's voice in my head about not visiting anymore, but I wasn't going to give up.

"You okay?" Jim asked as we walked into Dad's room. Even if our marriage felt like it was falling apart, I was grateful that he'd come to support me today. "If it gets too much, we can leave," he said.

We found Dad staring blankly at a wall. "Hi, Dad," I said. He turned toward us but didn't say anything. "Gia sends her love." Silence again.

"It's good to see you," Jim said, placing his hand on Dad's arm. Dad had always loved Jim and would greet him with a huge bear hug—a hug so tight Jim could barely breathe—and the two of them would end up laughing until Dad let go. Dad didn't acknowledge Jim's touch. Jim looked at me, sorrow in his eyes.

I became desperate to get my dad to say anything. "Have you had lunch, Dad? Have you seen Charlotte? Did you watch

Wheel of Fortune last night?" I asked question after question and got no answers. I turned to Jim. "What am I doing?" I asked.

"Not giving up."

"Is that crazy?"

"No. You love him."

"It's just so depressing. Let's go," I said. We crossed to the door, and as I reached for the handle, I heard Dad's voice strong and clear and full of life.

"Your mother is not here."

"What?" I said, turning quickly.

He looked me square in the eye, recognition in his eyes and his expression. "Your mother is not here," he said again.

"No, Dad, she's not," I said, moving toward him. "But I'll get her. I'll call her right now." I grabbed my phone and dialed. Shoot, voice mail. I left a message. "Mom, call me right away, or better yet, come to Dad's place. He remembers you, and he wants to see you. Call me back." I walked outside his room to see if I could find a nurse or a doctor to tell them Dad was lucid. Before I could find anyone, my phone rang. It was Jerry.

"Jerry, do you know where Mom is? Dad just asked for her," I said excitedly. Jerry didn't say anything, so I thought we had a bad connection. "Jerry, can you hear me?"

"Mom had a heart attack," he said.

"What? Where is she? Is she okay?"

"She died on the way to the hospital a few minutes ago."

CHAPTER 19

———— ⚜ ————

The scent of fresh grass and fertilizer filled the crisp morning air. It had been raining lightly, which would've made Mom happy. She believed the Victorian superstition that rain at a funeral procession was a good thing, because it meant the deceased was going to heaven. I didn't get how anything could be good at a funeral.

The rabbi recited the *Al mekomah tavo veshalom* in Hebrew over my mother's grave.

I didn't understand a word, but his tone sent chills through me. Even in a foreign language, the sounds of a life having ended were loud and clear. I was never comfortable at funerals, not that anyone was, but normally I would come late and hide in the back. Today, there was no hiding from my mother's cold metal casket. Next to it was a picture of her from Gia's middle school graduation. She looked beautiful, relaxed, and suntanned. Dad was still able to walk then, and they had flown in the night before from one of their cruises.

After the prayer was over, one by one our family and friends threw dirt on her grave. The ritual was supposed to be healing, but when it was my turn, it felt as though I was trying to bury my feelings with her. I had only thrown the tiniest bit of dirt, but I was worn out, as if I'd buried her entire casket alone.

I hated talking at these things, but Jerry had spoken inside at the service, so it was my turn. I owed it to all the people who showed up, and to my mother.

"Thank you all for coming today. My mother would've loved this turnout. I've thought a lot about her life, which ended far too early. She was a successful person, but if I'd said that to her, she would not have agreed. She didn't think anything she did was important or worth mentioning, but if she wanted to do something, she never did it halfway, whether that was learning at seventy to drive a stick shift or finding the perfect dress." A few people chuckled the way people do at funerals. Not a hardy guffaw, a quieter knowing laugh. "Before my mom met my dad, she was a flight attendant, and for three years she traveled the world, until my father took one of her flights. He fell in love with her when she woke him up to put his tray back for landing. I know this because she told me, repeatedly, and they were still in love until the day she died."

My father was staring through me. Two days earlier, Jerry and I told him what had happened to Mom. Dad didn't say a word, but the tears streamed down his face. Now he was staring blankly, and I didn't think he knew where he was or why. I envied him.

I went on to talk about my mom's life and what a good friend she had been to so many people and how my father, brother, and I would miss her. After I finished, I placed a rose in the dirt on top of her casket. Friends and family began to move away from the gravesite. I stayed put. I leaned down and spoke quietly. "Mom, how could you leave before I could really get to know you? Our relationship wasn't easy, but I had hope that we would find each other and connect in a way we hadn't before. That hope is gone. You loved Gia with all your heart and were an amazing grandmother. I wish you had accepted me the way you accepted her. Without judgment. I will do my best to take care of Dad. We'll all miss you, and I'm sorry if I took you for granted. I thought you'd always be there to change my hairstyle, to rearrange my cabinets, and to give me your recipe for roast chicken. I'll miss each of those things every day."

I collapsed into a folding chair. Some of my high school and college friends came over and expressed their support, which I couldn't take in right now. Ellen and Sam came over to see how I was, and we ended up crushed together in this uncomfortable group hug. The two of them left quickly, the way everyone does after a funeral is over. We're all trying to outrun death.

"This sucks," Jerry said, sitting down beside me. It was the first time we'd agreed on anything.

"What's going to happen to Dad now that she's gone?" I asked.

"I'll figure it out," he said.

"What do you mean, *you'll* figure it out?"

"Mom made me the executor of her will and gave me instructions on what she wanted if anything happened to her. I'll be making the decisions about Dad's care," he said.

"Why did she pick you? I'm the oldest."

"She didn't think you'd be able to make the hard decisions that we were going to be facing. She thought you'd be burdened with guilt."

"I would've done anything he needed, even if it was hard."

"I know, but Mom wanted to make things easier for you. We're also going to have to put her house on the market."

"I don't want to sell the house."

"Dad's never going to live there again, and his care is expensive." I didn't think I could take one more thing, and then Jerry handed me a sealed, padded envelope. "Mom wanted you to have this if something ever happened to her," he said.

I took the envelope but didn't open it. Maybe I was in shock, or maybe I'd never feel anything again. My legs were unsteady, and I was numb. I needed to get away from everyone. "Can you drive Dad and the nurse back to Brooklawn?" I asked him. People were coming back to my house after the funeral, but I didn't think Dad needed to be there, considering he no longer remembered any of them anyway. Jerry helped the nurse get Dad in the car, and they left.

The only people still at the gravesite were Jim and Gia and two men standing thirty feet away next to a backhoe, talking quietly. They were subtly looking at us, waiting to finish burying my mom's casket. I didn't want them to cover her up, because then she'd really be gone. Both my parents had disappeared, even though only one of them was deceased. How was I going to survive?

"I can't believe Grandma's dead," Gia said, tearing up. "I don't know what I'd do if I ever lost you or Dad."

My heart broke, and I tried to assure her that we weren't going anywhere, but who knew what life was going to throw at us? When she stopped crying, I asked Jim to take her home. I had my own car because I'd driven Dad and his nurse to the funeral. I didn't want Gia around him in case he had a hallucination or yelled at her. It was hard to know what he was going to do anymore.

I opened the car door and tossed the envelope that Jerry had given me on the floor of the passenger seat. I was relieved to be alone. When I pulled out of the gates of the cemetery, I needed to turn right to go home. Instead I turned left, and in twenty minutes I was standing at the door to his apartment. *This is a bad idea. I'm a terrible person. I can't do this.*

Michael opened the door. "What're you doing here? Isn't today your mother's funeral?"

I didn't answer. I just took his head in my hands and kissed him. Not the kiss of seeing a friend, but a passionate, not-holding-back kind of kiss. He pulled me into his apartment and shut the door. I didn't want to think about my mother, my father, my marriage, anything. We fumbled our way to his couch, and my hands moved to his chest. Michael pulled away, breathing heavily.

"Are you drunk?" he asked. I didn't want him to question this. I just wanted it to happen. I pulled his shirt over his head and felt the tautness of his pectoral muscles. "This might be a bad idea," he said as I attempted to pull down my skirt without bothering to unbutton it. Pencil skirts weren't meant to be worn if you wanted to have sex. I finally yanked it off. Seeing me in my bra and panties must have shut him up. I lay back down on the couch, and he got on top of me, kissing my neck, the pressure feather light. I began to quiver. He moved his lips to my ear, his tongue circling my earlobe. He whispered something, but I had no idea what, because my brain had left my body. I guided his face up to mine, and we began kissing. Deep, hard kisses that left us breathless. He stood up and took his pants off, then got back on top of me, and I melted into him. His fingers brushed over my bra and across my breasts so gently I wanted to scream for more. As he reached down and looped his fingers around my panties and began to take them off, my phone rang. It was Gia's ringtone. I was so startled I fell off the couch.

I came screeching back to reality. I had to get a hold of myself. I was married. "My mom died," I exclaimed.

"I know," he said, helping me up off the ground and easing me back onto the couch. "This will ease your pain."

"No, I can't." I stood up and pulled my skirt over my hips, not caring if the zipper was in the front or back. "I have to go," I said, picking up my purse and running out. As I drove away, I realized there were fifty people at my house eating potato salad.

The rain was coming down hard and pounding on my windshield as I pulled into the driveway. I ran to the front door without using an umbrella. I didn't deserve to be dry. I walked in disheveled and soaked. My makeup running, my skirt wrinkled, and my shirt untucked.

My ninety-six-year-old great aunt approached me. "I'm so sorry about your mother, dear." She handed me her plate of food with a half-eaten chicken leg and a quarter of a potato pancake. "You need to eat something."

"Thanks, Aunt Stella, but I'm not hungry."

She patted my hand, took her plate back, took a bite of the chicken leg, and crossed over to sit with the other mourners.

"You're soaked. Did you take a walk in the rain?" Jim asked, coming up to me.

"No, I forgot my umbrella in the car," I said.

"Where were you?" he asked.

"I needed time alone."

He got a towel from the bathroom and wrapped it around me. Around the mess that had just cheated on him, that had been cheating for months. I'd become a person I would've judged, a person I never would've respected.

After I had dried myself, Jim took the towel and handed me a glass of water. I'd forgotten how sweet he could be when I needed him. I went to the bathroom so I could pull myself together. I smoothed my skirt, tucked in my shirt, and redid my makeup. Over the next hour I talked to distant relatives and friends of my mother's I'd never met. I'd had no idea how many people's lives she had touched.

After everyone had finally left, Gia went to bed, and Jim and I were left in a room filled with empty coffee cups and used paper plates. "You go upstairs. I'll deal with this mess," he said.

"I'd rather help." We cleaned side by side in silence, both in our own worlds. After the house was in relatively good shape, we went upstairs. Jim fell back on the bed, not even taking off his suit jacket. I lay down next to him. "I never would have gotten through all this without you," I said.

"You would've been fine."

I helped him take off his jacket, then opened his belt.

"You must be really tired," he said.

"I'm all right." I began taking off the rest of his clothes. I was tired of being subtle. I wanted my husband tonight. I needed him. I stood up and removed every inch of my clothing until I was completely naked. Then as gracefully as a naked ballerina, I climbed on top of him and rested my chest on his. As our hearts were beating in unison, I felt safe.

"I'm really worn out," he said.

I started kissing his chest and then his neck. "Are you sure you're worn out?"

"I can't tonight."

"Oh, okay," I said, not masking the hurt and feeling lonelier than I'd ever been. I rolled off him. He turned away from me and put on a sleep mask. I grabbed my sweats out of the hamper and went downstairs to eat as much chocolate as I could find.

CHAPTER 20

※

Early the next morning I came downstairs to a painful silence. I thought of how many times that stillness was pierced by my phone ringing. My mother could never wait until a decent hour to tell me some inane piece of news about her life. It drove me crazy. I missed those calls.

I heard a strange slurping sound and found Theo on the couch licking the cushions. Someone had spilled Caesar salad all over, but I was going to pretend it wasn't there. The same way I was going to pretend my mother hadn't died, my father knew who I was, and I hadn't just almost had sex with another man. I plopped myself on a chair, draped my feet on the ottoman, and made no move to stop Theo. Jim came in, his pajama bottoms hiked up above his waist and his T-shirt on backward, the label at his collarbone.

"Can you believe someone spilled—"

"I know about Michael," he said.

My heart stopped. "Who?"

"Don't do that."

"Do what? I don't know what you're talking about." What did he know?

"Don't play games. I'm not stupid," he said. "Who is he?" He was calm, but his presence standing over me felt intimidating.

I was caught. "A guy from the gym."

"You met him at the gym? What a cliché. How long has this been going on?" Hurt and anger settled on his face.

"Nothing is going on. He's just a guy at the gym."

"Just a guy at the gym who you want to leave me for?" Where did he get that idea? "How long?" he asked.

"I told you, nothing's going on."

"How long?" The anger in him was building.

"A few months. I didn't cheat on you."

"What would you call it?"

I put my hands to my head and rubbed my temples. "It was more of a flirtation, and it's over."

"What's over if nothing happened?"

"I'm not going to see him again."

"Why? Did he dump you?" he said with such venom it scared me.

Theo, sensing the tension, sat down on my foot. He raised his paw and put it on my knee. "I realized that spending time with Michael wasn't helping our marriage. I was telling him things I tried to talk to you about, but you weren't listening."

"I know I've been distracted, but if you were that unhappy, you should've told me."

"I did, many times. You would say you'd try harder, then you'd shut down again."

"You have no idea how hard it is for me to be present with you right now. Just getting up in the morning and going to work is killing me. What more do you want?"

"Someone who doesn't think spending time with me is a burden." I wanted him to tell me I was wrong, that he loved spending time with me. I watched him for a response, but he looked away. "You should've been honest with me about your job."

"I was. You didn't want to hear it," he said. He was right.

"Even if I didn't want to hear it, you should've made me see how much you were going through." I began cracking my knuckles.

"So, it's my fault that you went off with some other guy."

"I didn't mean for it to happen, but Michael was giving me attention that you weren't."

"What are you, four?" He kicked one of the dog toys across the room so hard that it hit the wall. Theo raced after the dinosaur and began chewing so enthusiastically that our conversation was punctuated by squeaking.

"How did you find out?" I asked.

"I found your pros and cons list crumpled up under your desk."

"Oh. That was Ellen's idea of a joke."

"Great, so Ellen's in on it?" he said.

"There's nothing to be in on."

I held out my phone and told him he could look at my texts. I knew full well that I'd been deleting them as they came in. He refused to take it from me; then he slumped down onto the couch as if his legs could no longer hold him up. He looked broken. I felt horrible.

"How long have you known?" I asked.

"Since the day your mom died."

"You should've said something."

"You had just lost your mother."

I looked down at my lap.

"If I hadn't caught you, would you have told me?" he asked, then started cracking his knuckles too. It was a cacophony of pops and clicks.

"No."

"That's the first honest thing you've said." He stood up and started walking away.

"Where are you going?" I asked, getting up to follow him.

"To pack."

"Don't let my one stupid mistake ruin a twenty-year marriage."

"Mistake? You didn't *accidentally* fall into his arms. It's been going on for months."

"I said I was sorry."

"Actually, you didn't. You've been too busy making excuses."

I was breathing so hard I thought I might hyperventilate. He walked out of the room, and I went after him. "I am sorry." I reached out to touch him.

"Don't follow me and don't touch me."

"What do I tell Gia?" I asked, starting to cry.

"Tell her I'm at a conference. I'll call her later." He went upstairs and loudly opened and closed drawers.

The sobs that racked my body were sobs I'd been holding in for months. I didn't want Jim to leave, but he also wasn't the man I married. I wanted that man back, the one I never would've thought of cheating on. Jim walked out the front door carrying a suitcase and a backpack without saying a word. I watched out the window as he got in his car. I hoped he'd turn around and come back, but he didn't. Snot ran down my face, and I grabbed a tissue. I was sure my face looked as if it had been through a washing machine.

What do you do when you just buried your mother and your husband walks out on you? I couldn't make breakfast as if it were any other morning. I didn't want to walk Theo because I wasn't sure my legs could hold up my trembling body. I sat back down on the couch, staring into space, but all I could imagine was a judge decreeing my divorce final. Finally, I picked up the front page of the newspaper. I hoped someone else's miseries would make mine not feel as bad. I still couldn't concentrate on anything when Gia came downstairs an hour later.

"Hi." I tried to keep my voice natural. She got a Pop-Tart out of the pantry, then opened the refrigerator and reached for a carton of orange juice.

"Where's Dad? I need to talk to him," she asked.

I pondered whether to talk to her about what was going on but thought it would only upset her right now. "He had to go to a conference," I said.

"Right after Grandma's funeral? What conference?" She couldn't have known anything, yet she sounded suspicious. Or was I reading something into it?

"What do you need to talk to him about?"

"There's just something I want to tell him."

She looked at me. She was almost eighteen, so maybe she would understand that her dad and I needed some space. "I think we should talk," I said.

"I know what you want to talk about, and I don't want to."

Had she heard Jim and me arguing? Or worse, had she also seen the pros and cons list? Whatever I said now could determine if she ever spoke to me again. I took a big breath. "Sometimes in a relationship there are things that happen . . ."

"I know, you don't have to lecture me. Jason and I figured it out."

I didn't see that coming. I just dodged a bullet. "Figured what out?" I asked.

"It's fine. We got back together."

"I didn't know you had split up?"

"It doesn't matter. If you talk to Dad, tell him his advice worked."

"What advice?"

She grabbed her jacket from the closet.

"Where're you going?" I asked.

"To meet Jason."

I watched her leave and prayed she'd have better relationships with men than I did.

JIM

———— ⊹ ————

"I left Maggie," I say to Sam as he opens his front door.

"What?" Sam looks as if I slapped him. "Because you hate your job? That's not a reason to leave."

"She cheated on me." Just saying those words is enraging and humiliating. How could she do this to me?

"She had sex with someone?" Sam asks.

"She says it didn't go that far."

"Who was it?"

"Some guy at the gym. Ellen knows all about it."

"She didn't tell me."

"I'm sure Maggie swore her to secrecy."

"This is crazy." I follow Sam into his kitchen and sit at the island. He puts a bag of potato chips and a beer in front of me, the comfort food for men. "What're you going to do?" he asks.

"No idea."

"Where are you staying?"

"Probably the Hyatt on Main Street."

"No, you're not. You're staying here, in our guest room."

I don't want to intrude on his life, but I also don't want to stay at a hotel. I look around the living room. How many times had Maggie and I come over for poker games, to drink wine, or to just hang out and complain about our daughter?

"Where's your stuff?" Sam asks.

"In the car." He follows me to my car and then takes me to a small room off the kitchen. I've been in the house a million times but have never been in this room. It's small but warm. The bed is neatly made, with a faux-fur throw at the end. There's a television and a bookcase filled with biographies of old actors. It's so clean it's as if it's ready and waiting for me. I stand awkwardly holding my suitcase as Sam shows me the bathroom and where to find extra towels. He takes my suitcase from me and drops it on the bed.

"Stay as long as you want," he says.

"Thanks."

Ellen calls out to Sam from their bedroom, and he goes to her. I can hear whispered conversation. He comes back, bringing Ellen with him.

"Hi," I say to Ellen. I try not to be mad at her—I know her loyalty is to Maggie—yet this is uncomfortable for both of us.

"Hi," she says, as if it's perfectly normal that I'm standing in her guest room with my suitcase.

"I hope it's okay that Sam invited me to stay." I feel like an intruder with the two people I'm the closest to other than my wife and kid.

"Of course," Ellen says. A look passes between them. Ellen and I've always had a brother-sister relationship, and now we barely make eye contact. "I'll get you another pillow," she says and walks down the hall.

"We're finally going to be roommates," Sam says.

"Right. You, me, and your wife."

"Don't worry, she won't get in the way." He smiles.

"Are you sure Ellen's okay with this?" I ask.

"She's fine. We never take sides, although I'm totally on yours."

Ellen comes back with another pillow and puts it on the bed. We stand in the tiny bedroom, none of us saying anything. I'm a forty-six-year-old man moving in with my best friend and his wife. How did I get here? I never thought after twenty years that the person I trusted the most would betray me. My whole world has been thrown up in the air and dropped down like a basketball hitting cement over and over.

CHAPTER 21

—◆—

"Gia, are you still there? I can't hear you." Jim's voice was booming through the speaker of Gia's phone, reverberating off the walls of the nail salon. The salon was filled with mothers and daughters laughing and talking, and Gia and I'd been sitting next to each other like two strangers on a bus. I thought the two of us getting manicures would be a good way to spend time together, but she would've rather been with Jason than getting her stupid nails done. Her lovely words to me on the ride over.

Over the last five days, Jim had called her three times, but he'd cut the calls short to avoid her asking too many questions. When she wondered why he wasn't calling more, I told her there was lousy cell service where he was. Hearing his voice through her speaker made me sad, but it also made me angry because he'd been ignoring all my calls. The other women at the salon were giving me the evil eye, and the receptionist began tapping on a sign that read, "No Cell Phone Calls in the Salon."

"Could you get off the phone? You're disturbing everyone around us," I said. Gia made no move to hang up.

"Where are you?" Jim asked her.

"Mom made me go with her to get a manicure."

"Gia's getting one too," I yelled toward the phone, gesturing with my hand, which caused my manicurist to nick me with her cuticle cutter. "Ow," I said, putting my finger in my mouth. "Can you watch what you're doing?" I was taking my frustrations out on her, but I didn't care.

"You've been gone almost a week. When are you coming home?" Gia asked him.

"I'm not sure."

"It's Saturday. How long is that conference?"

"I don't know," he said, stumbling over his words.

"How can you not know?"

"It's complicated . . . and you sound busy right now. I'll call you tonight. I love you." He hung up.

"He's not at a conference, is he?" Gia asked so loudly that anyone who hadn't already been staring at us looked over.

I lowered my voice to a whisper. "Let's talk about this in the car."

"No. Every time I ask you about him, you get weird. What's going on?" she asked at the same loud pitch.

"Nothing."

"You're lying." She pulled her hand away from her manicurist, causing her to mess up her polish. "Now look what you made me do," she said, scowling at me. The manicurist rolled her eyes.

"Excuse us for a second," I said to both manicurists. Then I took Gia by the arm. "Come with me." I pulled her to the corner of the room. "Everything's fine," I said. "Your father and I are working a few things out." I had no idea if that was true.

"What's that supposed to mean?"

"It means things will soon be back to normal."

"I don't believe you." She stormed out of the salon. One set of her nails had fuchsia polish and the other was completely bare.

She needed a few minutes to calm down, so I kept my head down and walked back over to my manicurist to finish my nails. The manicurist who had been doing Gia's nails handed me a bill and moved on to someone else.

When my nails were done, I left the salon hoping I'd figure out what to say to Gia on the ride home, but instead of waiting for me, I saw her getting into Taylor's convertible. The two of them drove off, their hair blowing in the breeze. I sat down on the curb outside the salon. It was hard and uncomfortable, which was fitting for what my life had become. I rummaged through my purse to find my phone, but since my nails weren't completely dry, I had to be careful, kind of like that game Operation where you're trying not to hit the sides. When I finally got my phone, I saw Michael had texted me again. He'd been texting me for days, but I hadn't responded. I called Ellen.

"Hi," I said.

"I've been worried about you. You haven't called me back, and when I text, the most you say is that you're okay."

"I wasn't ready to talk. Losing my mother and my marriage in the same week isn't something I'd wish on anyone. Can you meet for lunch today?"

"When?"

"Now."

I told her I was across the street from Friendly's, and she said she could be there in fifteen minutes. Friendly's was known for ice cream, but it had pretty good food, especially when you were looking for something fried. The restaurant wasn't crowded, as it was early for lunch and too early for ice cream. I didn't want to be that person sitting all alone in a booth, so instead I waited for her on a bench outside. Bad thoughts about what I'd done to my marriage and how much I'd hurt Jim were smashing into each other in my head and making me dizzy. I wasn't good at meditating, but I thought it was worth a try. I breathed in and out slowly and settled on a mantra. "This too shall pass, this too shall pass, this too shall pass. . . ." After the tenth time I had recited the phrase, I finally started to feel better. My heart had slowed down, and my breathing was even, until a crumb of a thought drifted in. *What if it doesn't pass?* And then that became my mantra until Ellen arrived.

"Why are you out here? Did they ban you from the restaurant?" She gave me a mournful and empathetic hug.

"I needed air."

We sat at a table in the back. I caught Ellen up on this morning with Gia. "And then Jim just hung up, leaving me to try to make excuses for why he wasn't there. This whole thing's a giant mess." Ellen didn't say anything, which was out of character. "What?" I asked.

"Jim's not the one who messed things up."

"No, but he made it easy for me to do it." The busboy came over to fill our water glasses and spilled ice on my lap. He apologized as I pushed the ice onto the floor.

"That's not an excuse," she said.

"Whose side are you on?"

"I'm not on anyone's side. I'm your friend, but I'm also Jim's friend, and I see what he's going through. I feel bad for him."

"It's not like everything is hunky dory in my world." I took a sip of water, and a piece of ice slid into my mouth. I deserved to choke on it, but it went right down.

"Yeah, but you created that world. I told you it was a bad idea to keep seeing Michael."

"I couldn't help it."

"It's not like he hypnotized you," Ellen stated.

Could he have? Could I have fallen victim to his charm and good looks, and they made me do things I wouldn't have normally done? The waitress came over to take our order. Ellen ordered a grilled chicken sandwich with extra tomatoes, and an iced tea with an orange instead of a lemon. I hadn't even opened the menu, but I ordered a tuna sandwich with extra mayo, and french fries. I might as well ruin my figure. I'd already ruined my marriage, my daughter's life, and possibly my friendship.

"Are you mad at me?" I asked.

"No. I mean, I don't know, maybe."

I couldn't believe it. She was my best friend, and she was supposed to support me no matter what stupid things I'd done. "That's not fair. Besides, if it wasn't for your stupid pros and cons list, he would never have known."

"Don't blame me for your mess."

"You're right. I got myself into this."

"So, what are you going to do to get yourself out?" Ellen asked.

"I don't know. Something has to change for both of us. I mean, what kind of marriage do we have if we shy away from important conversations and we don't have sex?"

"You could've had a real conversation about your sex life instead of pretending it wasn't going on, and you could've gone to therapy. There were plenty of things you could've done before turning to another man."

"How can you say that? You know I tried."

"You didn't try hard enough. You kept waiting for things to change as opposed to finding ways to change them."

The waitress came back with our food. Ellen took a bite of her sandwich before my plate of food had touched the table. "Excuse me?" she called to the waitress with her mouth full of chicken and extra tomatoes. "Can you tell the chef that if he put a little pesto on the chicken, it wouldn't be so dry?"

"I'll be sure to pass that along," she said. "He *loves* getting tips from our customers." She pulled our check out of her pocket and dropped it on the table.

"My fries are perfect," I called after her, my voice louder than I intended. Ellen took another bite of her sandwich.

"The only thing I know for sure is that you and Jim need to talk," she said.

"He won't take my calls."

"Then go to his office. Or show up at my house. Apologize, beg, do whatever it takes. You did cheat on him."

"I'm judging myself. I don't need you to judge me too."

"I'm sorry, it's just you and Jim were the most solid couple Sam and I knew. If you two get divorced, we'll never find another couple we both like." I felt the same way about her and Sam.

"This whole thing makes me sick to my stomach, which is why I haven't wanted to talk about it. I know you mean well, but I need to get out of here." I took a big bite of my sandwich, grabbed a few fries, dropped money on the table and left. As I walked past the waitress, I handed her a ten-dollar tip. "Thanks for your patience." I continued out the door. Everyone I loved was mad at me. I didn't want the waitress to be mad at me too.

In the parking lot, I called Jim and was surprised when he answered. "I need to know if you're coming home soon," I said. "If not, we need to tell Gia something."

"I'm not," Jim said.

"Not soon or not ever?"

He stayed silent. Was he saying he was never coming home?

After a few moments, he said, "Fine, I'll come over later today, and we can talk to Gia."

"What should we say?"

"How the hell should I know?"

"You're a shrink. You've been trained for this kind of thing. You must've given your patients advice on what to say to their kids if they separated."

"I think we should just be honest," he said.

"That's a dumb idea."

"Fine, then lie. You're good at that." He hung up on me. He had perfected that skill in such a short time.

I shoved my phone back in my purse and saw Ellen walking out of the restaurant. I didn't want to talk to her again, so I ducked down beside an SUV.

"Excuse me, that's my car," a woman said. She and her toddler had come up behind me.

"Mommy, what's that lady doing?" her toddler asked.

"I was just tying my shoes," I said and walked off quickly before she could realize I had on leather boots with no laces.

Normally visiting with my dad made me feel better, but I hadn't seen him since the funeral. I couldn't handle the reality that both my parents were gone, while I was dealing with my life falling apart.

When Gia got home that afternoon, I didn't tell her Jim was coming over. I wasn't a hundred percent sure he'd show up.

Later that evening, Jim did come through the door, and I tried to convince myself that everything would be okay, but as soon as I saw his face, I knew it wouldn't. He brushed past me and reflexively hung his keys on the hook next to the front door. Then, as quickly as they landed, he picked them back up and put them in his pocket. When Gia saw him, she hugged him tightly. She told him how much she missed him and how happy she was that he had come home.

"Why don't we sit down?" I said.

"Why do we need to sit down?" Gia asked.

"It's okay," Jim said and led her to the couch. Gia sand-wiched him between the arm of the couch and herself, probably so she could keep him from leaving again. I sat across from them, feeling as if I was on my own island. I waited for Jim to start, but he didn't.

"Your father and I are going to live apart for a little while," I said, ripping off the Band-Aid. "It doesn't mean we aren't still a family or that you did anything wrong."

"I know I didn't do anything wrong," Gia snapped.

Great, I was off to a good start. I cracked my knuckles while I waited for Jim to add something. When he didn't, I continued, "We both love you, and we can all still do things together as a family. It's just your dad and I need time apart to work on some stuff."

"What stuff?" Gia asked, her voice cracking. Neither of us said anything. "You aren't going to tell me. You don't think I'm old enough to handle the truth."

"It's not that," Jim said.

"Are you having a fight?" Gia asked.

"No. We need to work on issues in our lives separately right now," I said.

"That's bullshit. You're getting a divorce."

"No one said anything about divorce," I said. Jim didn't say anything; he just looked down at his shoes.

"I don't want to be from a divorced family," Gia said.

Now I was close to tears. It broke my heart to see my daughter so torn up. "I said we aren't getting a divorce."

Jim put his arm around her. "I won't be living here, but it'll be okay, I promise. I'll see you a lot. I'll take you out to dinner, and we can see movies on the weekends."

Gia scooted even closer to Jim, which I didn't think was possible. "Are you ever coming back?" she asked, looking at him with eyes welling up with tears.

"We'll see," Jim said.

"Where will you live?" Gia asked.

"He's staying at Sam and Ellen's," I said.

"Not anymore. I just rented an apartment," he said.

"You did?" I said. Had it gone that far? Was this permanent? "Did you sign a lease?" *Please say no.*

"It's month to month." He didn't look in my direction.

"I'm going to go live with Dad." Gia wiped her runny nose with the back of her hand. "Dad, will you help me move?" Why didn't she want to stay with me?

"I don't have a bed in the second bedroom yet," Jim said. "It would be better for you to stay here for now." For now? He was taking her over my dead body.

"When can you get me a bed?" Gia asked.

"We don't know how long your dad will be in the apartment. He may not need to buy one," I said.

"Stop lying. Dad's never coming home." Gia ran out of the room, hysterical.

I turned to Jim. "You rented an apartment? Does that mean you don't want to try to work things out?"

"Right now, no," Jim said, standing up. "I have to go."

"You're going to leave me here to deal with all this?" I was incredulous.

"There wouldn't be anything to deal with if it wasn't for you." He took his keys out of his pocket and walked toward the door. "I'll talk to Gia again on the drive to the city."

"You're taking her to New York?"

"Yeah, for the weekend. It's a surprise. I'm taking her to see *Hamilton.*"

"You got tickets to *Hamilton*? Are you freaking kidding me? You knew I wanted to see that show, and you said the tickets cost a fortune?"

"She really wanted to see it." Was he trying to buy her off? How transparent. Why didn't I think of that? "Have her pack a suitcase. I'll pick her up Friday after school." He walked out.

I'd been suggesting we go to *Hamilton* for months, but he said it was too expensive and New York was filled with muggers and dirt. I was seething. I took a pillow off the couch and pounded the living hell out of it. How dare he put our entire marriage on me? He was just as much at fault for our issues as I was.

Over the next couple of days, Gia pouted or stayed in her room most of the time and didn't bring up anything about Jim and me. All she talked about was how much fun she was going to have next year on her own. I wasn't sure if she was trying to convince herself or punish me because she knew how much I was going to miss her. Why was she blaming me more than her dad for our problems? It wasn't as if she knew anything about Michael. Moms always got the brunt of everything when dads were in the clear.

Before I knew it, it was Friday afternoon, and Gia and Jim were driving away. I was alone in the house. Not alone for the afternoon, but completely alone. Gia wasn't calling me from upstairs, she wasn't asking for food, and she wasn't interrupting me. I hated it. I needed my daughter, I needed her noise, I needed a mojito. I'd never made one before, but if I was going to be on my own, learning a new skill would be good. I searched the internet for the ingredients: rum, soda water, lime juice, mint, and sugar. I had everything but the mint. I had curry, but that didn't seem right. If I added a few extra teaspoons of sugar, would it really be that noticeable? I put the ingredients I had in a shaker and shook it for all it was worth. Then I poured my concoction into a highball. It was tart and sweet and felt good going down my throat. It wasn't the best mojito, but the rum was doing its job.

When I put the liquor back, I saw that Gia had shoved a bunch of her favorite candy in the back. Her favorite was also my favorite. She was always coming up with new places to hide it from me, and now I couldn't unsee the candy. It was calling to me. Would she really notice if I ate a piece or two? A moment later, I was drinking my faux mojito and stuffing my face with Reese's Peanut Butter Cups. How sad I must've looked. Maybe if I invited someone over, I wouldn't look so pathetic. I could call Ellen, but she was at her office, and she might still be mad at me.

Michael didn't work at an office, and he wasn't mad at me. Jim was the one who'd moved out and asked for the separation. It wasn't as if I'd wanted it. But if we were separated, then why shouldn't I see if Michael wanted to spend time with me? Besides, Jim went to see *Hamilton*, so there was that.

I sent a text: *Hi. Sorry I left so abruptly last week and haven't answered your texts.*

It's okay. Your mother just died.

Thanks for understanding. I'm sad, but I think I'm mourning a mother I wish I had, not the one I had, if that makes sense.

It does.

You are the only person I've admitted that to.

You can trust me.

I do. Okay, here goes. *Are you free tonight? Jim and Gia are out of town.* I was glad he couldn't see me right then. Wearing sweatpants, eating stolen candy, and drinking a mint-less mojito.

He wrote: *Sure. 7:30 at La Cucina?*

I couldn't go to La Cucina with him. Angelo would ask too many questions. *How about Le Petit Chateau?* A French restaurant was far sexier than an Italian one anyway.

Great, c u later.

I was going on a date, a real date. I hadn't been on a real date since Jim and I got together. Would I know what to do? I supposed we'd talk and drink and . . . Wait, what would come after talking and drinking? Would he expect me to invite him to my house? The last time I'd seen him, we'd almost had sex. I didn't know if I was ready for that, but just in case, I should have a good bottle of wine. I checked the refrigerator and the wine rack, but nothing said *I'm classy and might possibly want to have sex.* I would need to go to the market for that.

As soon as I approached the electric doors of the market, I regretted my decision not to change out of my sweatpants. Three of the mothers from Gia's school were standing just inside. They looked as if they'd just walked off the runway, and I hadn't even brushed my hair. I was turning to leave when the doors automatically opened, and Jessica saw me.

"Hi, Maggie," she called out. Ugh, I was stuck. Jessica gestured to the women with her. "Do you know Emma, Amanda, and Susan?" she asked, as if our daughters hadn't been in school together since kindergarten.

"Sure, hi," I said.

"Hi," they all said with all the phony enthusiasm of high school cheerleaders. I was suspicious of their friendliness, since they never gave me the time of day at any class events.

"Sorry to hear about you and Jim," Emma said.

"What do you mean?" How could they know anything? We just told Gia a few days ago.

"We heard you two separated," Susan said.

"Where did you hear that?"

"I saw Jim moving into my apartment building," Jessica said.

"It's so sad, especially for your daughter," Amanda said. "Divorce is toughest on the kids."

"I don't know what I'd do if my husband ever divorced me," Emma said.

"We aren't getting divorced, just taking a break," I said. The three women nodded at each other, as if I were delusional about my own life.

"It's okay, we won't tell anyone else," Jessica said.

"There isn't anything to tell. I better get going. I'm in kind of a hurry," I said. Now I really needed that wine. Or maybe vodka.

"Bye," the cheerleaders said in unison.

I crossed to the liquor aisle, where rows and rows of wines were displayed in front of me. White or red, chardonnay or cabernet? What did one pick for the man that she broke up her marriage for? As I picked up a bottle of merlot, I felt an arm drape around my shoulders. It was Jessica.

"It's okay, you can talk to me. I get it. Being a single mother's not easy," Jessica said.

"I'm not a single mother."

"There's no shame in accepting it. The first time you say it out loud is so hard, but you'll get used to it. Say it with me: I am a single mother."

I didn't say anything. All I wanted was for this insane woman to get her stinking arm off me and go away. We were not the same. I was not, nor would I ever be, one of those single mothers who was totally alone at dinner parties or their daughter's wedding. If Jim and I got divorced, I would be . . . I would be . . . Oh my God, I'd be one of those single mothers.

Jessica was still droning on. "We should go out for drinks together and pick up men. And don't worry, I'd meet you somewhere so you wouldn't run into Jim at his apartment. Especially if he had a date over. That would be very awkward, wouldn't it?" she asked.

"Yes, it would be," I replied as I was planning my escape, although I wasn't going anywhere without my wine.

"Unless, of course, you're dating that cute guy I saw you with the last time I ran into you."

"We're just friends." At least until after tonight.

"Okay," she said. I said goodbye and turned to make my getaway when she called after me, "If you're not dating him, can I have his phone number?"

CHAPTER 22

———— ·✦· ————

I had a habit of always being early, so at 7:22 I was sitting in my car in front of Le Petit Chateau. I was nervous, and I couldn't keep my eyes off the clock as the numbers turned from 7:22 to 7:23 to 7:24. If Jim hadn't left me, I wouldn't be about to go on a date with Michael. I was more than willing to work things out with Jim, but he wasn't. So if Michael and I had sex, it would be Jim's fault.

I was wearing a silk shirt, with the buttons open perfectly at my cleavage. This was my go-to shirt when I wanted to feel sexy without trying too hard, even though I was trying hard. I pulled down the sun visor and admired myself in the mirror. My heart was beating into my throat. Oh no, what if I had a heart attack and died right now? Would the paramedics think, *Wow, she looked sexy?*

I cracked my knuckles and twirled my wedding ring around and around on my finger. I needed to give up these bad habits. I admired my ring; I did love it. What would it be like not to wear it anymore? Jim had surprised me on our fifteenth anniversary by trading in my original diamond and getting me this bigger one.

It was beautiful. I slipped it off my finger and dropped it into the side pocket in my purse. Being without my ring felt weird and naked and like a neon sign screaming, "Stop pretending you're not married." My fingers started rubbing together incessantly. Why were they tormenting me? I put my ring back on as I spied Michael walking from his car toward the restaurant.

He was in black jeans and a black sport coat over a white T-shirt. Jessica would've eaten her heart out. I was eating my heart out. I waited another minute before getting out of my car and going inside. Michael was talking to the hostess, who was flirting with him, but when he saw me, he whistled under his breath. The hostess shot me a look. She looked as though she was wondering how someone like me could get a man like him. Or maybe she was admiring my shirt. I wasn't sure which.

"You look amazing," he said.

I leaned in for a hug, and he kissed my cheek. I was lucky that my first official date after separating was with a man like him. My friend Monica had told me horror stories about the men she went out with after her divorce. Men who shaved ten years off their age, men who lied about what they did for a living, and men who said they were too busy to ever text during the week. Michael told me all the time how much he liked being with me. He laughed at my jokes and empathized when I talked about my dad's dementia. He was sensitive and caring to my needs.

The hostess took us to a table at the outside patio under a heater. It was like being in a café in the French countryside. There were white linens, red chairs, and chandeliers hanging from potted trees. There was also an outdoor fireplace in the corner, and our table looked out on Long Island Sound. The moon lit up the waves as they silently broke. It couldn't have been more romantic if it were a movie set.

"What a beautiful view," I said. "The hostess must like you."

"Or maybe she likes you," he said, taking my hand in his. "I know I do." He gazed into my eyes, and my nerves did belly flops. I was so jumpy.

"Can I get a mojito?" I called out to a busboy who was walking by.

"I'll tell your waiter," he said, barely stopping.

"I'll have one too," Michael called after him. The hand he was holding began to sweat, and I worried that he would think I had a glandular problem. I casually let go. He put his hand back in his lap, probably to wipe my sweat off.

"So, where did Jim and Gia go?" he asked.

"New York City to see *Hamilton*."

"And you didn't go with them?"

"I've already seen it," I lied.

"Well, New York's loss is my gain."

"You're such a charmer," I said, smirking.

"I was glad to hear from you. The last time I saw you, you ran out of my apartment. What happened that day?" he asked.

"I got scared."

"Well, I can't stop thinking about you. We would've had amazing sex. I would've had fun taking those silk panties off you." He said this as the waiter put down our drinks on the table. I was flustered and noticed the waiter grinning. I realized with my peek-a-boo blouse and my need to get drunk, he probably thought I was a slut. Then again, if I was paying for the crime, I might as well go all in. I took a long, slow sip of my mojito. The scent of mint and alcohol and the tartness of the lime juice made me braver. This was so much better than the one I made at home.

I took a breath. "Jim found out about us and moved out."

"Really? Well, now there's nothing in our way."

I had been telling myself that I was separated over and over the last few days, but I didn't think I had really understood what that meant until now. Hearing him say that out loud threw me off-balance.

I needed a moment, so I excused myself and picked up my purse and went to the bathroom. I looked in the mirror and dabbed a little more concealer under my eyes and lightly rubbed it in with my pointer fingers. Then I used a Q-tip to wipe off a little mascara that had run. After I was satisfied, I put my hands under the waterspout, but nothing happened. Like a wild woman, I started waving them around until a trickle of cool water dribbled out. Two seconds later, the water stopped. When I waved my hands under the spout again, I noticed a woman and her four-year-old daughter had come out of a stall and was watching me.

"Mommy, can I play in the water like that lady?" the little girl asked.

I smiled at the woman and dried my hands. As I walked back to the table, my mind was racing in all directions, and I forgot where we were sitting. I looked around until Michael waved me over.

"You okay?" Michael asked when I sat down.

"There was a long line," I said. I reached down to pick my napkin up off the floor.

When I sat back up, he was ogling me. "I hope I'm not making you nervous," he said.

"Maybe a little. I haven't done this before."

"I know, and I'm flattered that you wanted your first time to be with me." He took my hand and lightly kissed it. His warm lips made every muscle from my hand to my shoulder quiver.

"It's not my first time . . . I mean, I've had sex before. . . ." I said, blushing. "I mean it's my first time for this . . . whatever this is. . . ." I wondered if I was getting dementia. Then I realized it was just my hormones that were turning me into a babbling idiot.

"Well, now that Jim's gone, we can have fun, and you don't have to feel guilty."

"It's not that easy."

"Maybe not, but if we didn't see where this takes us, I think you'd regret it. You wouldn't want to wake up in ten years and wonder what it would've been like for us to have sex. I know I wouldn't."

I'd been thinking about it for months. I loved Jim, but he wasn't attracted to me anymore. This man was making it clear that he was, and I didn't want to live the rest of my life without sex. I was still young, and I deserved more than once-in-a-while intimacy.

The restaurant had gotten very crowded, mostly with couples. There were two men in their thirties flirting and teasing each other. They were celebrating their first wedding anniversary. I remembered when Jim and I celebrated our first wedding anniversary at La Cucina. We were young and giddy, and everything he said that night made me laugh. He had thought I was adorable, and I could tell he wanted to rip my clothes off. It made me sad that we weren't those two people anymore.

To my right were an elderly man and his wife holding hands across the table. They weren't saying a word, just looking into each other's eyes. What did people think of Michael and me? Did they think we looked good together? Could they tell I was a lot older than him?

Michael asked me a question, but the music and the murmur of voices made it hard to hear him. I leaned in closer, and when his eyes darted down, I knew he had gotten a glimpse of my breasts. I didn't know why I felt the need to adjust my shirt. It was just a preview of what he'd be getting later.

"Are you ready to order, or would you like to hear our specials?" the waiter asked, interrupting Michael's gaze.

"I'll have the lamb chops with the potatoes au gratin," I said.

"I'll have the same, but I'd like my lamb chops completely pink inside."

The waiter headed off. "Can you believe that French accent?" Michael said. "I could do a better one than that." He mimicked the waiter.

"You make an adorable Frenchman," I said.

"*Merci beaucoup, ma chérie.*"

"I've always wanted to learn French."

"Well, we can practice our French together later," he said suggestively.

I looked out at the Long Island Sound. There was one small fishing boat drifting in the water. The boat bobbed up and down, not seeming to move in any one direction, as if the captain had no idea where he wanted to go. Was I like that captain? What direction was I going? Michael asked what I was looking at. I'd opened my mouth to answer when I noticed that the boat had vanished. Where did it go? Had it been there?

When the food came, Michael ate quickly, like someone who was eager to get to the next course, which was probably me. I ate more slowly, savoring every bite. After we'd both finished, he put his fork down and wiped his mouth. "So . . . would you like 'dessert'?" he asked seductively.

Should I suggest we have "dessert" at my house? If Jim moved back in, our "dessert" would make things weird and gross, and I'd have to throw away my bed. Because I wasn't ready to answer, I asked, "How's your mother doing at Brooklawn?"

"She's fine. And now that she's settled in, I convinced her to sell her house and give me my inheritance early."

"Really?" I said, surprised he was pushing his mother to give him money.

"Yeah," he said, mistaking my surprise for approval. "I need the money now. I backed my van into one of those poles at the gas station. I was so mad at myself. It was so stupid."

"We all do stupid things."

"I guess. I told the insurance company that it was a hit and run, so I wasn't at fault. So, with the money they give me to fix it and the money my mom gives me, I'm going to be able to buy something new."

I wasn't sure if I opened my mouth what would come out, so I nodded. I'd never seen this side of him, but I didn't know what it was like to be desperate for money. Maybe he didn't know what else to do. I pushed down any negative thoughts. I didn't want to ruin the night.

"How's your writing going?" I asked, changing the subject.

"Good. I have one article to finish before I leave."

"Leave? Where are you going?"

"My editor liked the story I did on the tamarin monkeys. He assigned me a series on how animals are treated at various zoos in other countries."

"Oh. How long will you be gone?"

"Around three months."

"That's a long time." When was he going to mention he was going away? After we had sex? If I wanted someone to disregard me, Jim was already good at that.

"It's going to be a lot of travel in a short time. Kind of like I'm going on tour with my band, except there won't be any instruments or groupies. Unless you want to be my groupie?"

"I can't leave town for three months. I have a daughter, and I couldn't leave my dad for that long either."

"It's not like he'd know you were gone," Michael said.

"Excuse me?" I was shocked he said that.

"I just meant you said he was pretty out of it. If you were gone for a little while, what harm would it do?"

Before I could react, he excused himself to go to the restroom, leaving his phone on the table. After a minute his phone started ringing. I saw a picture of a pretty, very young woman in a lace bra and panties. I stared at it and realized it was Gia's friend Taylor. Oh my God, Michael was the older guy she was dating. Jesus, she was nineteen! He said he'd stopped dating young girls. I was disgusted, and I was mad, but I wasn't sure if I was madder at him or myself. Was I so desperate for attention from a good-looking man that I had ignored red flags? I started shaking. He wasn't interested in me; he was only interested in feeding his ego. Any woman who flashed her eyes at him was fair game. I couldn't believe I'd almost had sex with that man. I started pulling little hairs out of my eyebrows. When he got back to the table, I could barely look at him.

"Would you like coffee or dessert?" the waiter asked, holding our check.

"Neither," I said emphatically. "Just the check, please." As the waiter was putting the check on the table, I pulled out my credit card and handed it to him. Michael didn't say anything about me paying. Was he saving his money for his dates with Taylor? He must've thought an older woman would be desperate enough to put up with anything.

While I waited for the check and my credit card to come back, I pretended to look at my phone. When the bill came, I signed it and stood up. I needed to get out of there before I freaked out.

Michael seemed oblivious to my change in mood. "I'm looking forward to the rest of the night," he said, standing up.

I pulled my coat off the back of my chair. "I'm tired."

"So, let's go to your house and be tired together."

"I don't think so." I walked toward the entrance quickly, Michael trailing a few feet behind me.

"You're just going to go home?" he asked, confused.

"Yes." I walked to my car without turning around. I couldn't believe I had given up my marriage for this jerk.

CHAPTER 23

It was 5:52 a.m., and I was alone in the middle of my king-sized bed. I closed my eyes, hoping to go back to sleep, but my mind was racing with all the mistakes I'd made. I had denied what was happening with Michael for so long, and then when I couldn't deny it any longer, I'd rationalized it. I told myself that if Jim was going to ignore me, then it was okay if someone else found me sexy and interesting. I didn't think about how devastated and betrayed he'd feel if he found out. I was short-sighted and selfish, and I'd hurt him deeply. I regretted that more than anything. I didn't know if he'd forgive me, but I had to try to make it up to him and fight for my marriage. As I got out of bed, I checked myself out in the mirror. Sheet marks had taken up residence on my face. I hoped they'd move out soon.

I made two poached eggs, bacon, toast, and coffee and took it out to the table on our back deck. As the morning sun was lighting up the woods behind our house, the scent of marigolds wafted over me. It was spring, although my mood was far from springy. The neighbor's garage door rattled as it went up, then down, and his motorcycle reverberated as it traveled down the street. I barely ate anything, and the slippery yellow yoke on my plate was making me queasy. After I'd washed the dishes and cleaned up the house, I needed to do one thing before Jim and Gia got home in order to move on.

At ten o'clock, I was standing in front of Michael's apartment. As I was debating whether to ring the bell or knock, he opened the door to get his newspaper. He had on shorts and the same Captain America T-shirt he'd been wearing the first time I saw him, and the tattoo on his arm was on full display.

"I'm glad you're here," he said and motioned for me to come in. I sat on the couch, as far away from him as I could. He sat next to me. I took a throw pillow and placed it between us. "You're so confusing," he said. "One minute we're about to have sex, the next you're running out the door. Last night, the way you were dressed, the way you flirted with me, you wanted me as much as I wanted you. Are you just a tease?"

"No. Last night your phone rang while you were in the bathroom, and I saw it was from Gia's friend Taylor." I was going to stay cool and see what he had to say.

"That's why you were weird?" he said. "She's just somebody I met at the gym."

"Funny, I don't wear a bra and panties when I work out."

"I wish you did," he said and moved the pillow from between us. He inched closer to me and put his hands on the buttons of my blouse.

I moved away from him. "You can't really think I'm going to sleep with you."

"You're going to give up the opportunity to fulfill your fantasies with me because of one stupid girl?"

Right now, my fantasy was running him over with my car. "I would never be with someone who's sleeping with other women."

"So I date other women. It's not like we're committed to each other. And you didn't seem to care before Jim moved out."

"Taylor is one of Gia's friends. And she's nineteen!" I said loudly, hoping that he didn't know her age.

"I told you a long time ago I dated younger." He clearly knew her age.

"You're a thirty-four-year-old man dating a nineteen-year-old girl, and you don't see anything wrong with that?"

"She's an adult," he said emphatically. I was hoping that he'd feel bad, but that was obviously not in his repertoire of emotions.

"I can't believe you said that," I said. I knew what the expression "hot under the collar" meant. Not only was I hot under the collar, but my whole body felt feverish. "My husband is a far more honorable man than you are!"

"The same man who's been ignoring you since we met?"

"I'm not going to discuss that with you." I softened my voice. "This isn't how I wanted this conversation to go."

"Really? How did you think it would go?" he asked sarcastically. "Like I was going to stop seeing all the young, beautiful women in my life?"

He was so arrogant. How did I make this guy out to be someone he wasn't? I had sunk so low. "I only came here today to say goodbye and thank you for being there for me the past few months. No matter what, you helped me through a tough time," I said.

"Well, it didn't get me laid." He was showing his true colors, which made me confident that coming here had been the right thing to do. I walked to the door, and he followed close behind. "You're so lost—you have no idea what you want," he said.

As he reached in front of me to open the door, the words of his tattoo were almost in my face: *Death Before Dishonor.* I laughed and then looked him in the eyes. "You're an immature, vile, crude, loathsome scumbag." Adjectives were flying out of me. "Don't call or text me ever again," I said.

"No problem. Even the nineteen-year-olds I date are more together then you are."

As I walked over the threshold, he shut the door quickly, leaving me standing on his doormat with the word *welcome* staring up at me. I felt stronger and more self-assured than I had in a long time. If I had the strength to do that, then I had the strength to get my marriage back on track.

When I opened my car door, I saw the padded envelope that Jerry had given me at my mother's funeral wedged in the corner. I reached across the seat, picked it up, and held it in my hands. When I tore open the envelope, a small square box fell out, along with a letter. It was handwritten on my mother's butterfly stationary.

> *Dear Maggie,*
>
> *When your father got sick, I realized that if something were to happen to me, there were things I'd never been able to tell you. I wish I could have opened up to you more, but you and I had a tough time doing that. I hope by the time I die, I will have told you this in person. But just in case, I wanted you to know how sorry I am that I wasn't the kind of mother you deserved. I regret that I didn't make you feel special or good enough. I should have hugged and kissed you more and told you how important you are to me, but I was never comfortable showing that kind of emotion. My parents didn't teach me how, but I should have*

tried harder. I'm thankful that your father could give you that, but envious of the bond you two had. I wish you could have loved me like that.

You've been faced with struggles in your life, and over the years you'll be faced with more. Never doubt that you can deal with whatever obstacles are put in your way. You're a strong, intelligent woman with great instincts, who I've always admired and had faith in. I want you to know how much I love you and how proud I am that you're my daughter.

I asked Jerry if I were to die, to give you this letter and something else that was important to me. Something your father gave me on the day you were born. I love you, Maggie, always know that, and I hope your life is as fulfilling as mine was.
Love, Mom

I read the letter twice. I wished she would've said all that when she was alive. Now there was no chance anything could ever change. I opened the box, and inside was a gold bracelet with little diamonds around it, the one my mother would never let me borrow. It was her most valued piece of jewelry. I turned it around in my hands and noticed an inscription I'd never seen: *Thank you for such a precious gift, your loving husband.*

I drove to Brooklawn, and went straight to my father's room and climbed on his bed. I laid down next to him the way I used to when I was a little girl. Dad was staring at the ceiling. It reminded me how, in second grade during class, I used to stare at the ceiling and count tiles. At the last parent-teacher conference of the year, my teacher told my parents I was unable to focus in class. She said I wasn't going to do well in third grade. Dad was so mad he told her that if she taught in a less boring way, I'd be more attentive. He was always sticking up for me. As I looked into his eyes, I became Daddy's little girl again.

"Dad, you have to help me," I whispered. "I did something really bad." I put my head on his chest. He didn't say anything, but I felt his heartbeat quicken. "I got involved with a man, and Jim found out and left me." He didn't take his eyes off the ceiling. I turned over on my side and looked at him, but I couldn't read his expression. Even if he understood what I was saying, he wouldn't have admitted that he was disappointed in me. He would've found a way to excuse my behavior.

And then I began to shake. Sounds came out of me but no tears. It was as if there was an earthquake inside, and the tremors were causing damage, but the dam wasn't breaking. "Your perfect little girl screwed her life up," I said. "I need your help. You always knew what I should do." He moved his hand so it rested against my side. And then the dam broke. He could've been comforting me, or he just wanted me to stop getting his sheets wet. "Dad, I miss you so much. I don't know how to be without you. Please come back to me." I continued to cry as I realized I didn't have a dad, I didn't have a mom, and I didn't have a husband.

"Mr. Rubin, are you ready for lunch?" a young nurse said as she carried in a tray of food. "Oh, sorry, Maggie, I didn't see you there." She seemed embarrassed when she noticed what an emotional mess I was. "Your father hasn't been able to eat in the dining room lately," she said.

"Can you come back in a few minutes?" I choked out.

"Of course." She put the tray on the bedside table. The smell of macaroni and cheese wafted through the room, making my stomach churn.

I got off the bed and got a tissue to wipe the mascara streaks from under my eyes. "Dad, I wish you could say something to make it all better."

"I love you," he whispered without turning his head toward me. Hearing him say that made me feel safe. He knew I was there, and he knew who I was. As I was about to tell him I loved him too, he said, "I keep telling you, young lady, you need to go. And take all the squirrels with you." I kissed him on the forehead and walked out.

When I got home, I took a shower. I wanted a clean start to my marriage. It might take a lot of work, but Jim would someday forgive me. We could get back to where we were a year ago, when we were happy and having sex.

I needed to be more direct if things were bothering me, and he needed to be more communicative and not worry what my reaction would be. He would realize that we were better together than apart and that our marriage was worth fighting for. We could go to couples therapy, so we'd have help working through the hurt. I was nervous about seeing him but trying to be optimistic. Then again, he hadn't been breaking down my door to see me. What if he didn't want me back? He had loved me for years. Could he really stop so easily?

I gazed at my face in the bathroom mirror. The lines in my forehead had deepened. I dabbed a lot of concealer under my eyes to get rid of the puffiness. Then I highlighted underneath them with black eyeliner, but my hand was shaking so much I got eyeliner in my eye. I was smart and cute, and good makeup hid my age relatively well.

By the time I finished applying a coat of champagne eye shadow and waterproof mascara, my hair was close to dry. I used a curling iron to put in beachy waves, as if I'd just climbed out of the ocean. My hair was perfect, a big difference from the last time I'd gotten out of the ocean with frizzed curls and seaweed attached to the crotch of my bathing suit.

I put on a gray sweater dress, black tights, and boots. I was overdressed, but I wanted to look like I had when we were first dating. Now, what jewelry did one wear when they begged their husband to come home? I settled on the bracelet my mother gave me and the gold hoop earrings Jim gave me for my last birthday.

I was ready, but Jim and Gia weren't due home from New York for another half hour. Why the hell did I get dressed so early? If I sat down, I'd look rumpled. I leaned against the counter in the kitchen and read the newspaper, then I paced until I heard Jim's car pull up.

The two of them came in reminiscing about how good the hot fudge sundae they had at Serendipity at midnight last night was. I would've loved to be a part of that. Maybe after today, I could be. I hugged Gia tighter than usual and told her to go unpack. She kissed her father and ran upstairs. I walked toward Jim seductively, hoping he wouldn't be able to resist my charms. He looked me up and down like he did on our first date, then opened his mouth to say something but decided against it. Yes! Score one for tight sweater dresses.

I asked how *Hamilton* was. He said it was fantastic, which I knew it would be, but he didn't have to tell me in detail. I invited him to stay for a few minutes, and surprisingly he agreed. We moved over to the couch and sat down.

I was ready; I knew what I wanted to say. I'd been practicing my speech in the mirror all morning. I'd tell him how much I loved him and how we were destined to be together, and I'd never do anything like Michael again. I'd tell him I knew it would take him a while to forgive me and earn his trust back, but I was willing to work hard. I hoped he'd see how sincere I was, but before I could launch into my speech, Jim spoke.

"It's been hard being without you, and I've had time now to understand my part in everything. I miss you," he said. Well, that was easier than I thought.

"I miss you too," I said.

Jim's whole body relaxed next to me, and he took my hand. "I want to come home. We can work things out together."

As I gazed into his eyes, I saw a wonderful, caring man who was saying exactly what I wanted to hear. Those words made me happy, so what I said next surprised both of us. "I don't think you should come home."

He dropped my hand, and his relaxed expression turned to confusion. He began bouncing his right leg up and down, causing the couch to shake rhythmically. "I don't understand. I thought this is what you wanted."

"It was, it is, but not yet. If you come back now, nothing'll be different. You'll still hate your job, and I'll still feel unappreciated."

"We can work through that. Unless this is about Michael. Are you in love with him?"

"No, I never was. This has nothing to do with him. I'm never going to see him again." His shaking was driving me crazy. I put my hand on his leg, and he stopped. "I'm so sorry I hurt you. I was confused, and I regret all of it." I couldn't look at his face. I didn't want to see his disappointment.

"If you know why you did it, then we'll be able to move on," he said.

Before I started shaking my legs also, I stood up and paced around the room. "That's the problem. I don't know why. I have to figure out what's missing inside me. I'm ashamed that

I turned to someone else to distract me from my problems and fill my life with excitement. I need to figure out how I can be productive and useful when I don't have Gia to raise anymore. I need to find happiness within myself, and it can't be about anyone else."

"Can't you do that with me here?"

"No, I'm afraid if I don't push myself, I'll fall back into what's easy. I need to stand on my own for a while." I walked back over and sat next to him. "I know you haven't been happy either."

"That wasn't about you, or our marriage."

"So, your not wanting sex anymore wasn't about me?"

"No. I was just so stressed and tired all the time that sex wasn't ever on my mind."

"Well, it's been on mine."

"It will be different now. I know what I need to do to be less stressed," he said. "I'm going to keep my job and not work weekends anymore. Then we can have more time to relax and have fun together, and my sex drive will come back."

"It's not that simple."

"Maybe it can be."

I felt guilty that he was trying so hard, but I was strong in my conviction. "I don't want you staying in a job that makes you miserable. You need time to figure out if there's something else for you too."

Theo began howling at the sound of an airplane flying overhead. Jim whistled, hoping to get him to stop, but Theo ignored him. I sat down on the floor with my back against the couch. Jim got up and sat down next to me.

"How did we get here?" he asked.

"I don't know."

"I love you."

"I love you too."

"Do you want a divorce?" he asked.

"No, just time."

"How much time?"

"I can't answer that."

Jim's shoulders drooped. "What if I figure my stuff out, and I move on before you figure out yours?"

"I'll have to take that chance. If something bad happens to me, I don't want to regret the life I had," I said.

Jim got up and helped me to my feet. "I can't believe this is happening," he said.

"I'm so sorry," I said.

"So am I." He took my hand, and we walked to the door together. He put his hands on my face and gave me a slow, gentle kiss, then walked out the door.

ACKNOWLEDGMENTS

———·✧·———

I will forever be grateful to the following individuals, without whose contributions and support, this book would not have gotten started, let alone finished:

This novel was a labor of love and took me a little longer to gestate than it took to have both my kids. To Hunter and Jake, whose creativity has been a source of inspiration to me. Being their mother has been the best job I have ever had, even though the pay has been exceptionally low. To my husband, Bruce, my first editor and the most talented writer I know. I'm grateful for his undying support, his patience in listening to my fears that I didn't know what I was doing, and his encouragement to keep going. The three of you are my family, a family I love and would not want to live without.

I am eternally grateful to Miriam Trogdon, the first person to take a chance on me by helping me get my first script in television comedy. Because of her, even at a time when there were not a lot of female comedy writers, I got my foot in the door. And thank you to Elliot Webb, my first agent, who believed in my writing and whom I adored.

To the writing workshop I took led by the warm and gifted Linda Schreyer. Writing a book had been on my to-do list, but I don't know if I would've followed through if it hadn't been for Linda's workshops. She steered me through the book from the first page to the end of the first draft. And to Debi Pomerantz for her friendship, our weekly talks, and her notes on my writing. She has been a godsend.

I want to thank Joanne Kimes and Melissa Gelineau, the only readers I trusted with my first draft. Not only were their notes insightful and honest, but they completely understood the story I was trying to tell, and their wisdom helped me improve my second draft by leaps and bounds. I am grateful for their talents and their expertise.

To the Kauai Writers Conference 2018 for a memorable and educational experience. Especially to Christina Baker Kline, Kristin Hannah, and Josh Mohr. The lessons I learned from their workshops propelled me to perfect my final draft.

Thank you to Dr. Annette Swain, the neuropsychologist who took time out of her schedule to give me information on Lewy body dementia. Her knowledge helped me create a realistic picture of what Maggie's father was going through. I am also grateful to the Facebook support group for Parkinson's with Lewy body dementia. I appreciate their willingness to grant me admission so I would have an acute understanding of this horrific disease, how it affects the people suffering from it, and the strength of their caregivers.

I also want to acknowledge the Burbank Animal Shelter for all the good work they do and for letting me be a part of their volunteer operation.

To the enthusiastic team at She Writes Press, headed by publisher Brooke Warner. They are passionate and enthusiastic and I'm grateful they believed in me and my book. I also want to acknowledge my project manager, Samantha Strom who was an excellent guide through the whole process. And thank you to the PR team at Booksparks, Crystal Patriarche, Keely Platte and Paige Herbert for shining their light on my debut novel.

A shoutout to my dearest friends, who have stood by me and cheered me on. Cayla Schneider, Jill Campbell, Kim Abrams-Grove, Lori Wilson and Erin Semper. I couldn't have more loyal friends, and they have gotten me through the tough things in life.

I want to thank my parents, Katherine and Howard Rieder, who showed me what a good marriage should look like, and I'd especially like to thank my mom, who was more excited about my book being published than anyone else. To my sisters, Linda Gardner and Dee O'Reilly, I am blessed to have their love and support. Dee for making me laugh when things were hard, and Linda for always being there for me and for picking up the phone when I needed to vent for the thousandth time. I am fortunate to have both of them in my life.

And lastly, to all the moms who are left with an empty nest and a journey to find themselves once again. This book is for you.

ABOUT THE AUTHOR

L eslie Rasmussen was born and raised in Los Angeles, California. She graduated with a bachelor's in communications from UCLA and went on to write television sitcoms and is a member of the Writers Guild of America, West. She wrote for Gerald McRaney, Burt Reynolds, Roseanne Barr, Norm McDonald, Drew Carey, and Ralph Macchio, as well as *The Wild Thornberrys* and *Sweet Valley High*. After having children, she earned a master's degree in nutrition and ran her own business for ten years. Most recently, Leslie has written personal essays for Huffington Post, MariaShriver.com, and SheKnows.com. Leslie loves dogs, and besides having two adorable Labradors, she is a member of the Alliance of Therapy Dogs and has volunteered at the Burbank Animal Shelter in Burbank, California. Leslie lives in Los Angeles and has two sons and a husband she has been with since college. This is her debut novel.

Author photo © FotoJennik

SELECTED TITLES FROM SHE WRITES PRESS

She Writes Press is an independent publishing company founded to serve women writers everywhere. Visit us at www.shewritespress.com.

Duck Pond Epiphany by Tracey Barnes Priestley. $16.95, 978-1-93831-424-7. When a mother of four delivers her last child to college, she has to decide what to do next—and her life takes a surprising turn.

Play for Me by Céline Keating. $16.95, 978-1-63152-972-6. Middle-aged Lily impulsively joins a touring folk-rock band, leaving her job and marriage behind in an attempt to find a second chance at life, passion, and art.

A Tight Grip: A Novel about Golf, Love Affairs, and Women of a Certain Age by Kay Rae Chomic. $16.95, 978-1-938314-76-6. As forty-six-year-old golfer Jane "Par" Parker prepares for her next tournament, she experiences a chain of events that force her to reevaluate her life.

A Drop in the Ocean: A Novel by Jenni Ogden. $16.95, 978-1-63152-026-6. When middle-aged Anna Fergusson's research lab is abruptly closed, she flees Boston to an island on Australia's Great Barrier Reef—where, amongst the seabirds, nesting turtles, and eccentric islanders, she finds a family and learns some bittersweet lessons about love.

As Long As It's Perfect by Lisa Tognola. $16.95, 978-1-63152-624-4. What happens when you ignore the signs that you're living beyond your means? When married mother of three Janie Margolis's house lust gets the best of her, she is catapulted into a years-long quest for domicile perfection—one that nearly ruins her marriage.

Center Ring by Nicole Waggoner. $17.95, 978-1-63152-034-1. When a startling confession rattles a group of tightly knit women to its core, the friends are left analyzing their own roads not taken and the vastly different choices they've made in life and love.